I0804919

The Storm Testament II

Lee Nelson

Council Press
Springville, Utah

ISBN 13: 978-1-55517-657-0

Published by Council Press, an imprint of Cedar Fort, Inc., 2373 W. 700 S., Springville, UT, 84663
Distributed by Cedar Fort, Inc. www.cedarfort.com

LC CONTROL NO.: 2004000628

Cover design by Nicole Williams
Cover design © 2008 by Lyle Mortimer
Page design by Lyndsee Simpson Cordes

Printed in the United States of America

10 9 8 7 6 5 4 3 2 1

Printed on acid-free paper

To Sharon

Chapter 1

Caroline Logan didn't know what to think when she read the note from Henry Sears of Sears & Chadwick Publishing Company. Sears & Chadwick was a successful Philadelphia book publisher, and Caroline was a writer, but not a book writer. Yet Mr. Sears wanted to meet with her to discuss a special project. She had no idea what that project might be.

In fact, it was just within the past few weeks that one of Caroline's articles had finally made the front page of the *Philadelphia Inquirer.* She had been working there almost a year, one of three female writers covering social events, weddings, garden shows, and lawn parties—the typical topics covered by female writers. Her front page story, however, was a totally different kind of article.

It was late in October 1844, a year of strife in Philadelphia, as native-born Protestants clashed with immigrant Catholics from Ireland and Europe. The development of coal mines west of Philadelphia in the early 1800s had opened the door for industrial development. Philadelphia industries produced clothing, iron, locomotives, machinery, ships, shoes, and textiles.

The rapid industrialization had attracted thousands of German and Irish immigrants. Competition for jobs between the newcomers and those already in the city, both blacks and whites, was fierce. More than thirty people had been killed in riots and street battles.

It was by a stroke of luck that Caroline had been drawn into the conflict and had been able to interview Catholic rebel leader Sean O'Connor. Sent by the paper to Germantown to cover a harvest festival, she had retreated to the secluded area at the rear of one of the exhibit tents to write her story when young Sean burst in on her, quite by accident, scattering her papers on the ground.

Although Caroline had never seen the Catholic militant before, she recognized him immediately from the numerous "Wanted" posters throughout the city. Her first reaction was to scream, but she hesitated when the young man put his finger to his lips, signaling for her to be silent. He had scampered into the tent in an effort to avoid three constables walking through the exhibit area.

It was probably O'Connor's bright smile more than anything else that prompted Caroline to hold back her scream. And he had plenty to smile about, too. Caroline was a handsome woman, taller than most, with long blonde curls tied behind her ears with a light blue ribbon. Her eyes were blue and clear, her complexion, smooth and healthy. She was twenty years old and had a trim but full figure. She was accustomed to men turning to look at her.

The obvious absence of a wedding ring on her finger had nothing to do with lack of opportunity. In fact, she had developed a rather cool disposition toward men in an unconscious effort to discourage romantic interest.

As a gangly teenager, she had been silly about boys like the rest of her friends, but her first job changed all that. She was the only child in her family, and both parents worked from daylight until dusk in the textile mills, leaving Caroline with a lot of free time on her hands. Her earliest memories involved writing letters to everyone she knew, and often fictitious letters to people she didn't know. She became a prolific letter-writer.

At first, Caroline's father figured her letter writing a useless hobby, child's play. But he suddenly changed his mind when at fifteen Caroline landed a job copying letters for Lucretia C. Mott, head of the American Anti-Slavery Society. It wasn't long until Caroline was composing letters and working on anti-slavery flyers. Her writing skills developed quickly, but even more important, she had been exposed to a cause, a life and death struggle for freedom.

A seed of idealism had been planted.

Caroline seemed to sense that a marriage to one of her childhood sweethearts would pull her back into a routine, hand-to-mouth existence like that of her parents. No, she didn't want that. Not after a glimpse of what seemed to her a much more meaningful and exciting world.

Four years later, when she took the job as a reporter for the *Inquirer*, she moved closer to her work, into a brownstone apartment in Germantown. She was determined to keep men out of her life as she developed herself as a writer. Caroline hated covering garden shows and lawn parties but figured a price had to be paid as she developed her writing skills. She kept reminding herself that someday she would write something great.

Then she stumbled onto Sean O'Connor, or he onto her. The beautiful, educated, well-dressed female journalist was face to face with the most notorious ruffian of Philadelphia—a young bull, indomitable, crude in his dress and manners, unwilling to take his hat off to any man. He was the Catholic worker who had led his companions, armed with clubs and knives, into street battles with Protestant workers, resulting in the deaths of more than thirty men. Sean O'Connor was a wanted man, a fat prize for the approaching constables.

But Caroline didn't scream. She had another idea, and was suddenly very interested in the young rebel, more interested than she had been in any man for a long time. It wasn't a romantic interest but a professional one. In the young Irishman she saw a story, one that could further her career as a writer, one that could get her out of the society pages and into the important part of the paper, maybe even the front page.

None of the male reporters had ever been able to interview Sean O'Connor. It was doubtful that any had tried very hard. The young Irishman had a quick temper and a reputation for punching people who didn't agree with him or who asked hard questions.

There was electricity in the air as Caroline looked into the eyes of the young ruffian. He didn't look away, and neither did she, as she wondered how she might get him to answer her questions. Should she appear timid, perhaps frightened by his presence? Or should she be bold and confident? Should she just be herself, hoping his interest in her as a woman might keep him around long enough to answer her questions?

O'Connor was the first to speak.

"What kind of a lass is this?" he whispered, more to himself than to Caroline.

"Not plain like the working lasses," he continued, finally taking his eyes away from hers to inspect the rest of her.

"Might you be a rich lady?" he asked, obviously impressed with her dress.

"No, a reporter," replied Caroline, "and in your clumsiness you just scattered my notes all over the ground." She wanted to sound firm, but not bossy.

"I'm so sorry," he said, not sounding like he was sorry at all. He made no move to pick up the notes.

"Could I ask you some questions?"

"Why?" He cocked his head to one side and removed his hat, obviously enjoying the conversation.

"You are Sean O'Connor, leader of the Catholic workers."

"So the lass knows me name, does she?"

"You have not yet been interviewed in the papers. The people want to know what you are like, what you are thinking, why you do what you do."

"And you will help me tell them?"

Caroline nodded. "Many reporters are afraid of you."

For the first time, O'Connor showed a look of surprise. "Afraid. Of me? Why?"

"They know about your temper. They are afraid you might hurt them."

"Me?" said O'Connor, as if he were finding it hard to believe that all other men weren't brave and bold like he was.

"Can I ask you some questions?"

"No."

Caroline suddenly became tired of what seemed like senseless banter. At the same time, some of O'Connor's boldness seemed to be rubbing off on her.

"Then get out of here so I can pick up my papers and get back to work." She turned away from O'Connor, dropped to her knees, and began to gather the papers, guessing that he wouldn't leave.

Almost before she realized what was happening, the young Irishman was on his knees beside her, helping with the papers. She started to protest but decided to remain silent.

When he handed her the last of the papers, she looked up into his face, hoping some of the stubbornness had disappeared.

She tried to jerk back, but it was too late. The young Irishman caught her by surprise, kissing her quickly on the mouth, before leaping away with the agility of a cat to avoid the blow she delivered too late.

Caroline was about to scream for help when she suddenly realized her advantage. Getting back on her feet, she said, "Mr. O'Connor seems to have forgotten why he came into this tent."

The Irishman didn't respond, not understanding what she was getting at.

"There are three constables not fifty feet away, sitting on a bench at the concession, drinking iced tea. A cry from me and they will be upon you."

"You wouldn't, lass."

"I will, if you won't answer my questions, or if you take one step toward me."

Sean O'Connor reached into his belt and retrieved a silver-bladed knife. He ran his finger over the blade, then looked up at Caroline.

"I could throw this into that beautiful belly of yours before you could blink."

"And I could scream loud enough for the constables to hear. They would hang you for sure."

"A waste, a real waste." He was still fingering the knife blade. "Would you give the Catholic workers a fair story?"

"If I didn't, would it be very hard for you to find me?"

O'Connor put the knife back under his belt, nodding for Caroline to begin with the questions.

Twenty minutes later, Sean O'Connor slipped under the back side of the tent and disappeared down an alley.

Caroline gathered together her notes and headed out the front of the tent, looking quickly back at the empty bench where the iced tea was being sold. She wondered how things might have turned out had O'Connor peeked under the tent to catch her in the lie about the tea-drinking constables.

The interview with O'Connor was a smashing front-page success, winning for Caroline the envy of the other journalists. Of course, she left out the part about the kiss and even the lie about the constables. The editor paid her five dollars instead of the usual two dollars per article. Caroline felt that her career as a writer was starting to blossom. Who should she interview next?

A week later she received the letter from the Sears & Chadwick Publishing Company, inviting her to discuss a "project" with Mr. Sears. Certainly a writing project, maybe a book. But why would anybody want her to write a book?

Chapter 2

It was a sunny afternoon in early November when Caroline hired a carriage to take her to 315 South Warsaw Street, where the Sears & Chadwick Publishing Company was headquartered. She was wearing her best dress, one of peach satin with a modest neckline and full skirt, the popular style of the day. Her blonde curls were held back with a black ribbon, and a white shawl was draped lightly about her shoulders.

The streets were lined with maple and sycamore trees, already red and yellow from the first fall frosts. The noisy clatter of iron-rimmed buggy wheels on the cobblestone streets was frequently muffled by a matted blanket of newly fallen leaves. The sky was blue, the air cool and crisp but pleasant, thanks to the afternoon sun.

It was a perfect day for a buggy ride, but Caroline didn't notice. She was deep in thought, still trying to figure out why Henry Sears wanted to see her. Since receiving his letter asking her to come and see him, she had thought of little else. A hundred questions had been going through her mind. Why had Mr. Sears written to her? Did he want her to write a book? Why her? She was only twenty years old and just beginning a career as a newspaper reporter. What kind of book could she write? She had only been writing newspaper articles for a year, and she had only made the front page a few weeks ago, with her Sean O'Connor interview.

An older person would have been more patient, hoping for good news about a great opportunity but ready for the disappointment of being offered a secretarial or errand-girl position. In her twenty years, Caroline had learned the value of persistence and hard work, but patience was not one of her virtues. She was a young woman in a hurry. Still flushed with the success of the O'Connor interview, she was looking for more of the same and had convinced herself that this meeting with Henry Sears would open the door to another exciting opportunity.

Henry Sears greeted Caroline in the front office. He was a short man, maybe five and a half feet tall. His body had a thick, sedentary look from too many hours behind a desk, but his brown eyes were clear and bright, his smile spontaneous. He wore a brown tweed suit, glossy black shoes, and a white shirt with a stiff collar and ruffles down the front. What he lacked in hair on the top of his head, he made up for with thick, curving sideburns extending to the middle of his pink cheeks. His chubby hands were white, freckled, and soft like those of a pampered woman. Caroline couldn't help but contrast him with the daring, strong Sean O'Connor. The refined book publisher seemed no match for the Irish street fighter, certainly not as interesting to a woman—at least not at first appearance.

Henry Sears was a warrior of a different kind, one whose weapons were ideas and words—in the end much more powerful than Sean O'Connor's fists and clubs. Men like Henry Sears pulled the strings and made the decisions, while men like Sean O'Connor died on the battlefield.

Henry Sears was not in a hurry to uncover his reasons for inviting Caroline to see him. After the initial greetings were exchanged, he took her on a tour of the print shop and bindery, where they had to step carefully among the glue pots, then to the storage barn where the twenty-six titles published by Sears & Chadwick were stacked in neat, well-cared-for piles. Caroline was awed at the sight of so many new books.

"Why is he doing this?" she kept thinking. "Why doesn't he just get down to business and tell me why he wanted to see me?"

Mr. Sears seemed very confident, like he knew exactly what

he was doing, like there was a good reason for her to see his entire operation before he sat down with her to discuss business.

It must be pretty important, thought Caroline. *He wouldn't go to so much trouble if he didn't have something heavy on his mind.*

Caroline's heart beat faster. Her cheeks flushed with the conviction that this meeting with Henry Sears was really going to be something big.

He ushered her into his high-ceilinged office and closed the door, asking his secretary to hold all disturbances.

After guiding Caroline to her place on a velvet-cushioned chair beside a huge mahogany desk, Mr. Sears made himself comfortable in the big chair behind the desk. Before saying anything, he bit the end from a new cigar and proceeded to light it with a wooden match. He didn't offer one to Caroline. That would have been rude.

Henry Sears puffed on the cigar, looking into Caroline's face, still not saying anything. She was beginning to get nervous but was determined not to let it show.

"You're a beautiful woman, Miss Logan," was his first comment.

"Thank you," she responded, trying to be nice but annoyed that he wasn't getting to the point of the visit.

"In fact," he continued, "I think you are the most beautiful writer I have ever met."

"You didn't bring me all the way over here to tell me that."

"Your good looks have a lot to do with me inviting you here."

"I'm a writer, not a mistress," said Caroline, getting up to leave.

"Let me assure you, my intentions are honorable," he said with a burst of sincerity that pulled her back. "I have only business to discuss with you, nothing else."

"Then let's talk about business," said Caroline with a boldness that surprised her. "Why did you invite me here?"

Mr. Sears snubbed out the cigar and leaned forward, placing both forearms on the mahogany desk, his hands clenched into fists.

"For several months now, our company has been looking for someone to take on a very exciting writing project. We think you might be that person."

He paused to let his words sink in. Caroline remained silent. There was nothing for her to do but listen.

"We have been looking for a woman writer, one with good looks and courage. I was beginning to think that such a woman did not exist in Philadelphia. Then I saw your interview with that rascal Sean O'Connor. That took courage."

"Thank you," responded Caroline, choosing not to tell him that her meeting with the Irish rebel was accidental.

"How much do they pay you for those articles you write for the *Inquirer*?"

"As much as five dollars each, usually less."

"How would you like to write a book that would sell thousands of copies, with you receiving a fifty-cent royalty on each copy sold?"

"Of course I would like that," responded Caroline. "But you know as well as I do that I'm just a beginning writer. I have never even started a book. Why did you ask me to come here? You certainly can't tease me into believing I am a likely prospect to write a best-seller."

"Don't worry about your writing ability. It's good enough. Besides, we have editors that can help."

"Please tell me what you have in mind."

"We want you to write a book about the Mormons."

"Ridiculous. I don't know anything about the Mormons."

Mr. Sears placed a black cloth-bound book on the desk and pushed it over to Caroline. Caroline picked it up and opened to the title page.

She read, *The History of the Saints; Or, An Exposé of Joe Smith and Mormonism,* by John C. Bennett, Boston, 1842.

"That book has sold nearly ten thousand copies," explained Sears, "making Mr. Bennett a nice little fortune in royalties. It could very well become the best-selling exposé ever written on the Mormons."

"The reason this book has sold so well," he continued, "is because Bennett got inside. He was one of them for a while, found out what was really going on.

"The thing in this book that really has people excited," he continued, "is this polygamy business. Also, the political talk about the Mormon plan to conquer the whole world, overthrow governments, and that kind of thing."

"What is it you want me to do?" asked Caroline.

"A few months ago we got to thinking that if we could get an attractive female writer to go to Nauvoo—the Mormon city on the Mississippi—in disguise, as a schoolteacher or something, and live among the Mormons, she just might get a marriage proposal to become a plural wife to one of the Mormon leaders."

Caroline was speechless, finding it hard to believe Mr. Sears was serious.

"Naturally the woman would be curious, wanting lots of questions answered before entering such a relationship. She would get the whole story, not only the polygamy stuff, but the revolutionary information too, and who knows what else."

"Is that what you want me to do?"

"Yes," he responded in a matter-of-fact manner. "I see a first-person story, you telling every detail of your adventure, climaxed with your escape just before the plural ceremony is to take place. You would be a national heroine. You would make a fortune in royalties."

"I don't know," said Caroline. "Sounds like a dirty job, not something I'd be proud to write home to Mother about."

"Dirty!" he exploded, standing up. "Those Mormons with their plural wifery are striking a vital blow at the very institution that made this country great—the family. And they would overthrow our government, too, with their 'Kingdom of God.'

"By exposing the Mormons you would be exposing a great evil," he continued. "You would be a heroine, a patriot. What do you think?"

"Sounds kind of risky," responded Caroline, wishing Mr. Sears had proposed something else for her to write. "You're asking me to be a spy, to make friends under false pretenses, to deceive people who have never done anything to me. I don't know."

"I don't want you to do it if you don't feel good about it," said Mr. Sears. "But should you decide to do it, we are prepared to give you a two-hundred-fifty-dollar cash advance and a ten-percent royalty on every book sold."

Caroline had never seen two hundred fifty dollars at one time in her life. She had not made that much money her whole first year at the *Inquirer.* Maybe the project wasn't so bad after all. She decided to ask another question.

"It could be dangerous, don't you think?"

"I agree. The Mormons probably wouldn't take kindly to discovering a journalist spy."

"In order to ensure your secrecy," he continued, "I have arranged a contact for you across the Mississippi in Iowa. A plantation owner with a strong dislike for Mormons. You can't trust the mail in Nauvoo. When you need to get a message to me, or send some of the manuscript, you can do it through this contact."

He sat back down in his chair, leaned forward, and looked into Caroline's eyes.

"Will you do it? For your country? For the sacred institution of the family? To further your career as a writer? For the money?"

He made it sound so appealing, so easy, so right. Still, Caroline felt uneasy. So many unknowns, so risky. But would she ever get an opportunity like this again? And a two-hundred-fifty-dollar advance! She could buy her own carriage, make a down payment on a new house or a farm . . .

She caught a brief glimpse of herself, disguised as a schoolteacher, interviewing Brigham Young himself. By comparison, the Sean O'Connor interview was child's play. Could she take such a big step and not stumble?

"Could I have a few days to think it over?" she asked.

"Why don't you stop in day after tomorrow, same time," said Mr. Sears as he stood up to escort Caroline out of the building to her waiting carriage.

"Is there anything else you would like to know?" asked Mr. Sears as he helped Caroline into the carriage.

"No, I can't think of . . . yes, there is one thing," Caroline said. "Who is this contact I would be working with? Are you sure he can be trusted, that he won't betray me to the Mormons?"

"You won't have any worry there," laughed Sears. "I know the fellow personally. He would never willingly aid the Mormons. His name is Boggs. Dick Boggs."

Chapter 3

When Caroline boarded the *Osprey* at St. Louis for the last leg of her trip to Nauvoo, she was surprised to see the paddle-wheel steamer so crowded. It was the spring of 1845, and she soon learned the reason for the crowd. Her arrival in Nauvoo would coincide with the laying of the capstone on the Mormon temple, an event expected to attract thousands of spectators.

Circulating among the passengers, Caroline heard gossip that the temple would never be finished. The capstone ceremony meant that the walls were completed up to the square, but the roof and spire still needed to be built, as well as all the inside woodwork and plastering.

Being a handsome woman, some of the male passengers went out of their way to make conversation with Caroline. She took full advantage of the situation to learn all she could about Nauvoo and the Mormons. One fellow said the Mormons would be expelled or exterminated before the temple could be completed. Another suggested that a single match could settle the temple question once and for all.

Some of the passengers scoffed at the Mormon belief that once the temple was completed the Saints would receive supernatural powers through the mystical bestowal of endowments.

It soon became apparent to Caroline that the protests were too vehement, too loud. The gentiles were reacting too strongly to the upcoming completion of the temple. She concluded that they really were afraid the Mormons might receive some magical powers.

Nevertheless, most of the passengers were in agreement that the Mormons wouldn't be around long enough to finish their temple. There were rumors that Brigham Young was going to lead his people west, possibly to California.

The thing that seemed to bother people most about Nauvoo and the Mormons was the lawlessness in the area. They felt Nauvoo was a haven for counterfeiters, horse thieves, killers, and organized banditti.

After Joseph and his brother Hyrum were killed the previous summer, the Illinois legislature had revoked the Nauvoo charter. The biggest city in Illinois, a frontier city at that, no longer had any legal peace-keeping machinery—no police, no courts. It really was a haven for criminals. The gentiles in the neighboring towns blamed the Mormons for the lawlessness. The Mormons blamed the state legislature, which had taken away the charter and its power to enforce the law.

When the Mormons reorganized the Nauvoo Legion under the direction of Hosea Stout in an effort to keep the peace and reestablish law and order, the neighboring communities feared the Mormons might be preparing to avenge the death of their prophet. The gap between the Mormons and their neighbors only widened. The Nauvoo Mormons were in a no win situation.

There was talk about a trial going on in Burlington, Iowa, just across the river from Nauvoo. Two Mormons, the Hodge brothers, were on trial for killing and robbing a Mennonite minister and his son-in-law. The conversation among the passengers was how many other Mormons were engaged in these kinds of acts and not getting caught.

When the steamer stopped at Warsaw, only two stops away from Nauvoo, Caroline obtained a copy of the *Warsaw Signal,* the local newspaper, and retired to her cabin to brief herself on the local news. She was surprised, even shocked, at the bluntness of the front page article about Nauvoo. The *Philadelphia Inquirer* didn't publish those kinds of stories, not regularly, anyway.

The story, by Tom Sharp, blasted the Mormons for running counterfeiting operations in Nauvoo. It accused them of having three coin presses and quoted the dead prophet as having bragged in public that his own mint produced better coins than the U.S. Mint.

Caroline read the paper from front to back, hoping there might be something on polygamy at Nauvoo, the subject of the proposed book. There was nothing.

She pondered the city Nauvoo, the biggest city in Illinois, with a population of more than twelve thousand people. Five years earlier it had been nothing but a swamp. She wondered about the mysterious temple, why the Mormons would put so much time and money into a building they would soon have to leave behind. She remembered reading about Joseph Smith's murder the past summer, how his death was expected to bring about the end of the Mormon movement. To everyone's surprise, the Mormons pulled together, stronger than ever, under the forceful direction of Brigham Young, a man with only eleven days of formal schooling, who misspelled his own name on his first marriage application.

There were a lot of mysteries about Nauvoo and the Mormons, many unanswered questions. One thing she did know: Nauvoo was a mighty interesting place, teeming with opportunity for an enterprising journalist. She was on leave from her newspaper with the understanding she would send in articles on the Mormons and Nauvoo under the pen name of Carol Austin. But even more important was the book contract with Sears & Chadwick Publishing Company.

Nauvoo was the place to be, where things were happening, where history was being written, possibly the most exciting place on the North American continent in 1845. And Caroline was going to write about it.

Chapter 4

When the *Osprey* stopped in late afternoon at Keokuk, Iowa Territory, the last stop before Nauvoo, Caroline was one of the first passengers to go ashore. She wanted to make contact with Dick Boggs, the man who would serve as her liaison with Sears & Chadwick in Philadelphia. She also hoped he would be willing to relay her stories to the *Philadelphia Inquirer.*

Knowing she would be entering Nauvoo as a spy, Caroline sensed an urgent need to establish a home base, a place of retreat, a haven where she would be safe. She needed a place where people accepted her for what she really was, a place where people were sympathetic to what she was doing. Henry Sears had made arrangements for her to establish a contact with Dick Boggs, who lived on a plantation not far from Keokuk. Sears had never met Boggs, but he assured Caroline that Boggs could be trusted and depended on not to betray her to the Mormons.

Holding her skirts just high enough to keep them out of the black mud, Caroline walked into the little town to inquire as to the whereabouts of the Boggs plantation.

Keokuk was the first real frontier town Caroline had ever visited. The buildings were made from logs and rough-hewn planks, chinked with white lime, rags, grass, or the black mud from the streets. There were no sidewalks and no apparent pattern to the scattered buildings, half of which seemed to be saloons.

Keokuk was at the southern tip of a section of land known as Half-Breed Tract—hundreds of square miles established by a sympathetic U.S. Congress to provide homesteads for the offspring of white frontiersmen and Indian women. No sooner had the half-breeds claimed their free homesteads, however, than they began trading their holdings off for whiskey, guns, horses, and cash. It wasn't uncommon for the same piece of property to be sold as many as a dozen times by the same party.

The half-breed tract was a wild, untamed melting pot for homeless Indians, outlaws, horse thieves, real estate swindlers, and hoodlums. But the concentration of ruffians had been diluted some when the Mormons began settling on, twenty thousand acres north of Keokuk at Montrose, just across the Mississippi River from Nauvoo. Joseph Smith had bought the land on contract at a price just under two dollars an acre, with annual payments for twenty years at no interest. Though the Mormon settlers thinned the mixture of ruffians and outlaws, they certainly didn't put a lid on the lawless, frontier spirit of the land. Not yet.

Nevertheless, Keokuk wasn't the kind of place where an attractive young lady from Philadelphia would walk the streets without an escort, as Caroline was doing.

Caroline realized she was being stared at from all directions as she approached the general store to ask directions to the Boggs plantation. She felt very uneasy in this frontier town, partly undressed, unsafe. She had never thought about it before, but in Philadelphia people seemed to have an ingrained respect for rules and tradition. There were many invisible lines that simply were not crossed, except by an occasional outcast or criminal.

Caroline had only been in Keokuk a few minutes, but she already sensed that the Philadelphia rules were not in effect. She longed for a male escort, a strong one with a rifle over his shoulder.

She was glad when she entered the store to find herself alone, away from the eyes of gawking strangers. She was the only customer in the store. Not even a clerk was in sight. Caroline looked about and wasn't surprised to find the line of merchandise for sale very different from what she was accustomed to seeing in similar stores in Philadelphia. Instead of ribbons, bows, multicolored umbrellas, and dozens of jars of candies and sweets, the walls were lined with guns, saddles, lead, powder, Indian blankets, barrels of beans and flour, and animal traps of all kinds, mostly of the claw variety with double and single clamps. She liked the smell of the store—saddle leather, whiskey, and fresh dill.

There was a little bell on the plank counter. She rang it.

A big half-breed suddenly appeared in the doorway to the back room. He had to duck his head as he stepped toward Caroline. His hair was long and black, his beard at least a few weeks in the growing. He wore a red homespun shirt and leather trousers. His piercing black eyes, aquiline nose, and dark features had an intimidating effect on Caroline, soon disarmed by a friendly smile. A closer look revealed a well-fed, contented air about the big half-breed that made Caroline feel even better.

"Boat must be in," he said, figuring correctly that this attractive young woman must have been brought in by a river boat. "What can I get for you?"

His appearance was Indian, but his English was as good as any she had heard since leaving Philadelphia.

"Could you give me directions to the Boggs plantation?"

A look of surprise appeared on the face of the half-breed, a look of disbelief. He asked, "You mean Dick Boggs?"

"Oh, you know him. Good."

"You have business with him?"

Caroline was getting worried. She hadn't expected this kind of response to her question. A plantation owner should be a respected member of the community. There shouldn't be anything surprising about a plantation receiving guests from a river boat, yet this half-Indian seemed stunned that she was inquiring about the Dick Boggs plantation. What did he know that she didn't?

The half-breed pointed out the window to the west. "About two miles, following the creek. Road's pretty bad. You want to go there?"

"Yes. Is there anything wrong with that?"

"Well, no. Just not used to ladies, city folk anyway, wanting to see Boggs. He doesn't get many visitors."

"Do you know who might take me there? Where I might rent a wagon?"

"Road's a little tough on wagons this time of year, mud and all. We'll be closing down here in a little while. I'd be glad to take you out on horseback, if you can ride."

Caroline looked hard at the big half-breed. He seemed nice enough. Could she trust him? Why had he been so surprised about her wanting to visit the Boggs plantation? Well, she would just have to find out.

Swallowing her hesitation, Caroline said, "Thank you very much. Do you have a place where I can change into something suitable for horseback riding?"

Chapter 5

The tall half-breed introduced himself as Peter Weaselhead as he handed Caroline the reins to a buckskin gelding. He was already mounted on a lanky black mare.

As soon as Caroline was mounted, they headed west at an easy canter toward the Boggs plantation. The sun was getting low in the sky, and Caroline was a little concerned that they wouldn't make it back to town before dark. At first she thought she would spend the night at the Boggs plantation, supposedly among friends, but she wasn't sure now, remembering the surprised look on the half-breed's face when she announced she wanted to go there.

Having heard much about the stoic silence of Indians, Caroline was pleasantly surprised at Peter's willingness to talk about himself. His mother belonged to the Mandan tribe; his father was a French trapper he had never seen. When he was twelve, his mother had died of smallpox, leaving Peter to be raised at a Catholic mission near St. Louis. He worked there as an apprentice in the mission general store.

Years later when the Half-Breed Tract in the Iowa Territory was opened for settlement, Peter claimed 620 acres, which he promptly sold to a white man for enough cash to open his own store in Keokuk. He was not married, nor did he have any family.

When Peter asked Caroline if she was a Mormon—a natural question with so many moving into the area—she assured him she was not. She told him her first name, but not her last. She figured the less he knew about her, the better. She said she was a schoolteacher on vacation, traveling up the river. She was stopping to see Boggs at the request of a mutual friend in Philadelphia.

It didn't take long to cover the two miles to the plantation. As the two riders reached the crest of the last hill, getting a first look at the Boggs kingdom, Caroline suddenly realized why the half-breed had been surprised at her wanting to go there.

This was not the kind of plantation Caroline had envisioned—a white mansion with tall pillars, sweeping lawns, and orchards cared for by well-dressed servants. Instead, she saw a single log cabin—a small one at that—a log barn, corrals, pig pens, and a row of crude huts which she supposed to be slave quarters. There were no lawns, shrubs or white fences—just dirt, weeds and makeshift rail fences. Caroline felt Henry Sears had deceived her. The place was at best a run-down homestead, not a plantation by anybody's definition.

No one was in sight, not even the slaves, who apparently were still in the fields working. There was a tired-looking gray gelding tied to a post in front of the cabin.

"Will you be staying the night, or would you like me to escort you back to town at the end of your visit?" asked the half-breed.

A few minutes earlier, Caroline would have hesitated at that question, but after seeing the place, she knew she didn't want to spend the night. She asked Peter if he would wait for her while she visited Boggs, then accompany her back to town. She was glad when he dismounted and made himself comfortable under a tree on the hill overlooking Boggs's place. She was relieved he wouldn't be around to overhear her conversation with Boggs. She rode ahead in eager anticipation of meeting the man she suspected might be the most famous Mormon-hater of all, next to his cousin Lilburn, the former governor of Missouri.

It wasn't until Caroline had dismounted and was tying her horse to a fence post that the door to the cabin opened. She looked up to greet the man she had traveled so far to see.

Dick Boggs limped into the evening sunlight to greet his attractive visitor. He was a squat, heavyset man. The top of his partly bald head was white and sweaty like a big chunk of pig fat. He squinted through small black eyes at Caroline. His eyes were too close together, and the red of his puffy lips was barely visible through his thick brown beard. His clothing consisted of full-length red homespun underwear, gray trousers with wide brown suspenders, and cowhide boots. His clothing was soiled and greasy. His broken teeth were milky brown from constant tobacco chewing. He certainly wasn't the plantation gentleman Caroline had expected.

Caroline quickly noticed the source of Boggs's limp, a wooden stump in place of a boot on his right foot. She couldn't help but wonder what kind of violent deed had caused this, and if the injury had anything to do with the man's hatred for Mormons. She figured she would find out soon enough.

Boggs looked at Caroline in disbelief as if she were the first white woman he had ever seen. She certainly was the first one to visit his farm. He just stared at her, up and down, taking in every detail, not thinking to say anything. Caroline was the first to speak.

"Mr. Boggs?"

He seemed even more surprised. He wasn't used to this "Mister" business. The names he went by were Boggs, Masser, and sometimes Dick. But "Mister," that was something new.

"I'm Caroline Logan," she continued. "Henry Sears said you could help me. I'm writing a book."

Finally Boggs came to life, his mouth breaking into a broad grin, exposing more of the crooked, tobacco-stained teeth.

"Cousin Lilburn told me you might be coming," were Boggs's first words. "But I never thought you would really come, not here. Come in."

Caroline stepped toward the cabin door, taking a last look at Peter Weaselhead seated beneath the tree on the hill. It made her feel better, safer, to know he was there.

"Meet Frank Worrell," said Boggs to Caroline, as she stepped into the darkness of the cabin. The air was heavy with the stench of unwashed bodies and dirty clothing. It was dark compared to the outside sunlight, and it took Caroline's eyes a minute to adjust.

"Frank led the charge on Carthage Jail the night Joe and Hyrum Smith were shot trying to escape," continued Boggs, in an apparent attempt to impress Caroline with the caliber of his friends.

Frank was a thin weasel of a man who remained seated at the plank table while Boggs stumbled through the introductions and offered Caroline a dirty chair across the table from Frank.

When all were seated, Boggs spoke to Frank. "Caroline is going to spy on the Mormons, write a book about all the corrupt stuff going on in Nauvoo. Cousin Lilburn sent her to me. I'm going to help her."

"How?" asked Worrell.

"This place'll be her base, where she brings her stories. I'll send 'em away to Philadelphia through Cousin Lilburn. Too many Mormons in the post offices to risk sending hot stories by regular mail."

"Mormons'll make catfish bait of you," said Worrell, suddenly turning to Caroline, "if they catch you. For sure."

"Catfish bait?" asked Caroline, not sure what he was talking about.

"They put you in a skiff and take you to the middle of the river," he continued, "then slit open your belly, slip a couple of rocks inside so you won't float, then over the side with you into the cold black water, never to be seen or heard from again."

"Can't be too careful," said Boggs.

"Well, I just wanted to stop by and meet you on my way to Nauvoo," said Caroline, feeling like she wanted to leave as soon as possible. "I guess I'd better get going. Want to get back to Keokuk before dark."

"Did you ride out alone?" asked Boggs.

"No. Peter Weaselhead, the storekeeper, came with me. He's waiting on the hill."

The two men looked at each other as if there were things they would like to discuss, but couldn't in Caroline's presence.

She stood up and was almost to the door when Boggs and Worrell simultaneously scrambled out of their chairs to follow. In an effort to prolong the conversation, Boggs asked if she was planning to be in Nauvoo for the capstone ceremony.

"I plan to catch the next boat to Nauvoo," responded Caroline.

"Hope you get there in time for the fireworks," said Boggs, winking knowingly at Frank.

"Fireworks?" asked Caroline.

Boggs looked around, as if making sure no one was listening.

"If you want a hot story . . ." began Boggs, seeming pleased with some underlying humor in what he was saying. "If you want a hot story, stay close to the temple for a few days. You just might get a chance to report the biggest fire in the history of Illinois."

Caroline remembered the discussion she had heard aboard the *Osprey:* the concern that if the temple were finished the Mormons would never leave, the underlying fear of supernatural powers that would accompany the completion of the temple.

It hadn't occurred to her that people like Boggs and Worrell might try to stop the temple from being completed, but now it seemed obvious that they would. Certainly the Mormons wouldn't sit back and let their temple be burned. Whether Boggs and Worrell—and others like them—succeeded or failed, she would have a good story.

And how many other stories would she uncover as the conflict between the Mormons and the mobs escalated? Maybe coming to Nauvoo had been the right thing after all.

She would have to find a better way to get her stories out, however. She felt the less involvement she had with Boggs, the better off she would be. She figured Henry Sears had made a mistake in lining her up with Boggs.

Offering a pleasant good-bye to Boggs and Worrell, she climbed aboard the buckskin gelding and galloped toward the hill where the half-breed Peter Weaselhead was waiting.

Chapter 6

The first time I saw Caroline Logan was on the afternoon of May 23, 1845, the day before the capstone ceremony for the partially completed Nauvoo temple. I was on the highest scaffold, helping the stone mason Patrick O'Riley maneuver huge slabs of limestone into place. My .50 caliber Hawken rifle was a few feet away, leaning against the scaffold.

My primary responsibility was that of temple guard, having established myself as one of the best marksmen in Nauvoo, in company with Bill Hickman, Porter Rockwell, and Hosea Stout. I was usually assigned to help the workers on the highest scaffold, a place where I had the best view of the surrounding countryside. With the increasing amount of carpentry work going on in and about the temple, there was concern that the mobs would try to set the temple afire.

I enjoyed working with Pat—liked his friendly, freckled smile, his constant cheerfulness. He was about my age, unmarried, from Ireland. When not setting stone at the temple, most of his time was spent courting Nauvoo's young women. The object of his affections, and words, on this particular day was schoolteacher Sarah Lange. She had come out from Boston about a year earlier. She was prim and proper as schoolteachers ought to be, but as Pat would say, she was a looker too. Friendly and smart. Pat was one of many interested in Sarah.

Occasionally Pat looked away from his work at the tables below where women were preparing the midday meal.

"Sarah's on the food committee this week. Let me know when you see 'er," commented Pat. In recent months the food committee consisted of about twenty-five women. The Church provided the food from the tithing warehouse—beef, turkeys, potatoes, carrots, apples, etc. The women prepared and served it to the nearly two hundred workers, most of whom toiled in the quarry, chipping and sawing the huge limestone blocks and slabs that were carried to the temple in big-wheeled ox carts.

A year earlier there weren't nearly as many men working on the temple. There was much unrest among the Saints then. People were concerned about the polygamy rumors and Joseph's efforts to reintroduce consecration. Most people didn't want to give up their property. Some of the most influential members were in open rebellion, even William and Wilson Law and Oliver Cowdery. With all the confusion and dissension, it was tough keeping temple construction on schedule.

That all changed when Brigham Young, as president of the Quorum of the Twelve Apostles, took over. The people were ready to forget their bickering and get to work. The deaths of Joseph and Hyrum were like mortar, cementing the people together in an unbreakable bond.

I'll never forget the public viewing of the bodies in the Mansion House. The line must have been at least a mile long, ten thousand people waiting in the hot summer sun to get one last look at their beloved prophet. All day and into the night, the mourners filed quietly past the open caskets.

The heat inside the building was unbearable. Emma had fired up the wood stove in the kitchen to boil herbs. She was trying to fill the air with a camphor smell to cover up the stench of rotting flesh. The bodies were decomposing quickly in the June heat. Bottle flies were buzzing about the uncovered faces of the two dead men and were constantly being shooed away by the attendants and viewers. The floor below the caskets was stained with drippings from the dead men's wounds.

There was a look of new determination in every tear-streaked face leaving the house. The former bickerings and dissensions were forgotten. The Mormons had a martyr now. The prophet who had commanded them to build a temple had shed his blood for the cause.

In the weeks of confusion that followed, the people felt a growing force, a swelling of pent-up energy seeking an outlet. The special feeling created by the martyrdom worked among them like yeast. The people felt a growing tension, like the force of a volcano seeking to burst through the ground.

Some tried to harness the new force for their own benefit. Emma claimed her son was the rightful heir to the presidency of the Church. Sidney Rigdon argued that as first counselor in the presidency, he was next in line to take over. Turncoat John C. Bennett produced a letter, supposedly written by Joseph, naming him as successor. James Strang, leader of a group of Saints in Wisconsin, produced a similar letter. Out of the past came David Whitmer, who claimed to have been ordained by Joseph in Kirtland, with Oliver Cowdery and Martin Harris as counselors. And, of course, the Quorum of the Twelve Apostles claimed to hold the keys to the kingdom.

The Saints were restless and unsure until that fateful day when Brigham Young, just returned from a mission to the eastern states, stepped to the pulpit and preached a sermon that would never be forgotten. The words weren't as memorable as the sound of the voice and the look on Brigham's face. It wasn't Brigham that the people heard and saw, but Joseph. The voice and face were transformed as if the murdered prophet had risen from the dead. The people had the sign, the heavenly direction they had been looking for. Brigham was their new leader.

He told them it was time to finish the temple. The force that had been smoldering beneath the surface suddenly had an outlet. Finishing the temple became an obsession.

In addition to the regular full-time worker missionaries like me, hundreds of volunteer workers began showing up daily at the quarry and the building site. Most of the men in Nauvoo spent one day a week working on the temple. More work had been completed in the last nine months than during the entire first three years of construction. The women handled the preparation and serving of food for the workers. Children mixed mortar and picked up after the workers.

On that May afternoon as I worked with Pat O'Riley, the major stone work was almost finished. The front capstone, the large rock that would hold all the smaller stones together, would be set in place the next day. A big event was called, the capstone ceremony.

"There she is, in the green dress," whispered Pat, interrupting my contemplation of the temple.

"Who's the new lass with her?" he continued. "The one with the yellow curls. Let's get down and wash up."

I didn't know it at the time, but the new lass with the yellow curls was Caroline Logan, newly arrived in Nauvoo.

Chapter 7

I grabbed my rifle before climbing down from the scaffold behind Pat. As a guard, I was expected to keep the rifle beside me at all times, even during the dinner break. One never knew when the mob would strike. Besides, the rifle served as a constant reminder that my responsibilities were different than those of the working men I rubbed shoulders with throughout the day. It reminded me that my job was to be constantly on the lookout for danger and mischief.

The desire of the mob to stop the work seemed to grow in direct relation to the desire of the Saints to finish the temple. The Mormons expected the dedication to be accompanied by heavenly manifestations and fire from heaven, as was reported at the dedication of the Kirtland temple almost ten years earlier. The mob seemed truly concerned that the spiritual manifestations might really occur. Why else would they try so hard to stop construction of the temple?

The first thing they did was sneak into the quarry one night and saw partway through several of the axles on the ox carts used to carry the limestone blocks from the quarry. Then it was strychnine in the workmen's water barrel and the disappearance of a shipment of nails from St. Louis. Once a worker was shot from the scaffold by a hidden assailant. But with the recent commencement of carpentry work and the accompanying deliveries of lumber, the biggest concern was fire. While only two or three guards watched the temple during working hours, the number was doubled after hours, holidays, and Sundays. Every precaution was taken to make sure the temple didn't go up in smoke.

What the Church lacked in wages for the men who worked on the temple, it made up for in food. After Pat and I sloshed away the lime dust in a wooden watering trough, we headed for the tables where the food was served.

The breeze from the west had prevented the smell of the food from reaching us at the top of the scaffold, but our appetites suddenly became ravenous at the aroma of hot food. I slung the rifle over my shoulder and joined the men moving down both sides of the serving tables, piling my plate high with roast turkey, boiled beef, fried potatoes and onions, homemade bread with butter and honey, fresh boiled greens, sliced dill pickles, radishes, and onions. At the end of the table I was handed a canning jar full of chilled buttermilk. A true feast for working men and guards.

It being a nice day, Pat and I headed for a stretch of sloping lawn on the south side of the temple. No sooner had we stretched out and begun our meal than Pat mumbled, his mouth full of boiled beef, "Here they come, Sarah and that new lass."

From the look in Pat's eye, I could tell the women were approaching from behind me. Not wanting to turn in an obvious stare, I continued looking at Pat, who shoved a big piece of turkey in his mouth.

"The new lass. Looks even better up close. Good enough to make a man want to go back to school. Lad, you better team up with 'er while I'm chatt'n with Sarah."

In the six months I had known Pat, he had always seemed intent on "teaming" me up with someone of the opposite sex. It seemed unnatural to him, the way I kept to myself, pretty much avoiding social contact with the young women of Nauvoo.

Pat let me alone for a few weeks when I told him that I was a widower, that my wife, Red Leaf, a full-blooded Ute Indian, had been killed by the Comanches, and that I was not in the mood to court another woman, at least not yet. But now he was back to his old ways, having convinced himself that I needed a new woman to cure what he figured to be a well-disguised grief.

"Please, don't get up," ordered Sarah, as she and her new friend stopped behind me. I put my plate on the grass and looked around as Sarah introduced us to Caroline Logan, Nauvoo's newest schoolteacher.

I have to admit that as the two women seated themselves beside us on the grass, I was somewhat taken in by Caroline's blonde curls and blue eyes. There was no doubt that she was one of the most handsome women I had ever seen. But as we sat there making small talk over a big lunch, the thing that interested me most about Caroline was her apparent lack of interest in me.

She wasn't cold or unfriendly like some of the more vain women are when trying to discourage potential suitors. I hadn't said or done anything to make her feel that way, anyway. Neither had Pat, who had eyes only for Sarah. Caroline was unlike so many of the other young women, who seemed so enthralled with male companionship.

She had questions about everything. Mostly the temple, how it was being built, when it would be finished, why we needed all the lumber for a stone building. She wanted to know where the money was coming from to build the temple. She had a good appetite, too, chewing enthusiastically on beef and turkey between questions.

I answered her questions to the best of my knowledge, thoroughly enjoying her intense curiosity. I told her how the sisters in Nauvoo saved a penny a week each to buy nails and glass. I told her about several of the sisters who donated family china to be ground up in the plaster to make the building sparkle.

I figured she must be a new convert when she asked about the endowments that would be performed after the building was dedicated. The endowment was not something to be discussed outside of a temple, and until the temple was completed, it was a subject not discussed at all, at least not by the rank-and-file Mormons. At that time I didn't know anything about the endowment, not having experienced the ceremony, but I did know eternal marriages were performed in temples and was beginning to think this Caroline

Logan was the kind of woman that most men would be proud to take to the temple. She certainly had an active mind and a generous supply of wholesome good looks to go with it.

When I hesitated, not sure how I should respond to her questions about the endowment, she quickly changed the subject, asking me about the capstone ceremony the next day.

As I explained how the weight and size of the capstone held the other lesser stones in place, I balanced my rifle across my fingers to illustrate how the capstone worked.

"Why do you carry a rifle?" she asked suddenly, her tone more sober.

"I'm a guard," I explained, slapping the butt of my rifle with fondness. "My rifle Old George (named after my old friend Beaver George) and I do the guarding."

"Against what?"

"Mobs. They'd do anything to keep the temple from being completed."

"Like what?"

"See all that lumber?" I asked, looking into her face. "That's enough to make a bonfire that would warm the heart of every mobber within fifty miles."

She looked away, asking, "Do you really think they would try something like that?"

"If we give them half a chance. No doubt about it."

It seemed like a long time before she said anything else. After all the other things I had told her, I couldn't help but wonder why Caroline seemed so upset over the idea of the mobs wanting to burn the temple—like being upset over a cat wanting to eat a mouse. Mobs were part of everyday life in Nauvoo. Yet she seemed so surprised.

I wanted to ask her a few more questions. I was curious to know what was on her mind. But it was time to get back to work.

Springing to my feet and cradling my rifle under my arm, my parting words to Caroline were, "Don't worry, nobody's going to start any fires around here, not with George and me around." She didn't respond.

"Pat, let's go," I called to the Irish stone mason. He had been more intent on holding hands than forks; his dinner was only half eaten. "Got a lot of stones to lay before dark."

As I climbed the ladder to the highest scaffold, I couldn't help but think about Caroline's reaction to such a commonplace idea as the mob wanting to burn the temple. She certainly wasn't a naive person. Why had she seemed so alarmed? She certainly wasn't the frightened-child type.

Then I wondered why I was so concerned about what this woman was thinking. Had her blonde curls and blue eyes influenced me more than I cared to admit? No way.

"Come on, Pat," I called. He was still holding Sarah's hand at the bottom of the ladder. "Let's get those rocks in place."

Chapter 8

The capstone ceremony began at 6 AM on Saturday, May 24, 1845. Most of the Twelve Apostles were present, including Brigham Young, who was conducting. In spite of the drizzling rain, thousands of Saints gathered to watch the big flat slab of limestone set on the northeast corner of the wall.

I was standing on the highest scaffold, rifle ready, keeping a sharp lookout for mobbers and would-be law enforcement officers with writs or warrants for the arrest of Church leaders. Since the capstone ceremony had been announced weeks ago, no one would have been surprised to see a sheriff show up to serve papers on one of the leaders. Papers were impossible to serve at other times because the leaders simply could not be found.

But the Mormon crowd had a way to deal with paper-serving sheriffs and deputies. As soon as one was spotted, the Mormon who saw him first began to whistle, a signal to nearby Mormons that an enemy had entered their midst. The nearby men also began to whistle as they gathered around the hapless officer. As they whistled, they pulled out their knives and began to whittle on sticks. They did not threaten the officer with the knives, but the sight of several dozen flashing blades always had a very calming effect on the officer. Of course he couldn't continue his journey through the tangle of whistling whittlers. While this was going on, the leaders had plenty of time to disappear.

The barrel of my rifle was pointed down to prevent water from entering the barrel and dampening the powder. Pat was seated on the temple wall nearby, just in case he was needed to help with the capstone.

The ceremony began with the brass band playing "Nightingale," a favorite song in Nauvoo. The band was one of the busiest groups in town. It played at the arrival of river boats, frequently at worship services in the grove, and at weekly dances. The Mormons loved their band.

At exactly eight minutes after six, Brother William Player began spreading the mortar, preparing the base for the capstone, which was being lifted with pulleys secured to the highest scaffold. Brigham Young had already climbed the ladder to the top scaffold.

As soon as the stone was swung into place and the ropes pulled away, Brother Brigham stepped onto it. The vast audience was hushed. Brother Player handed Brigham a large beetle, the largest of the wooden mallets used to tap the stones into place. Tapping the slab here and there with the beetle, Brigham worked it into its final resting place. He finished at 6:22 AM. The capstone was pronounced set. The band played the "Capstone March," composed for the occasion by William Pitt.

When the band finished, Brigham Young stepped to the edge of the scaffold and said in a loud booming voice for all to hear, "The last stone is now laid upon the temple, and I pray the Almighty in the name of Jesus to defend us in this place and sustain us . . . until the temple is finished and we all have our endowments."

The whole congregation then shouted, "Hosanna, Hosanna, Hosanna, to God and the Lamb, Amen, Amen, and Amen."

Brigham Young then dismissed the workmen for the rest of the day. The exterior walls were completed. Work on the roof, doors, windows, and interior would begin Monday. The congregation was dismissed, too.

Normally we worked six days a week, Sunday being our only day off. It was a real treat having a free Saturday. And it was only six thirty in the morning.

Pat and I headed back to the log cabin we shared, about half a mile north of the temple. In exchange for our work on the temple, the Church had given each of us a town lot a year earlier with the agreement that a free and clear deed would be registered in each of our names when the temple was completed. We had built the log cabin on Pat's lot with the understanding that we would build another on my lot when either of us married, or whenever we decided not to continue sharing the same cabin.

As we joined the throngs of people heading back to their homes and businesses, I didn't think to check to see which of the guards were remaining behind to guard the temple.

As we were sloshing back to the cabin, I suddenly became aware that Pat was more silent than usual. His normal good humor was missing.

"What you thinking about?" I asked.

Pat didn't say anything for awhile, then responded, "I've been thinking maybe it's time to begin that second cabin."

I loved his subtlety. "You making an announcement?"

"The lass hasn't said yes, but I think she will," he said with a wink.

"Wouldn't want an old pal sleeping in the rain," he continued. "Let's get the cabin started."

I remembered the first time I had visited the lot on the day it was given to me. It was about one acre in size, and it didn't take but a few minutes to decide exactly where the cabin should be built. There was a little knoll on the west of the lot where one had a perfect view of the new temple to the south, the Mississippi River to the west, a hardwood forest to the north, and seemingly endless fields of corn and wheat to the east.

Pat didn't agree with my selection of a cabin site. He pointed out that in his opinion the best place would be on the opposite or east side of the lot near the road access. There would be fewer problems getting out in the winter, more protection from the wind off the river, and probably a better chance of getting a good well close to the house. It didn't occur to him that it was my lot and my cabin. We were partners of a sort, living and working together, and he felt his opinion carried as much weight as mine.

We had discussed the matter on frequent occasions, each of us only becoming more entrenched in our conflicting opinions. As we approached the lot on that rainy morning in 1845, we both realized the difference would have to be resolved soon if we were to begin my cabin.

"We're going to build it on the knoll," I said firmly. "It's my lot, my cabin. That's where I want it."

"Let's get the logs cut and dragged in; then we'll decide where to build," said Pat, sensing the time wasn't right to talk me out of the knoll location.

When we reached the cabin we gathered our logging tools—axes, crosscut saw, and file—in preparation for heading to a nearby grove to cut house logs. With all the land being cleared for farming purposes, there was plenty of free timber for the taking. But we couldn't find the wedge, the tool for making sure the saw didn't bind or the tree didn't fall in the wrong direction.

We couldn't find it anywhere and were just finishing the second inch-by-inch search of the cabin when Caroline and Sarah suddenly appeared in the open doorway. They had attended the early morning capstone ceremony too, though we hadn't seen them in the huge crowd. They didn't have any teaching duties, it being Saturday.

Sizing up the situation immediately, Pat was the first to speak.

"Show Caroline your building lot, Dan," he began, obviously groping at the first idea that came to mind that might get him some time alone with Sarah. "See if she doesn't agree with me that the best building spot is on the east."

Suddenly I saw an opportunity to settle the building site problem once and for all.

"If she agrees with me that the west side, the knoll, is the best spot, will you agree that that's where the cabin will be built?" I asked, knowing he was in no mood to discuss such insignificant matters, not with Sarah Lange standing in the doorway.

Seeing I had no intention of leaving until he responded, and knowing I would continue the discussion if he didn't go along with my suggestion, Pat nodded his agreement that if Caroline liked the knoll, the discussion would end.

I headed out the door, inviting Caroline to come with me. Her boots were already muddy from the walk through the streets, so we headed straight out across the lot to the knoll.

The rain had stopped and the clouds were thinning, taking definition as the May sun tried to shine through. The rains had left the air smelling fresh and clean.

I told Caroline about our continuing discussion as to where my cabin should be built. I told her I hoped she would endorse my favorite spot on the knoll.

"And if I don't?" she challenged.

"Have you ever had your face pushed into the black Illinois mud?" I responded, enjoying the playful interchange. In fact, it was the first time since Red Leaf died that I found myself really enjoying the company of a woman.

"But I know you will like it," I assured her, as I took her hand to help her jump across a marshy puddle at the base of the knoll.

Just as we reached the top of the knoll, the morning sun found an opening in the thinning cloud cover and cast a brilliant glow over the rain-washed countryside. Ahead of us to the west, the Mississippi River glistened like a fat silver ribbon in the morning sun. A magnificent rainbow beginning on the glassy waters of the great river spanned over two-thirds of the horizon before disappearing in a dark green hardwood forest to the north. To our left the white limestone walls of the partially finished temple glowed in the new sunshine. Everywhere the fields and groves were green and fresh. Even the neighboring houses looked freshly washed. It was a perfect morning to gulp in the freshness of spring.

But something about the temple was different, something I couldn't quite put my finger on. Of course the workers had the day off, but something about the empty scaffolds made me feel uneasy.

I looked at Caroline. She too was looking at the temple, but rather than enjoying the beauty of the majestic structure in the morning sunshine, she had a worried expression on her face.

"Why aren't there any guards on the scaffolds?" she asked.

Suddenly I realized what was different about the temple. The guards were gone. When Brigham Young had dismissed the workers for the remainder of the day, apparently there had been a mix-up in assigning guard duty. The assignments for the day had not been made. I remembered that nobody had said anything to me about the guarding assignments over the weekend. That was unusual.

"Maybe the guards are on the other side of the building where we can't see them," I suggested, doubting that there was any truth in the idea. I felt a little chagrined that as one of the regular guards, an obvious oversight in duty assignments had to be brought to my attention by a pretty schoolteacher.

As we walked back to the cabin, I couldn't help but wonder why Caroline would be so aware of the guard situation at the temple. She was no ordinary woman.

"Well?" said Pat to Caroline in a cheery voice as we entered the cabin. "Don't you agree that the knoll is the wrong place to build a cabin?"

"I like the knoll," she responded without hesitation. "The view of the temple and river is breathtaking. That's where I would build, if it were up to me."

I liked the decisive nature of the statement, leaving no room for interpretation. Pat was beaten fair and square. The cabin would be built on the knoll.

Caroline didn't allow me any time to relish my victory.

"Don't you think you should do something about the guards not being on duty?" she asked in a serious tone. Again I found myself wondering why a pretty schoolteacher would be so concerned about guard assignments at the temple.

"You're right," I said, "I need to check it out." Then to Pat, "Did you find the wedge yet?"

"No," he said, and it was obvious that he and Sarah hadn't been looking for the wedge. It was obvious, too, by their nervous dispositions that they still had not reached a decision about the engagement.

"Come on, Caroline," I said. "Let's walk up to the temple to see what's happened to the guards. While we're there we'll pick up a wedge." There were several in Pat's tool box on the scaffold.

Caroline led the way out of the door into the muddy street.

Grabbing my rifle from behind the door, I followed.

"See you in about an hour," were my parting words to Pat and Sarah, both of whom seemed pleased that we were leaving again. Maybe they would have this engagement thing worked out by the time we returned.

While we were walking side by side up the muddy road, Caroline asked if the Mormons were practicing polygamy.

The question caught me by surprise. One just didn't talk about such things in Nauvoo. Sure, the turncoat John Bennett, and others, were selling books containing all kinds of lies about the Mormons and the so-called practice of spiritual wifery. But nothing had ever been said from the pulpit. Some of the young women were refusing to see young suitors for reasons no one could understand. But young women often did strange things, anyway.

"I don't know anything about polygamy," I said, and I was telling the truth. "I suppose that if the Lord commanded it, the Mormons would do it, but I haven't heard of any commandments like that."

"Are you sure you're not hiding something from me because I'm not a Mormon?" she asked directly.

"You're not a Mormon?" I asked in surprise.

"You didn't know?"

"Of course not," I said. "Why would anyone want to come to Nauvoo if they weren't Mormon?"

She walked along for a moment, gathering her thoughts, then responded in what appeared to be a very honest manner.

"I was writing for a newspaper in Philadelphia and just got tired of it. I wanted a change, and having heard so much about Nauvoo the last few years, how your people cleared an unwanted swamp to build the second largest city in the state, and all that stuff about the mobs and persecutions, the extermination order by Governor Boggs . . . Nauvoo sounded like a very exciting place, so I just decided to come here."

"No kidding!" I said. "Just like that! No wonder you are so different. No wonder you have so many questions about everything. Do you know much about the Church, the doctrine, I mean?"

"Just what I've read in the papers, but I'm learning quickly."

"I'd be glad to try to answer any questions you might have. In fact, I'd be willing to bet that with all your curiosity, you'll be joining the Church—if you stick around long enough," I ventured.

"Could happen," she responded without any particular tone in her voice. "But before I join, I'd sure like to know if there was any truth to all the talk about polygamy."

"Well," I said, spotting a chance to catch her off guard. "I suppose you'll find out soon enough—a long time before I'll know anything about it, for sure." I winked at her.

"And what do you mean by that?" she asked.

"You're a handsome woman," I explained, expecting to really stun her with my next comment. "Sufficient enticement to lure even the most secretive of polygamists out of hiding."

I had expected her to be outraged, offended, or at least a little embarrassed by my comment. Instead, she just looked calmly ahead, without comment, as if I had just made a very commonplace statement, something so old that it had already gone through her head a hundred times. Maybe it had. And she wasn't even a Mormon!

As we turned into an alley between several stores, taking a shortcut to the temple just a few hundred yards away, I wondered about Caroline Logan. She certainly was different than any woman I had ever met.

At the back of the alley our attention was attracted by three hot, steaming horses—two bays and a sorrel. They were just catching their breaths from what must have been a hard, fast ride. It was unusual that they were tied in the back of the alley. Anyone patronizing the stores would have tied their horses in front where riders could dismount directly onto the wooden walkway. Then it occurred to me that the stores were closed, as were all the businesses in town, to celebrate the setting of the capstone.

To make matters even more curious, the horses were tied very loosely to the rail, no knots, just a few loops of the reins. No one would tie a horse so loosely unless he intended to return soon, yet the stores were closed.

Determined to satisfy my curiosity, I walked closer to the horses, confident the muddy ground would tell me where the riders had gone. To my surprise, the boot marks didn't lead to one of the nearby buildings, but along a hedge of small trees toward the temple. Caroline and I followed, not for any particular reason other than that we were already headed in that direction. Soon the tracks were lost in the thousands of tracks left behind by those attending the capstone ceremony.

I had just begun to climb the ladder to the scaffold where Pat's tool box was resting, Caroline waiting at the foot of the ladder, when I smelled coal oil. The fact that the temple had not been guarded for several hours, the memory of the three steaming horses, the tracks leading to the temple, and now the unmistakable smell of coal oil led me to an undeniable conclusion that gave me a very sickening feeling. Arson!

I pointed my rifle in the air and pulled the trigger. Not only would the crack of my rifle be a call for reinforcements, I hoped it might scare off the arsonists before they had a chance to ignite the coal oil which I assumed was being poured over the piles of lumber.

Not wanting to waste precious seconds scampering down the ladder, and seeing I was only ten or twelve feet above the ground, I leaped free of the ladder.

Even before I hit the ground, falling to my knees in the soft mud, I knew exactly what I was going to do. Pushing the surprised Caroline against the temple wall, ordering her to be as inconspicuous as possible, I headed down the hill as fast as I could run toward the three horses. Without the horses there would be no getting away for the arsonists.

Upon reaching the hedge, I looked back and wasn't surprised to see three men running along the side of the temple toward me. There was no way they could catch me before I reached their horses unless they gunned me down, but none of them appeared to be carrying rifles, and I was far enough away to be a very unlikely target for their pistols. When they saw me they stopped, realizing they were cornered.

I leaped upon the nearest horse, a bay, urging it into the others. Pulling their reins free, the horses galloped out of the alley and down the street. By this time, Mormons were coming from everywhere to see what all the commotion was about.

"Mobbers trying to burn the temple!" I shouted, turning the horse up the street at a full gallop. "Mobbers at the temple!" I shouted for all to hear.

Then I remembered Caroline. She was at the temple, too, cornered with the mobbers. I reined the horse back in the direction of the temple, urging it to run even faster.

Black smoke was billowing from behind the temple, but even more alarming, the three mobbers were climbing the scaffold, dragging Caroline along with them. They climbed onto the first scaffold, pushed the ladder away, and huddled behind some surplus limestone blocks for protection. All three carried revolvers.

Hundreds of men were racing toward the temple, many of them armed. Some raced to the back to help put out the fire, while others formed a semicircle around the cornered arsonists.

"Don't shoot," I shouted. "They have a hostage."

How could I have been stupid enough to leave Caroline behind? She was a prisoner and it was my fault. The Mormons around me were discussing whether or not they should try to pick off the mobbers with their rifles. They didn't seem overly concerned with Caroline's safety, their biggest concern being to get the arsonists.

Soon the fire was out. Apparently they hadn't poured out very much coal oil when I sounded the alarm. That, combined with the wetness from the morning rains, saved the temple lumber. Those who had been fighting the fire gathered to the semicircle to witness the fate of the mobbers.

If they hadn't stumbled onto Caroline, I was confident a hundred riflemen would have filled the mobbers full of lead—just punishment for trying to burn the house of the Lord.

I was afraid the shooting was about to begin when Deputy Sheriff William Brown from Carthage announced that he had come to arrest the arsonists and take them to jail. Leading four horses, he walked up to the scaffold, single-handedly put the ladder back in place, and ordered the arsonists to come down.

I admired Brown's courage. He wasn't fooling anyone by his

law and order act. Everybody knew the criminals would be free within hours. But, whereas the Mormons were eager to gun down escaping arsonists, they were hesitant to shoot a deputy who was going through the motions of doing his job.

By this time, a Mormon authority had arrived and ordered the Mormons not to shoot. Leaving Caroline on the scaffold, the three arsonists mounted the horses and galloped away with the brave deputy.

Caroline was climbing down the ladder when I rode up to the scaffold. Figuring she didn't want to talk to the approaching men, I crowded the horse beside the ladder, allowing her to get behind me.

"Take me home, please," she asked in a loud but calm voice. "I want to be alone." The encounter with the mobbers certainly hadn't made her hysterical, as one might have expected.

After dropping her off, I headed toward the cabin. The bay horse was lively and well-behaved. I figured I'd keep him, and the saddle, too. I didn't figure anybody would contest my ownership, not around Nauvoo, anyway. Besides, I needed a horse to drag logs to my cabin site.

Chapter 9

It was easy to think about Caroline as I worked on my new cabin in the long summer evenings. Pat was supposed to help me as I had helped him with the other cabin, but now that he was engaged to Sarah Lange, he always seemed to have something that needed doing away from the cabin. I ended up doing most of the work by myself, but I didn't mind, and with the new bay horse to drag the logs, the cabin progressed quickly.

I knew I would miss Pat's cheerful company, and I didn't look forward to living alone. Knowing I had one of the most beautiful building sites in Nauvoo was comforting. The view of the temple, the river, and the distant fields and forests was always refreshing—but I felt an undeniable urge to have someone to share it with. A woman's touch would make my cabin a paradise. The right woman, of course. And as I worked, I found it increasingly easy to picture Caroline standing in the doorway to greet me when I came home from work. I could see her stirring a kettle of beef stew hanging from a kettle hook in the soon-to-be-built fireplace, fresh flowers in the window, a blue and white checkered tablecloth on the table. I could hear the humming of a contented woman, Caroline and I sitting on the porch after supper watching the sun set over the Mississippi River.

But it didn't take long to realize that something was wrong. After the narrow escape at the temple, Caroline avoided me, and I didn't know why. As I worked on the cabin, I supposed that something good might happen between us. We seemed to get along so well, and it was so easy to talk to one another. I was even beginning to feel that perhaps I had mourned Red Leaf's death long enough.

At first it was just little things. I would call on Caroline at the Lee House where she shared a room with Sarah. The first few times, she said she was behind on her lessons and needed to prepare for the next day of classes. I believed her. She was always polite and friendly, but somehow distant, a distance I hadn't noticed before the attempted temple burning.

Then one night when I stopped by to see her, she was already gone for the evening. I learned later from Pat that she had attended a party at the Parley P. Pratt residence. A few days later, she attended a party at John D. Lee's. The object of my affection had suddenly become a rising socialite. Through Pat and Sarah I heard that she was an excellent dancer, often twirling across the floor with some of the most prominent men in Nauvoo—men like John Taylor, Lorenzo Snow, John D. Lee, and even Brigham Young on several occasions.

Sometimes I compared my little, partially completed log cabin with the prominent homes where Caroline attended her parties—homes made from lumber and brick, with polished plank floors, large windows, gables, and long flower boxes. As much as I enjoyed building it, my little cabin wasn't much when compared to the nobler houses of Nauvoo.

I stopped calling on Caroline, figuring there was no sense in making a donkey out of myself. I figured Caroline and the prominent people of Nauvoo might look down their noses at my cabin, but I liked it. I had made it myself—felled, peeled, and worked every log into place. Someday maybe I would build a brick or frame house, like those where the parties were held, but for now I liked my little cabin. I only wished Caroline had similar feelings.

While working on the temple each day, I managed to keep up on the latest news of the exciting events occurring in and around Nauvoo—events that were making history and keeping the community in turmoil.

The attempted burning of the temple was quickly forgotten when the judge in Burlington, Iowa—above Montrose on the other side of the river—found William and Stephen Hodge guilty in the murder of a Mennonite preacher and his son-in-law. The Hodge brothers were Mormons, but they weren't the churchy kind. They spent more time in saloons than worship services, hanging out with the likes of Bill Hickman and Porter Rockwell. But whereas Hickman and Rockwell were defenders of the faith, using guns if necessary, the Hodges were more involved in their own version of the law of consecration. They consecrated cattle, horses, whiskey, guns, and anything else of value that Missourians and gentiles didn't keep a close eye on.

Before his death, Joseph Smith cautioned the people about stealing from gentiles. He said a man who would steal from a gentile would also steal from his brother—but his advice was not remembered by many, at least not by the Hodges.

I didn't figure Joseph's warning applied to horses belonging to mobbers in the act of burning the temple.

Reportedly the Hodge brothers killed the two Mennonites for a bag containing four hundred dollars. Mormons usually stuck together, protecting each other from the heavy and often unjust hand of gentile judges and lawyers. Most everyone was surprised when Brigham Young turned the Hodge brothers over to the Iowa authorities.

An interesting complication to the whole affair was the murder of Irwin Hodge, older brother to Stephen and William, on the streets of Nauvoo shortly after the guilty verdict had been reached. Just before his death he had warned the Iowa authorities that Brigham Young would be coming to rescue the Hodge brothers.

On the evening before the scheduled hanging in Burlington, I was seated on a stump beside my cabin, chisel in one hand and mallet in the other, splitting cedar shingles for the roof, when I was startled by a female voice. It was Caroline, and she seemed her old friendly self.

"I can't believe it's almost finished!" she exclaimed, sounding like she really meant it.

I showed her around, explained how the logs were notched together, how the joists were placed just right to keep the sides from bowing out, and how the newly split shingles would keep the bad weather out. She seemed pleased and even excited with the progress, as if it were her own cabin. Having already concluded that she wanted nothing to do with me, I was totally bewildered by her behavior.

"Caroline," I said, pausing a moment to get her to look at me and give me her full attention. "Why did you come here?"

She looked surprised, not sure how to respond.

"You never have time to see me when I call," I continued. "You're attending every party in town. Why are you here?"

She just looked at me, not responding. She seemed taken aback, surprised—as if she suddenly realized something about me she hadn't known before. I began to regret that I had spoken so bluntly.

When she finally spoke, she was as forward as I had been. She didn't make excuses or apologies. She didn't attempt to explain her behavior—her avoidance of me, the parties. Her words were blunt and to the point, as mine had been.

"Will you take me to the hanging tomorrow?"

Chapter 10

Joseph Smith's warning that stealing from the mob was wrong was tough counsel to follow, especially for people who had seen their homes burned, their cattle driven off, their crops trampled, and their women ravished. When the Nauvoo Charter was revoked by the state of Illinois, shortly after the death of Joseph, and the Saints lost all hope of justice through the courts, Mormon men began to organize into secret bands. One of the best-known groups, called the Danites, was organized before Joseph's death.

At first the secret groups were mainly concerned with defending the Mormons from the mob, but they soon discovered it was next to impossible to provide an adequate defense—not knowing when and where the mob would strike. It was customary for the defenders to arrive after the damage had been done and the mob had disappeared into the night.

Frustrated at their inability to defend their people, the Danites and others began to seek revenge against suspected mob leaders and participants. And, of course, as they struck back, they found themselves confiscating enemy goods—guns, food, money, and other items of value that were then generally consecrated to the Church.

Some of the booty was dispersed among the raiders, first for expenses, then compensation for risk. As the Church received less and less of the stolen goods, the Mormon raiders experienced unprecedented prosperity. Stealing from gentiles was significantly more profitable than farming, and more exciting.

So it was with Stephen and William Hodge. They had "consecrated" a small fortune in gentile goods, a good portion of which was hidden in the river bottoms near Nauvoo, their robbers' haven.

It is hard to tell how long their little business would have prospered had they stuck to stealing, but when they murdered the Mennonite preacher and his son-in-law for a purse containing four hundred dollars, Brigham Young had had enough. He had commanded the people again and again to cease the stealing, but his admonishments were pretty much ignored.

The people needed a stronger sermon than could be preached from the pulpit. When the Iowa authorities asked Brigham Young for help in extraditing the Hodge brothers to Iowa, Brigham Young, to the amazement of both gentiles and Mormons, cooperated with them and the Hodges were taken to Burlington to stand trial. Throughout the trial the Hodges claimed religious persecution, but they were eventually found guilty of the murder of the two Mennonites and sentenced to death by hanging.

The upcoming hanging of the Hodge brothers was a landmark execution in that the Mormons had willingly given up two of their members without the typical organized resistance. How many more such executions would follow, now that Brigham Young had opened the gate? Many wondered if Brigham Young might have a change of heart at the last minute and send in the Nauvoo Legion to rescue the Hodge brothers. The upcoming hanging was the single most talked about subject in the upper Mississippi.

Realizing the hanging was the biggest thing ever to take place in Burlington, city fathers gave Sheriff John McKenny an unprecedented four hundred dollars, plus an additional fifteen dollars for the finest hemp rope, with the orders that the hanging was to be the best ever in the Iowa Territory.

The city fathers weren't disappointed. The sheriff erected the gallows in a hollow west of town on the Mount Pleasant Road. The valley formed a perfect amphitheater, the gallows in the center, in perfect view for those seated on the surrounding hillside. No movement could be made, or word spoken, that all could not see and hear.

Caroline and I arrived at the amphitheater about an hour before the hanging was scheduled to begin. We had left Nauvoo early that morning, before daybreak, on horseback. After crossing the river on a flatboat, we headed north along the Burlington Road.

To my amazement, there were already thousands of people there ahead of us. Most were gathered in small groups discussing the upcoming event. And more were arriving by the minute. A glance down the road toward Montrose revealed a steady stream of wagons and horses. I had no doubt there would be at least as many people in attendance as at the capstone ceremony, maybe ten or twelve thousand.

"Isn't it interesting to see how men will come so far to see men killed?" observed Caroline, as we dismounted and tied our horses to a dogwood tree.

"And women too," I added, as we made ourselves comfortable on the open hillside. Although the great majority of the people gathering for the hanging were men, there were a few women present. Most of the women, however, seemed to be of the dance hall variety from Montrose or Keokuk. None of the Mormon women from Nauvoo had come, at least not any that I had seen or heard about, except for Caroline.

"Why did you want me to bring you here?" I asked.

"I suppose it's the journalist in me," she responded easily, without any forethought.

"You going to write a story about it?"

"Probably not right away, but someday. History is being made here today. Kind of an ugly chapter, perhaps. Still, I want to be an eye witness."

"But why me?" I asked. "You've been meeting some pretty prominent Mormons. I'm sure many of them are here. Why didn't you come with one of them?"

Suddenly Caroline was smiling as she looked at me. I tried to remember what I had said that she might find amusing, but before I could reach any conclusions, she said, "Are you jealous?"

Her comment caught me by surprise, but I responded quickly. "Of course not. Why should I be?"

"You are jealous!" she concluded, putting her hand on my arm.

I looked away, upset with myself for being so stupid, feeling I was being played with, teased. I wished I could understand this Caroline Logan, and why I let her use me.

She apparently sensed my disgust and began to flatter me with how I made her feel safe, especially out in the wild . . . but I didn't hear anything else she said.

Not more than fifty yards down the slope from me hobbled a familiar form along the side of the hill. He used a hickory cane to compensate for a wooden stump on his uphill leg. He was better dressed than the last time I had seen him—the night he stepped into the bear trap I had tied to the rear wheel of his buggy. It was Dick Boggs.

Chapter 11

When the bear trap that was tied to the rear wheel of the buggy clamped shut on Dick Boggs's leg and the buggy horse stampeded, dragging Boggs off into the night, I didn't expect to ever see him alive again. Six years had passed, but suddenly there he was, not fifty yards away, hobbling across the hill, a wooden stump in place of the foot that had been caught in the bear trap.

My mind flooded with old memories—the election day in Gallatin when Boggs tried to castrate me with his knife, the escaped slave Ike and I running through the woods with Boggs and his dogs on our trail, and the day Boggs gunned down my cow on the streets of Far West. But I had had my revenge. Setting that bear trap next to his buggy had been a mean trick. But when the steel jaws clanked shut and the horse ran off, dragging Boggs behind it, I felt like he was only getting what he deserved.

I wondered if he would recognize me as the kid who had lured him out of his buggy and into the trap. I was only sixteen at the time and had changed a lot since then. I was a man now, able to whip him soundly in a fair fight should the occasion present itself.

He hadn't changed at all, except for the wooden leg and better clothes—including a white shirt, black coat, and beaver hat. A hanging was a special occasion; a man had to dress his best.

There was no doubt in my mind that Boggs would try to kill me if he recognized me. But at fifty yards, and after six years, I didn't figure there was any chance of a confrontation.

"See that man down there with the wooden leg?" I asked Caroline, pointing to Boggs.

"Yes," she said somewhat guardedly, then asked, "Do you know him?"

"Name is Dick Boggs. Killed my cow at Far West when I was sixteen. Meanest Mormon-hater you'll ever see."

She didn't say anything.

"He'd try to kill me if he knew I was here."

"Why?" she asked cautiously.

"I did it—the wooden leg."

I expected her to be very curious about how I had caused him to lose the leg, but all she said was, "Oh."

Caroline wasn't her usual curious self when it came to Dick Boggs. I wondered why, but not for long. The hanging was about to begin.

By now the natural amphitheater was crowded with people, mostly men, mostly gentiles, although I recognized some familiar Mormon faces. There must have been nearly ten thousand in attendance, and a good number of them were still wondering if Brigham Young would attempt to free William and Stephen Hodge.

As I mentioned earlier, Sheriff McKenny was determined to make the hanging one of the most spectacular events in the short history of the Iowa Territory. He wasn't about to just hang the Hodges and send everyone home.

First, a local preacher led the congregation in the singing of a hymn, followed by an opening prayer by another preacher.

Then the prisoners emerged from the back of a covered wagon that had carried them to the amphitheater. There were chains on their hands and feet, but the gasps of surprise that echoed from hill to hill were caused by something else.

The brothers were dressed in strange white robes.

"Temple robes," were the words being whispered through the crowd.

I hadn't seen temple robes before, but I knew the women in Nauvoo were busy sewing the special temple clothing that would be used once the temple was completed. The people who had been through the Kirtland temple were buried in their temple robes, so most Mormons were familiar with the look of the robes. But to see two thieves wearing the sacred garb on the way to the gallows was a shocking sight. The brothers surely were insistent in trying to convince everyone that they were going to the gallows for religious reasons, not for any crime they committed.

Stephen Hodge was brought forward first, not to be hanged, but to speak to the crowd.

"You are sending two innocent men to an ignominious and shameful death. You are hanging us because we are Mormons," were his last words.

The prosecuting attorney spoke next, detailing the murder of the two Mennonites. His speech was followed by another hymn. Then one of the preachers gave a fiery sermon on the evils of Mormonism. Last of all the mayor spoke, among other things thanking everyone for coming to Burlington and putting his growing town on the map.

After two hours of speeches and songs, it was finally time for the hanging. The Hodge brothers were led to the top of the scaffold and blindfolded. There was a long moment of silence as if someone was waiting for the Nauvoo Legion to come to the rescue. But nothing happened. Apparently Brigham Young agreed with the court findings that the Hodge brothers really were guilty of the murders and deserved just punishment.

The nooses were slipped over the blindfolded heads and pulled tight. When the sheriff gave the signal by dropping his hand, the platform gave way beneath the two brothers. As soon as the kicking stopped and the bodies were still, the crowd began to disperse.

A big man seated next to us was one of the first to get to his feet. After brushing off the seat of his pants, he said that this was by far the best hanging he had ever seen, and he had attended many.

Caroline didn't put her hands over her face as I thought she might when the brothers were dropped through the scaffold. She was a brave girl, taking in every detail.

In silence we moved with the crowd toward the waiting horses.

While contemplating the events of the day, a strangely familiar voice called Caroline by name.

I thought it was one of her friends from Nauvoo until I spotted Dick Boggs pushing through the crowd. He didn't see or recognize me, or even seem to notice that Caroline and I were together. She wasn't holding onto my arm or walking close to me.

Caroline was looking ahead as if she hadn't heard him speak, but there was no question but what he was pushing through the crowd toward her.

My first reaction was to turn my back and disappear among the nearby men, but there was no way I could leave Caroline alone with the likes of Dick Boggs. Besides, I was very curious to find out how he knew her.

"Caroline, it's me, Dick Boggs," he said, when he finally got in front of her.

She just looked at him, without saying anything, a look of disbelief on her face.

Then Boggs looked at me, realizing for the first time that I was with Caroline. First, there was a questioning look on his face, then one of recognition.

"Frank," he called back through the crowd. "Get the boys, quick."

Then he reached under his coat. I wasn't even sure he had recognized me, but I wasn't about to wait and see what he was reaching for. Instead of trying to jump out of the way, or lunging upon him as a white man might have done, I instinctively used a trick taught me by the Ute Neuwafe. Keeping one foot firmly on the ground for balance and thrust, I struck Boggs with the other foot, a forceful blow to the belly, driving him to the ground. While he was still gasping for air, I leaped upon him and wrestled away the pistol that he was trying to get out from under his coat.

I shoved the pistol barrel under his chin and waited until he caught his breath, then growled, "Next time I see you, I'll kill you."

I could see the fear and hate in his reddened eyes as he looked into my face.

"And if you ever show your ugly face in Nauvoo, you can plan on feeding the catfish with the rest of your ugly carcass," I continued, surprised at how mean and threatening I could sound.

Then I stood up, not sure what to do next. A few men had gathered around, expecting they might see a fight, but apparently not very many had noticed the fracas. Caroline was gone. Then I spotted Frank Worrell and two other men racing toward me.

Tucking Boggs's pistol in my belt, I headed for the horses as fast as I could run.

"Stop him!" shouted Worrell.

"Shoot him!" screamed Boggs.

People stopped and looked, trying to figure out what was happening. Only one man tried to stop me. I shoved him out of the way without hardly slowing down.

Upon reaching the horses I discovered that Caroline was already mounted and holding my horse's bridle. I leaped into the saddle, and soon we were weaving our way at a full gallop through the wagons and riders. It wasn't long until we were out of range of the shouting Boggs.

I could hardly wait until Caroline and I were alone and I could ask her some questions—like how she knew Dick Boggs and why she hadn't said anything when I first pointed him out to her before the hanging.

Chapter 12

There was a stiff breeze from the west keeping our horses cool as we galloped down the road toward Montrose. Occasionally I looked back to see if we were being followed, but after four or five miles—and still no sign of Boggs or Worrell—we slowed our pace to a brisk walk, allowing the winded horses to catch their breath.

We were alone on the road now, having established a substantial lead on the rest of the people coming home from the hanging. The hanging had lasted longer than expected, and we hoped we could make the river crossing before dark.

Caroline didn't wait for me to ask her about Boggs and how she knew him. She explained that Boggs's name had been given to her by a friend when she left Philadelphia. The friend had asked her to stop and see Boggs at his plantation near Keokuk before going to Nauvoo. Her friend had been concerned about Caroline living among the Mormons and thought that Boggs might tip her off to some of the dangers in Nauvoo.

"Well, did he?" I asked.

"Oh yes," she responded lightly. "He warned me about spiritual wifery and how anyone who disagreed with the leaders could end up in the river as catfish bait."

"What did he say about spiritual wifery?" I asked, curious as to what Boggs would have to say about polygamy.

"Only that if a man started to court me, I'd better make sure he didn't already have a wife." She paused.

"Well?"

"What do you mean?"

"Have you been courted by any married men?"

"I don't know. Are you married?"

"I'm not a polygamist, if that's what you mean."

"Are there polygamists in Nauvoo?" she asked, suddenly getting very serious.

"The leaders have never admitted it from the pulpit or in print, but I suspect something is going on."

"Why?"

"All the books and articles being published all over the country must be based, at least partially, on the truth, I would guess. A lot of lies are circulating around, for sure."

"Would you take a second wife?"

"I don't have a first," I said, avoiding her question.

"Sarah said you were married to an Indian girl in the Rocky Mountains."

I was surprised she knew about my marriage to Red Leaf. I was surprised Sarah knew about it. I supposed Pat told her. I didn't talk much about Red Leaf. People, even most Mormons, found it hard to swallow that one could be happily married and in love with a "squaw."

"She was Ute."

"Was?"

"She died."

"I'm sorry."

We rode in awkward silence for a while. My thoughts were on Red Leaf and the horrible events leading to her death. I didn't want to talk about it, especially not with Caroline. Though friendly and warm on the surface, there was something cool and calculating in her nature. I couldn't put my finger on it. I had no reason to doubt her story about Boggs, but I had the unmistakable feeling that there were things—important things—about Caroline Logan that she was keeping from me.

Nevertheless, there were some things I liked about her, especially the way she handled herself after the hanging, when I got in the fight with Boggs. Had she not thought quickly, getting the horses ready for a quick retreat, I might have found myself with more trouble than I could handle. Red Leaf would have done something like that too, I figured.

It was nearly dark and beginning to rain when we reached the ferry landing, across the river and a little upstream from Nauvoo. The ferryman, a sour-faced fellow with a gray stubble face, was reluctant to make a crossing without a full load. He apparently had expected to collect some good fares from people returning from the hanging, but the event had lasted longer than expected, and we were the only ones to reach the ferry before dark.

"You'll have plenty of business tomorrow," I said, trying to cheer him up.

"I wish," he replied sourly. "They'll take the steamer rather than stay over in Iowa, leaving me empty-handed."

He finally agreed to take us, but he demanded two dollars, double the regular fare. Reluctantly I gave him the money and began to load our horses while he went over to the little corral to get his horses. The flat-bottomed ferry was powered by a team of horses walking on a treadmill.

As he was leading the team to the ferry, three riders suddenly appeared on the wagon path coming from the west. The rain had not yet washed away the white foam rings around the edges of their horses' saddle blankets. The horses had come a long way, in a hurry.

One of the riders was bigger, fatter than the others. Suddenly there was a sickening feeling in my stomach. Caroline and I hadn't hurried enough. Dick Boggs and his men had taken a different route in an effort to get ahead of us and cut us off before we reached the ferry. They had failed, but not by much. We were still in big trouble.

"Hey," I shouted to the ferryman, who had stopped to look at the approaching riders. "Hurry up, let's get going."

"Hold on," he shouted back. "Paying customers coming from the west."

There was no time for talk. With our horses already loaded on the ferry, there were no odds unloading the horses and trying to get away down the road. The boat was our only chance, and the treadmill horses were not in place.

I drew the pistol, the one I had taken away from Boggs, and pointed it at the startled ferryman.

"The catfish will be chewing on your carcass tonight," I shouted, "if those horses aren't hitched to the treadmill in thirty seconds."

He looked in my direction, an astonished look on his face, but he didn't move.

"Now!" I ordered, cocking back the hammer on the pistol.

He moved, but not like I thought he would. Instead of bringing the horses to the ferry, he dropped the reins and dove behind a hill of sand and dirt.

My first thought was to leap from the boat, get the horses, and hitch them up myself, but when I looked toward the west, Boggs and his men were just a short distance away and quickly closing in. There was no time to hitch the horses.

Caroline was one step ahead of me, already untying the ferry. As soon as the rope was free, we each grabbed a long pole and began pushing the ferry out into the river. The rain was coming down hard now.

We hadn't pushed out more than thirty or forty feet when the water became too deep for the poles to be effective. As the current began to sweep us downstream, I untied my horse and began to coax it onto the treadmill. It didn't want to cooperate, even when Caroline began beating it on the rear with her pole.

A glance toward shore revealed that Boggs and his men had arrived and were dismounting from their animals. Boggs was shouting something to me, but with the roar of the wind and rain, and the waves beating against the side of the boat, I couldn't hear what he was saying. I turned back to the horse, pulling desperately at the reins. It was almost dark.

The horse didn't budge until Boggs fired his gun. Then it reared over backwards, blood spurting from a hole in its neck. It landed on the railing, then rolled over into the river. The other horse panicked, breaking its reins and leaping over the railing behind its mortally wounded companion.

The antics of the horses nearly capsized the boat. All the movement made us an impossible target as two more shots were fired. Caroline and I dove behind the railing to avoid the bullets.

Another dozen shots were fired before the muddy Mississippi finally carried us out of range and out of sight in the rain-drenched darkness.

Chapter 13

The west wind pushed us away from the bank toward the middle of the river, then gradually subsided as the rain intensified. Our rain gear had been tied to the back of the saddles and had gone overboard with the horses. There being no shelter on the little ferry boat, we were soon soaked.

Fortunately the humid summer rains of the upper Mississippi River Valley aren't nearly as chilling as the rains in the Rocky Mountains. Nevertheless, both of us were soon shivering in the total blackness of the night storm.

In an effort to keep warm, we climbed onto the treadmill. With our hands on the rail we got the treadmill moving, just enough to keep us warm. If the night had been clear, allowing us to see either bank, we could have paddled the boat toward shore. But in the total blackness of the storm we lost all sense of direction. We couldn't tell if our paddle wheels were pushing us upstream, downstream, toward one of the shores, or if we were merely traveling in circles, but we kept it moving.

After a time it seemed the treadmill was becoming more difficult to keep going. At first I thought it just seemed that way because we were getting tired, but it wasn't until we decided to sit down for a breather that we discovered the bottom of the boat was covered with water—more than one would expect from the rainfall. Running my hands along the side of the boat near the water level, I quickly discovered two holes where Boggs's bullets had apparently passed through the side boards.

"We're sinking," I said. "Taking water through the bullet holes. Wish we had some buckets to bail the water out."

Caroline didn't respond. Things were looking bad for us, and I half expected her to start crying, as one would well expect a woman to do in such a desperate situation. I was ready to put my arms around her and comfort her as our boat sank. There was enough iron in the ferry—used in construction of the treadmill—that I didn't figure there was any way the boat would stay afloat once it filled with water.

While feeling for the bullet holes I had bumped against a floating wooden box, one that had been situated in front of the rudder as a seat for the ferryman when crossing the river. I figured that once the boat went down, Caroline and I could hang onto the box while waiting for the dawn, at which time we would swim toward the nearest shore.

Suddenly I became aware of the sound of tearing cloth, but before I could ask Caroline what she was doing, she said, "Take your boots off."

"Not about to start swimming as long as this tub is floating," I responded, thinking she wanted us to abandon ship.

"Take 'em off and start bailing while I plug up the holes with pieces of this handkerchief." Again I could hear the tearing noise.

I felt foolish. While I had been getting ready to abandon ship, Caroline had figured out a way to save the boat. I sat down on the edge of the treadmill, removed my boots, and began bailing out the water while Caroline leaned over the side of the boat and shoved wadded up pieces of her torn handkerchief into the bullet holes. I remember thinking how smart she was pushing the wads of cloth in from the outside, instead of the inside, so the pressure of the water would push the wads more firmly in place.

While the pieces of cloth didn't completely stop the flow of water into the boat, they decreased it sufficiently to make my bailing productive. Twenty minutes later, most of the water was back in the river.

After I had finished bailing out the water and was sitting on the edge of the treadmill, wondering whether or not to put my boots back on, Caroline sat down beside me, close. Her shivering had stopped. I was still warm from bailing out the water. I put my arm around her.

The rain continued, but with less intensity. There was still no wind.

"What do you think will happen?" Caroline asked in a concerned, but calm voice.

"I suppose we'll paddle this tub to shore, as soon as there's enough light to see where the shore is."

"Then what?"

"We'll probably find a nearby farm house just in time for breakfast."

"I'd like two pieces of bacon," said Caroline. "And three eggs, some fried potatoes and onions."

"And some toasted bread, spread thick with butter and huckleberry jam," I responded.

"And a big cup of buttermilk."

For the first time since boarding the boat, we both realized how hungry and tired we were. It had been a long day, with the lengthy ride to Burlington, the hanging, the fight with Boggs, the flight. We had enjoyed a brief snack on the trail while we were riding, but that was all. Just some buttered bread, apples, and boiled beef. Most of our food was in the saddle bags when the horses went overboard.

Sleep eventually comes, even to the cold, wet, and hungry.

Caroline and I were sitting on the treadmill, leaning against the side of the boat, dozing restlessly in the nighttime drizzle, when the front of the boat was suddenly struck by something hard. As we were thrown to the deck, there was the sound of splintering wood. The boat tipped sharply to one side, then all was still, except for the gentle rocking of the boat.

We could hear the lapping of water against a rock shore. Still unable to see in the blackness of the night, I carefully crawled over the side of the boat, my feet finding a rocky bottom under about a foot of water. Taking my hand, Caroline crawled out beside me, and together we carefully picked our way through the rocks, out of the water, and up a sandy beach into a thick grove of trees. Where the trees were thickest, we crawled into a bed of half-dry leaves and waited for the dawn.

Chapter 14

As soon as it was light enough to see, we crawled out of our bed of damp leaves and pine needles to see where we were. The rain had stopped, but the heavy, gray clouds still covered the sky. It appeared more rain might be coming.

Our clothing was still wet from the drenching the night before. We had slept little and eaten nothing. We were cold, hungry, and very tired.

The first thing I noticed was that the boat was gone. We had neglected to pull it farther up on the rocks the night before. Apparently, without its passengers, the lightened craft worked its way free of the rocks and was carried away by the muddy Mississippi.

The loss of the boat wasn't important until we discovered that we were on the upstream tip of a midriver island—over a half a mile of river between us and either shore. It was a small island, not more than two hundred feet wide, maybe three hundred feet long, and thickly wooded—maple, ash, dogwood, and a few pine trees. As far as we could see, both the distant shores were thickly wooded, too, with no signs of civilization—no cabins, roads, fields, or columns of smoke.

"What are we going to do?" asked Caroline, her voice still calm, but worried.

I didn't admit it to Caroline, but I was rather pleased with the situation. In the civilized society of Nauvoo she had played games with me, intimidated me, and even used me—and because of my feelings for her, I was an easy victim.

In civilized society she had a confidence I lacked. Part of it was my lack of education and part was my being away in the Rocky Mountains so long. When I returned to Nauvoo, I discovered there were a lot of things I didn't understand about civilized living. I made mistakes and quickly lost much of the confidence I had gained while living with the Utes. For example, it was a much-appreciated compliment to tell a squaw she looked plump and well-fed. It made her feel like her man cared enough for her to be a diligent provider. But the first and last time I offered the same compliment to a Nauvoo matron, I made an enemy for life and became the subject of many laughs from the men for weeks to come.

Caroline, on the other hand, was completely at ease in society. Her good looks and pleasant personality enabled her to use people like me for her personal gain. She was confident and sure of herself.

But now we were in my territory. The trees, the streams, the hills, and the animals were my friends. Even on this small island, the land would provide our basic needs for warmth, food, and shelter. Old memories of survival in the Rocky Mountains flooded into a dormant part of my being. In spite of the nagging cold and gnawing hunger after a mostly sleepless night, my mind became alert, my senses keen, and my heart happier than it had felt in a long time. It was that good feeling of coming home after having been away a long time. And Caroline was with me. That made everything better. My only concern was that we might be rescued too soon, before I had a chance to get acquainted with the real Caroline Logan.

"What do you think we should do?" she persisted, sounding more concerned than before. She was beginning to shiver in the cool morning breeze.

"First, we'll build a nice, warm fire," I explained with a friendly smile.

"But we don't have any matches," she protested.

"Then we'll cook some food," I continued, ignoring her mention of matches. I looked up at the clouds. "Then we'll whip together a nice warm shelter to keep us comfortable and dry in the next storm."

"Shouldn't we try to get to shore?"

"Our best bet, I think, would be to catch an upriver steamer as it passes the island. Would take us right to Nauvoo. Ought to be one coming along in a week or so."

"A week? But . . ."

"Come on, let's get that fire going." I took her by the hand, and we headed for the middle of the island.

The trees, brush, and grasses were soaked and dripping, and soon we were as wet as we had been the night before. But it felt good to walk, to stretch, to get the blood pumping. One could almost taste the freshness of the cool, rain-washed air.

Near the center of the island, where the forest was thickest, we discovered a small, grassy clearing, a perfect place for our camp. Letting go of Caroline's hand, I moved among the largest and bushiest trees, carefully examining the east sides for dry twigs and moss. The storm had come in from the west the night before, so I figured the east sides of the trees would be driest. It wasn't long until I had an armful of dry twigs, moss, and bark.

Borrowing one of Caroline's boot laces and using my pocketknife, I quickly built a bow with the accompanying spindle and notched baseboard. After fashioning a nest from the driest moss and placing a piece of bark beneath the notch in the baseboard, I began stroking the bow back and forth with increasing speed, the spindle whirling easily in the notch. I was pleased that I had remembered this primitive skill so well.

Caroline squealed with delight when a tiny stream of smoke emerged from the baseboard. I ignored her response, realizing the task at hand required all my attention and that the hardest part of the job was still ahead.

Faster and faster the spindle whirled, until a conical pile of ashes, about the size of a pea, had accumulated on the piece of bark. Suddenly I dropped the bow and spindle, carefully picked up the piece of bark, and dropped the spark into the nest of moss, quickly closing the moss around the spark. Then, holding the nest close to my lips, I puffed ever so gently.

At first there was no smoke, then just a little. I puffed a little harder. More smoke. Soon lots of smoke. I puffed harder and harder. Suddenly the nest burst into flame. Quickly I lowered it to a smooth spot on the ground and began piling on the dry twigs and bark. Soon we were warming our hands over a blazing fire. Caroline insisted on helping me gather a plentiful supply of limbs from the driest places beneath the biggest trees. Soon our soaked clothing was steaming before the comfortable warmth of the fire.

"What would you like for breakfast?" I asked lightly.

"Eggs, salt pork, buttermilk, toast, butter, jam . . ."

"How about some fresh catfish?"

"But we don't have any fishhooks and line," she protested, suddenly serious again.

"We didn't have any matches, either," I suggested, holding my hands closer to the warm fire. "Get yourself dry, keep the fire going, and I'll see if I can't catch us a little breakfast."

I headed into the woods, my destination the river. I followed the shore until I came to a partial inlet, about waist deep, clogged with fallen logs and other debris from the river—just the kind of place I was looking for. Without hesitation I waded in and began working my way along the bank, feeling carefully under fallen logs and in underwater holes in the bank.

The escaped slave Ike had called this kind of fishing "noodling" when he had taught me how to do it in the back-waters of Shoal Creek near Far West, Missouri, when I was fifteen. In the murky water, the fish didn't see you approaching their resting places, and if you touched them under the belly, they usually stayed still, enjoying having their undersides stroked.

Finding a fish, you gradually worked your hands toward the mouth and gills, tickling all the time, then suddenly grabbing the gills between thumb and forefinger and jerking the fish out of the water.

Ike had warned me about the dangers of noodling, too. Snapping turtles and eels hid in the same kinds of places. The turtles could take off a finger or thumb before you knew what was happening, and the eels could bite viciously with their slimy needle-like teeth. Such bites usually resulted in severe infection and swelling. Ike told me about a friend of his who reached under a floating log and grabbed a water moccasin by the tail. When he realized he had a snake, he let go. That was a mistake. The reptile shot across the top of the log and bit him on the neck. He died.

The water was too murky for spearing, and without hook and line, I had no choice but to noodle.

I hadn't been in the water more than a minute or two when I touched something alive and slippery under a washed out portion of the bank. Instinctively I jerked my hand back, waited a moment, then reached forward, very slowly. I touched it again—cool, slippery flesh. Still, yet alive. Slippery, yet firm. It was a fish, all right, and a big one.

I began gently tickling the belly with both hands while I slowly moved my body into position near its head. I didn't know what kind of fish it was, but from the firmness, I figured it was probably a catfish or bass. I began to worry that maybe it was too big. From the tickling I figured it to be almost two feet long, maybe ten pounds. Caroline and I could feast all day on this one fish, if I could only get it on the bank.

As soon as I was sure where the gills were, I took a deep breath, paused for a moment, grabbed with all my strength, thrusting my fingers into the gills. The fish exploded in an effort to break free, but my fingers had pushed through to the middle, and I was determined not to release my death grip. Using my free hand to control the thrashing of the fish, I scrambled for the bank, where I heaved the big catfish into the grass and leaves.

After knocking it senseless with a club and pushing a stick through one of the gills and into the soft ground to prevent it from wiggling back into the water, I knelt down by the water to wash the mud and blood from my hands and arms. I could hardly wait to show Caroline the big fish, and I had caught it so quickly. I knew she would be very pleased; we were both so hungry.

Then I wondered if this one fish would be enough to last us through the day. Maybe I should catch another before heading back.

Then I wouldn't have to search for food again until the next day. Two fish would be more impressive than one, anyway. I waded back into the water toward some logs where I had not yet fished.

Luck was with me. I felt something soft and slimy under the first log. Again, it didn't try to get away, but it was different. Softer. Maybe too soft.

I hesitated a moment, then began to pull my hand away. But I was too slow, too late. Two rows of needle-like teeth sank deep into my wrist.

I jerked my hand back, out of the water, and looked directly into the beady eyes of an eel. He was coated with slime and murk, like he hadn't moved from beneath that log in years. His cloudy eyes looked determined, like he wasn't about to let go of my wrist, but I grabbed the back of his head with my free hand, clenching my fist tight and jerking back and forth until he finally let go.

I swung him around my head once and slapped his soft body with all my might against the firm surface of the log. I did it a second time, and a third, before slinging the limp body out into the river.

Carefully I washed the slime from my hands, watching the blood ooze from the tiny holes. I remembered what Ike had said about the infection and swelling resulting from eel bites and hoped he was wrong.

I climbed back upon the bank, picked up the catfish, and headed back to camp, more sober than I had been just a few minutes earlier.

Chapter 15

When I saw how excited Caroline was about the fish, I decided not to tell her about the eel. The bleeding had stopped, and I hoped there would be no infection.

Without cleaning the fish, I filleted out one side and set the long strip of white flesh on a clean piece of bark, which I propped up beside the fire. Then I looked up at the darkening clouds.

"Rain's coming," I said.

"You've built fire without matches, caught fish without hooks," said Caroline. "Now tell me how you are going to build a shelter without materials and tools."

"Tonight you will sleep in comfort in a Ute war lodge," I responded, then proceeded to explain how we would build it starting with a large tripod consisting of three long, strong poles. Next we would cover the tripod with brush and strips of bark in a way that would repel the rain and wind. It would be similar to the wickiup that Red Leaf and I had shared at the foot of the great Mount Timpanogos.

Together we dragged three long poles out of the woods, lashed them together on the ground with green willows, then pushed them upward to form a tripod. The fire was on the east side where the opening would be. I explained to Caroline that Indians usually had the openings to their dwellings on the east to face the rising sun, but there was a practical reason, too—the prevailing storms usually came from the west, and it was good to have the storm at your back.

By the time the tripod was in place, the air was filled with the aroma of roasting fish. I pulled the steaming fish away from the fire, and together Caroline and I sat down in the mouth of what would soon be our Ute war lodge and began stuffing our mouths with tender pieces of white catfish. It seemed the more we ate, the hungrier we became. Some of the meat from the middle of the back where the fillet was thickest wasn't completely cooked, but we gobbled it down anyway, our hunger was so intense.

While Caroline was finishing up the last of the fish, I tossed the remainder of the catfish over to my resting place and began to fillet out the other side. I figured I'd get that cooking while we worked on the lodge. That's when Caroline noticed the eel's teeth marks on my wrist.

"What are all those red marks on your wrist?" she asked.

"Eel bit me," I responded matter-of-factly, like it was nothing more than a bee sting. "While I was fishing."

"But the marks are so red, and your hand seems to be swelling. We need to get you to a doctor. You should be resting."

I rather enjoyed the fuss she was making, but I responded, "First things first. A sore wrist won't be our worst problem if we don't soon have shelter. Let's get the war lodge built."

After placing the second fillet on the same piece of bark and pushing it next to the fire, Caroline and I headed into the woods to gather materials for our shelter.

A little over an hour later, the tripod looked like a huge pile of brush and bark, except for the high, wide opening above the fire. If the storms came from the west, as they usually did, even a heavy rainstorm wouldn't dampen our fire.

After covering the floor of our new dwelling with pine boughs and grass, we stretched out to give it the comfort test. It was cozy, all right, and would give us the protection we needed until we were rescued.

Caroline pulled the second piece of fish away from the fire and placed it between us. I wasn't hungry.

While building the lodge I made a special effort to keep my wrist out of Caroline's sight, but I watched it closely myself. Not only had it become more red, the skin was becoming increasingly tight with swelling. It was becoming more painful by the minute, and even though it was a humid summer day, I felt cold, yet thirsty. There were plenty of nearby rock formations where much of the last night's rain water had been captured in crevices and pockets. The fresh rain water tasted much better than the muddy river water, although I wouldn't have been opposed to drinking that had it been necessary for survival.

"Let me see your wrist," ordered Caroline, suddenly noticing that I wasn't eating the fish. Her mouth stopped chewing when I showed it to her.

"I didn't realize it was so bad," she said.

"It wasn't when we started building the lodge."

"But you should have been resting. I could have done the work on the lodge by myself."

"But you wouldn't have been finished before the rain started." It was just starting to rain. Just a sprinkle, but I could tell by the blackness of the clouds that it was going to get worse.

"Need to get in some firewood before it rains," I said.

"I'll get it. You stay here," said Caroline with authority as she jumped to her feet. This time I didn't try to help. Caroline had napped briefly while I had fished in the morning. Now it was my turn. After a sleepless night and a busy day, I was so tired that even the worrisome condition of my hand didn't keep me from closing my eyes and falling into a restless slumber.

When I awakened, it was dark. I could hear the quiet drizzle of the rain outside, but the lodge was dry and warm, thanks to the fire that Caroline had kept going. I felt weak and sick, like I might pass out at any moment. It took effort to focus my eyes. My hand hurt worse than ever, and when I held it out in front of me toward the fire, I could see that the swelling had spread up to my elbow and down into my fingers.

"Want some fish?" asked Caroline, noticing I was awake.

I shook my head to let her know I wasn't hungry. She came over beside me, and there was an unmistakable look of alarm on her face when she saw how weak and helpless I had become. I showed her the worsened condition of the hand.

"Caroline," I said, in all soberness. "I saw a man die once with an infected foot."

"You're not going to die," she objected, but there was a worried tone in her voice.

"His name was George Chesterfield III," I continued. "I called him Beaver George. He took a ball in the foot. We were camped on the Wisdom River, headwaters of the upper Missouri, the foothills of the Bitter Root Mountains."

"Was he a friend of yours?"

"More than that. He taught me how to be a mountain man. We were traveling together, him looking for beaver, me looking for Ike—the escaped slave I told you about."

Caroline stared at me intently, sensing that I was trying to tell her something.

"His foot started out about like my wrist, redness and swelling. His temperature kept going up until he was delirious. The black and the green. The smell. The pus."

Caroline didn't even blink at my gross description.

"I wanted to cut the foot off, but he wouldn't let me. Said a mountain man without a leg was no mountain man at all. Couldn't mount a horse if you couldn't put your foot in the stirrup. Couldn't wade across a beaver pond without the wooden leg sinking out of sight. Couldn't run from Injuns or stay on the trail of a wounded elk.

"Nope. He wouldn't let me touch that leg." I paused for a minute, looking into the fire, remembering every detail of Beaver George's death.

"I let the old cuss die . . ." My voice was suddenly filled with emotion, and it became hard to get the words out.

"I should have cut his foot off while he was out of his mind. Maybe I could have saved him."

"We talked about it before he went out of his mind. How I would tie a strip of hide above the infection and twist it tightly with a stick so the flow of blood would be mostly stopped. We discussed how I would heat the knife in the fire until it was nearly red. First, cut the flesh away. Then reheat the knife, hotter than before, and push the side of the blade against the raw flesh to sear it smooth so there would not be bleeding when the twisted band was released."

By this time Caroline knew what I was talking about, though she hadn't said anything. She knew that my life was possibly in her hands, as Beaver George's had been in mine. She knew I was suggesting that maybe she would have to amputate my hand.

"After the searing," I continued, "Beaver George told me how to chop through the bone.

" 'Take a solid stone, about the size of a goose egg, in your right hand. Hold the knife edge over the bone, then pound like hell until she's split in two—then cover the whole mess with hot melted pine pitch.'

"I had everything ready, but he wouldn't let me do it. Should have done it anyway."

I looked away from the fire, into Caroline's face.

"Could you do it?" I asked.

"Would you want me to?"

"If I was delirious, and if the wound was smelly with infection, and no sign of getting any better—I would want you to do it."

We looked into each other's faces for what seemed like a long time. She was the first to speak. "How can I get pine pitch on this island?"

"The trees where we cut these boughs. It should be running from the cut marks."

I stretched out on my back, exhausted from the intensity of our conversation. As I looked up at the flickering firelight on our brushy ceiling, I had confidence that Caroline would somehow do the right thing. It was no longer necessary to hold back the blackness. I passed out.

Chapter 16

Caroline sat cross-legged, Indian style, in front of the fire. At the back of the war lodge, constructed of limbs and branches and thatched with bark and grass, Dan Storm tossed restlessly on a mat of green grasses, delirious with fever, his hand and forearm red and swollen. He had not fully regained consciousness since passing out two days earlier. In his delirium he had said many things—calls for help to the escaped slave Ike, angry threats to Dick Boggs, and even words of comfort to the Indian girl named Red Leaf. Some of the things he said were in a strange tongue that Caroline figured must be a faraway Indian language.

With the coming of morning, his restlessness had only increased, along with the size of his hand. His forehead was hot and dry as his body fought the infection with an increasing temperature. During the night and early morning, Caroline had frequently wiped his hot forehead with a sponge made of tree moss dipped in cool rain water. Sometimes his restlessness would cease for a brief moment when she placed the wet sponge upon him. That was the only sign that perhaps the cool rain water was offering some relief. But now she had more pressing matters to attend to.

It was late morning; the rain of the previous night had stopped. There was no sunshine, but occasional blue holes in the gray clouds gave promise of a mild afternoon.

She was leaning toward the fire, a stick in her right hand, stirring the steaming contents in the inverted shell of a box turtle. As she stirred, the hard balls of brown pine pitch gradually softened, then melted into a thick, black syrup. With the point of her stick, she carefully fished the bits of bark and pine needles from the syrup and flung them into the fire. She wanted the pitch to be as pure and clean as possible.

Beside her on a mat of clean, green grass rested her surgical tools—a pocketknife with an open blade, a two-foot strip of boot thong, a solid stone the size of a large goose egg, a sponge of wet tree moss, and a scrubbed turtle shell filled with cool rain water.

When the pitch was melted, she pushed the turtle shell toward the edge of the fire so the sap could cool just enough to get a little thicker. When it was just the right consistency, she let go of the stirring stick and crawled to the back of the lodge to get a closer look at her patient.

There was no sign of let-up in Dan's delirium. His temperature was still high, and his reddened hand and wrist were double size—hot, hard, and smooth like the surface of a watermelon in the hot summer sun.

After sponging his face with the cool rain water, she hooked her hands under his shoulders and began dragging him, an inch at a time, toward the fire and her crude surgical tools—wondering if she would be able to muster the courage to do what needed to be done. She wondered, too, if the pain of the cutting would make Dan unmanageable. Once she began, would she be able to finish?

Once she had pulled him to the desired place beside the fire and her tools, she decided to tie his healthy hand tightly to his belt with a piece of the thong as a precaution. If the pain caused him to thrash about, at least his good arm would remain safe at his side.

She took the healthy hand in hers, looked down at the smooth sun-browned skin, felt the warmth, and sensed the latent strength and gentleness of the callused palm. It felt good, very good—the feel of Dan's skin against hers. She pulled the hand to her and pressed it firmly against her cheek and neck. Then, ever so gently, she kissed the back of the hand as her eyesight began to blur with new tears. The hand still smelled of fish and pine—a result of cleaning the catfish and cutting branches for the shelter. But she didn't mind the pungent smell on Dan's hand as she continued to hold it to her lips. She longed to cry, as she had done as a child, but knew she couldn't allow herself such luxury. Not now. Not with Dan's life hanging in the balance. She bit her bottom lip, hard, telling herself that a one-armed Dan Storm was better than no Dan Storm. His life was in her hands, and she would not let him down.

Carefully, she tied the healthy hand to the belt, then looked at the other hand—red, swollen, and deformed. She touched it, first gently, then probing, pushing. It seemed to be harder and hotter than when she had checked it a few hours earlier. It wasn't getting any better; the time of waiting was over. She must act, now.

Quickly she wrapped the remainder of the leather thong loosely around his forearm, just below the elbow, and tied the two ends into a knot. She slipped a smooth stick beneath the thong and twisted the thong in a tightening circle until she felt the flow of blood to the injured hand was reduced but not completely stopped. If necessary she could tighten or loosen the loop later.

After placing the knife on a stone with the blade pointing into the hottest part of the fire, she took another close look at the swollen hand. The teeth marks of the eel were barely visible. She wondered what awful poison would make the teeth of an eel so dangerous.

The hand looked and felt like it was about to burst—spewing forth pus, blood . . . perhaps even poison, the eel poison. Instead of bursting, however, inner pressure seemed to be pushing the pus and poison up the wrist.

Caroline hadn't received any professional medical training, but it somehow seemed logical to her that if she could remove the pressure and prevent the swollen hand from pushing the poison into the wrist, perhaps more of the wrist could be saved, maybe even the hand—but she didn't dare hope for that big of a miracle.

Using a pad of dry tree moss for insulation, she picked up the heated knife, and without giving it more than a few seconds to cool, made a quick puncture into one of the tooth marks. The relief of pressure was immediate as the creamy liquid oozed out. She made two deep slashes across the tooth marks. The wound was ugly as its juices poured out on the ground, but Caroline tried to tell herself there was still hope for a successful outcome. None of the flesh was black or green, nor was the smell terribly unpleasant. She squeezed the fingers and the wrist at the same time in an effort to force as much of the poison as possible from the open wound.

While the flesh remained swollen, the intense inner pressure was gone. The hand no longer looked like it might burst. As the oozing from the wound ceased, she rinsed it with fresh water in an effort to wash away as much of the poison as possible. Then she gradually loosened the thong. At first the blood flowed freely, but it quickly subsided. Again she washed the wound with the rain water. Then she covered the open wound with wet moss—partly as a dressing, partly to keep away the increasing number of flies being attracted to the blood and pus.

After replacing the messy grass and moss with clean grass, the long wait began—a wait in which Caroline's mind was filled with many thoughts, most of which centered around the welfare and care of Dan. But she also thought about the events that brought her to the Mississippi River valley—the promise of a best-selling book, a chance at fame and fortune, a once-in-a-lifetime opportunity. There was now no doubt in her mind that the Mormons were indeed practicing polygamy—and the friendliness of some of the married men gave her confidence that she would soon receive a proposal to become a plural wife. With that proposal she would get the information that would fill her book and bring fame and fortune.

Any man inviting her to join with him in plural marriage would be obligated to answer her questions—questions any woman would have when approached with such a seemingly outrageous proposal. How can plural marriage be justified in a Christian society? How can one be sure the leaders really endorse it? Can one speak to Brother Brigham about it, receive his sanction? Who else is doing it? Why is it so secret? How can lying about it be justified? Did Joseph Smith practice polygamy too, before he was killed? Who were his wives? Will there be more wives after me?

Yes, all of her questions would be answered, at least enough to fill a book. And she had a strong feeling that the answers would be coming soon. The mobs were becoming more insistent in their persecutions. There was increasing talk of fleeing to the West Coast or the Rocky Mountains, far from the hated mobs. Times were temporary, changing. And in the face of an uncertain future, while some men became more timid and fearful, others became more bold and daring.

Caroline had confidence in her good looks, charm, and intelligence. Her lack of membership in the faith didn't seem to be a deterrent to masculine attention. If possible, she didn't want to mock the sacred baptism of the Mormons to get what she wanted. She was living enough lies without adding that one. But her book would be an honest one, a candid one, uncovering many of the myths and secrets of Mormonism.

She had plenty of background material, written down meticulously during her several months among the Mormons. Things couldn't have gone better for her, except for her relationship with Dick Boggs. Instead of helping her, he had nearly killed her, having lost all reason in his intense hatred for this Dan Storm. In the future, she would avoid Boggs at all costs.

But what about Dan Storm? How did he fit into her plans? She vividly remembered the warm swellings in her heart as she held his unconscious hand to her cheek and lips. The harder she tried to suppress those feelings, the stronger they seemed to grow. On his hand, even the smell of raw fish was not offensive.

But Dan was a Mormon, and she was a spy among his people, a spy who planned to publish his people's most holy secrets. What would he do if he found out about her? Should she tell him? No. Never.

Maybe he wouldn't live, but maybe he would. With or without his hand, what possible hope could there be for a future together if she persisted with her book plan? Maybe she should back away from her plan. No. Never.

Chapter 17

When I regained consciousness, it was dark. The fading light of a dying fire cast an interesting network of flickering shadows on the thatched ceiling of the lodge. I looked at the shadows for a long time, feeling alert but very, very weak. Even the attempt to turn my head to the side required a determined effort. Caroline told me later that I had been delirious for more than four days. My strength was gone, but so was the fever and most of the swelling pressure in my arm.

The night was still. No rain. No wind. No sound except for the distant sloshing of waves on the rocky shore. Then another sound, deep breathing, in the direction of the fire. Caroline.

Mustering all my strength, I willed my head to turn toward the fire. The diminishing light from the glowing coals danced warmly on the sleeping woman. She was on her side, her tousled hair and head resting on an outstretched arm, her knees drawn close to her breast. Her breathing was deep, her sleep sound.

She had never looked more beautiful. The sleeping face, though somewhat soiled, was angelic, like that of a sleeping child. Watching her in the fading light was food for my hungry soul. Although she was several yards away, warmth and even strength seemed to be flowing from her to me. I remained silent, not wanting to disturb her rest.

It wasn't until the coals had lost their glow and the blackness of the night had closed in completely that my thoughts turned from

Caroline to my injured hand. I remembered the conversation we had had before I had passed out—about the time I had almost amputated Beaver George's foot.

A sudden thought brought cold chills to my spine and hot sweat to my forehead. I couldn't remember if Caroline had done anything to my hand—like cut it off. I was getting better. Could it be that my hand was gone?

My eyes filled with tears—not out of self-pity, but from the vivid picture in my mind of a bitterly determined Caroline, a stone in her fist, pounding the knife blade through the bones of my forearm. I couldn't remember if she had done it or not, but in my imagination I could picture her doing it.

It took a lot of effort, but I slowly moved my healthy hand across my body. The throbbings coming from the inflicted hand were not normal, and it was too dark to see, but I knew I could trust the touch of my good fingers. They would tell me whether or not the injured hand had been removed.

To my relief it was still there. Still somewhat swollen, and matted with moss over a deep slash where the teeth marks of the eel had been. I couldn't remember receiving the slash marks, but figured they had something to do with Caroline's treatment of the wound. I didn't know what Caroline had done, but I did know that with the decreased swelling and temperature, the hand was healing.

With my anxiety gone, I suddenly felt very tired and gladly let myself fall into a deep, peaceful sleep.

When I awakened, light and narrow shafts of bright sunshine were penetrating the thatched ceiling. To my surprise I felt stronger than I had felt during the night. There was soreness but no pain in my hand. The chills and high fever were gone. In fact, I felt pretty good, except for a gnawing hunger in my stomach. It seemed to be getting worse by the minute as my nostrils filled with the smell of something good cooking over the fire.

With a little effort I turned my head toward the lodge opening and the fire. Caroline, her back to me, was crouched over the fire, stirring whatever it was that smelled so good.

"What's for breakfast?" I asked cheerily.

Caroline spun around and faced me, the stirring stick still in her hand, the surprised look on her face quickly changing to a bright smile. Again I was taken back at how good she looked; even after I don't know how many days on a deserted island, she maintained a fresh, clean appearance. In fact, the extra sunshine had only enhanced her good looks and vibrant health.

"You're awake!" she exclaimed.

"And mighty hungry."

"When your temperature finally dropped last night, I figured you'd probably come to your senses soon—but I had no idea you would wake up so cheerful. Do you feel all right?"

"Half starved."

"You nearly died, and all you can talk about is food."

"Would you rather I said something more serious or profound?" I asked.

"It's such a relief to see you awake and healing," she said. "I guess I really don't care what you say. But if it's food you want, food you'll get." She turned toward the fire.

"Wait a minute, I want to tell you something," I said.

She turned toward me again, kneeling beside the fire.

"Come up beside me, please."

As she crawled toward me, across the floor of the wickiup, I tried to figure out the best way to thank her for the care that had saved my arm and possibly my life. But when I looked up into her face, the words I had been looking for didn't come. The silence was just beginning to get uncomfortable when I surprised both of us by saying, "Caroline, will you marry me?"

"What?" was her only response, after what seemed like a long pause.

Now that I had gone this far, I didn't see any sense in retreating.

"Will you marry me?"

"I don't know what to say," she said as she looked away.

"Say you will."

"I can't."

Another long pause. I knew, or at least I thought I knew, that she loved me too. But something was wrong, terribly wrong, something she didn't want to talk about. My timing had been bad. I had made a mistake, one that I didn't understand.

"What's for breakfast?" I asked, hoping to take our conversation back to where it had been a few minutes earlier and end an awkward predicament.

Without hesitation, she followed my lead, scooting toward the fire.

"Wait'll you taste it . . . been simmering for two days, just waiting for you to gobble it up."

Using what appeared to be a crudely fashioned wooden spoon, she stirred the contents of her now steaming cauldron one last time.

"Sure smells good. What is it?"

"Original recipe tortoise goulash," she said proudly.

I realized her blackened cooking pot was the inverted shell of a fairly large box turtle. Beside her was a smaller turtle shell, apparently my bowl.

"Lots of turtles on the island," said Caroline. "Easy to catch, good to eat."

I had never eaten turtle before, but figured that if it tasted half as good as it smelled, I was in for a real feast. Caroline filled the little shell from the big one and carried it to me.

"I was going to carve a spoon this morning," she said, avoiding looking into my face.

"I'll eat Indian style," I said, sitting up part way and taking the bowl in my hands.

"Indian style?"

"Anything you can't drink out of the bowl you eat with your fingers, then lick them clean when you're through."

The gravy was thick and brown and, except for the lack of salt, was as good as any gravy I had ever tasted—rich and flavorful. It wasn't until the gravy was almost gone that I began to realize why it tasted so good. The other items in the goulash began to appear. Lean chunks of turtle meat, wild onion bulbs the size of thumb knuckles, and lots of mushrooms, the spongy morel variety.

I had polished off the second serving and was about to ask for thirds when Caroline insisted that I not eat any more until I had given my body time to digest the first two servings. It sounded like good sense, but my hunger hadn't diminished at all, it seemed.

I stretched out full length on my grass mat, looking up at the thatched ceiling. I was still too weak to stand up, but my strength was returning quickly.

"I'm sorry," I said, referring to the marriage proposal.

"Please don't be," she said, looking away toward the woods.

"It's just that I thought you felt the same way about me . . ."

"Please don't make any conclusions about how I feel," she said, still looking away at the woods. "There are some things in my life that make it impossible for me to even consider a question like that at this time."

"Something in your past?" I asked, hoping she would tell me what it was.

"No. Something in my present and future, something I can't discuss with you."

I didn't say anything more, figuring I had played the fool enough for one day.

"Be patient with me, Dan. Things will change. Please continue to be my friend," said Caroline.

Suddenly I felt angry. Had I had the strength to stand up, I would have been tempted to shove her in the river. I turned on my side, facing the back of the wickiup, my back to Caroline. I was determined that as soon as I was strong enough to get on my feet I would whip together a raft and get us off this cursed island.

Chapter 18

The next morning I felt a lot better. My hand was still stiff and very sore but my general health and strength were much improved. My feelings toward Caroline were improved too—some of the sting of her rejection had worn off. I wanted to believe that she had a good reason for turning down my proposal of marriage, but I wondered why she was so firm in her refusal to talk to me about it.

Every time I would get to thinking that maybe she just plain didn't like me, it seemed she would bring me another bowl of that tortoise goulash or crawl over to check my wound—and our eyes would meet, or our fingers touch. During those moments, however brief, something unspoken passed between us, a mutual attraction, even a longing to be together. And I would wonder again why she was fighting it, why she refused to acknowledge or discuss this mutual feeling.

I remembered how different it had been with Red Leaf, my Ute Indian bride of years earlier in the Rocky Mountains. We had had a simple but brief life together. I had understood only the bare rudiments of her language, and she none of mine, yet our time together had been happy.

For years the memories of Red Leaf and a sense of responsibility for the events leading to her horrible death had prevented me from finding interest in other women, at least until Caroline came along. I was quickly learning, however, that this Caroline was not another

Red Leaf. Sometimes I wished she were, that we could just load up a pack horse with supplies and head for the Rocky Mountains, build a cabin in a scenic mountain valley and raise a bunch of kids, make friends with the local Indian tribes, and just enjoy the carefree life I had known among the Utes.

Even though I had committed myself to silence on the subject of marriage, I couldn't resist sharing this dream with Caroline. She was just returning from the woods with more mushrooms and another turtle.

"Come with me to the Rocky Mountains, Caroline," I began with an enthusiastic smile. She didn't turn away or ask me to stop.

"I know a valley surrounded by majestic peaks twice as high as any you have ever seen. So high they still have snow in August. So steep that even grass and trees can't grow at the higher elevations. So jagged and majestic that you would suspect they were fashioned by God himself. The streams come gushing down from the peaks with a roar of thunder, then spread out as clear as glass across lush meadows, jammed with beaver ponds and grass reaching to a horse's belly. The lake in this valley has fish as long as your arm, easy to catch whenever you're hungry. And the woods are full of the biggest deer and fattest elk you have ever seen.

"When you walk in the woods, it's like going into a brand new church or the temple—like you are walking on holy ground where no man or woman has ever walked. Everything is new, fresh, unused, the way God made it. No officials to tell you what to do and when to do it. Just Injuns. And they can be good neighbors once you make friends with them."

"Sounds like a wonderful place," said Caroline, a faraway look on her face. "Why did you come back?"

"Injuns can get awful mean and nasty, too. I told you about Red Leaf. After she was gone, I just had to leave. Seemed like the right thing to do. But I'm going back. Not sure when. But I want you to come with me."

"I know," was all she said.

I continued, "We could build a cabin in one of those beautiful meadows. There would be plenty of firewood and fresh spring water, and a view that would take your breath away. We could open a trading post for the Indians. And maybe later a school, when we had kids old enough to be part of it. You could be the teacher. It would be the beginning of a new town, a new state, and we would be the ones to start it all. Maybe others would join us by and by."

"Those are beautiful dreams," she said, again stirring the contents of the simmering turtle shell.

"I want to share them with you," I said.

"Please, Dan, I can't get involved in a discussion about a future with you, not now."

"And why not?" I said in anger, rising to a full sitting position for the first time since my unconscious delirium.

"I just can't." Her voice began to break, and tears filled her eyes.

Suddenly I felt bad at having pushed her too far. I was about to offer some words of comfort and apology when the air was suddenly filled with the distinct sound of splintering timber and the grinding of wood on rock, followed by the yelling and cursing of male voices.

Chapter 19

The three burly loggers were standing on the shore of the island cursing their bad luck at having jammed their huge log raft onto the upper tip of our island when Caroline stepped out from behind a tree and greeted them with a friendly smile. Their surprise was complete, as indicated by the sudden halt of their cursing and arguing and the long silence as they looked upon Caroline in astonishment. In 1845, one didn't expect to stumble onto a beautiful woman on uninhabited Mississippi River islands.

The men had been on the river several weeks, guiding and coaxing their huge pine log raft toward the St. Louis sawmills. The logs had been cut and dumped into the river in the pine country far to the north.

The three loggers did their best to keep the raft in midstream, where the current was swiftest. There was a platform with a tent and a cooking pit in the middle of the raft where the men slept and cooked their meals. There was also a little boat tied to one side that the men used to get to and from shore when necessary.

Had the raft hit the tip of our island to the right or left of center, the momentum would have spun it around to one side, allowing the powerful current of the Mississippi to carry it down either side of the island. As it was, the raft hit the tip of the island dead center and ground to a complete halt, pushing a good number of the logs upon the rocky shore.

The raft was forgotten, however, at the sight of Caroline, at least for the moment. She was the first to speak.

"Where are you gentlemen headed?"

They just glanced at each other in astonishment as Caroline explained how we had been marooned on the island.

A few minutes later, two of the men were helping me toward the raft. I was still too weak to walk by myself. Once Caroline and I were comfortably situated in the open-ended tent, they began to work the raft free by moving sections of logs from one side to the other until the force of the current was sufficient to turn the raft out into the main current.

As soon as the raft was floating again, the three loggers came to join their unexpected guests and get supper started. We learned that we weren't very many miles above Keokuk, the half-breed town near the Boggs plantation. The loggers agreed to row us to shore when we reached Keokuk. They said it would be sometime during the night.

Caroline told me about the half-breed Peter Weaselhead, the store owner who had been so helpful to her when she had first come up the river. She was sure he would put us up until we could catch a river boat back to Nauvoo.

Exhausted from the walk to the raft, I crawled to the back of the tent to get some rest while the loggers gathered around Caroline, falling over themselves to satisfy her every need—bringing her things to eat and drink, a more comfortable stool, shading her from the late afternoon sun. You would think the queen of England had come aboard their boat. Caroline seemed to enjoy the extra attention, and I rested peacefully, feeling relieved that we had been rescued from the island. But as I dropped off to sleep, I felt a little sad that a good time for Caroline and me had ended.

Chapter 20

It was almost daylight when we knocked on Peter Weaselhead's door. There was a pistol in the half-breed's hand when he finally greeted us. He recognized Caroline immediately and invited us in. Having been awake most of the night, we were anxious to get some rest. He showed us to the storage room, where he spread out a couple of buffalo robes over some sacks of grain. Soon we were fast asleep.

I awakened to the sound of a familiar voice. A number of vertical shafts of sunlight shining through tiny holes in the shingled roof told me the sun was high in the sky. I looked over at Caroline, who was still breathing deeply, her eyes closed. The buffalo robe had slipped from her shoulders. Gently, I pulled it back over her. She didn't stir.

Again I heard the familiar voice. It was coming through the partially opened door and had an unmistakable Irish accent. It had to be Pat O'Riley or his twin. I rolled out from under my buffalo robes, quietly slipped into my boots, and headed for the door. My body felt much stronger. And from the intense itching, I knew my hand was healing.

The face matched the voice. It was Pat, and he was busy at the counter buying a huge pile of merchandise—cooking utensils, garden tools, rope, candles, whitewash, and food staples.

"Pat," I called.

When he looked in my direction, a look of total astonishment covered his face. He dropped what he was doing and rushed toward me.

"The ferryman said you drowned when the boat sank. Where's Caroline?"

I pointed toward the back room.

"She's still asleep."

We moved to the back of the room and seated ourselves at a small plank table. I told Pat about the narrow escape from Boggs and his friends—the storm, the horses plunging overboard when Boggs started firing at us, the crash landing on the island in the middle of the night, the eel bite, the fever and delirium, the rescue by the loggers.

As I was finishing the story, Caroline joined us and Peter Weaselhead brought some breakfast—boiled beef, bread, butter, dill pickles, and apple cider. I was really hungry. It felt great, sitting at that little table with Pat and Caroline, eating and talking.

"Do you want the whole story?" responded Pat when I asked him what he was doing in Keokuk.

"Sure," said Caroline enthusiastically. "Peter says the next upstream boat won't be here until the day after tomorrow."

Pat leaned forward, placing both forearms on the table, his usual jovial manner suddenly disappearing.

"It all began the day you two went to the hanging. Ebenezer McConklin asked Sarah to come over to his office."

"Who's he?" I asked.

"President of the Nauvoo free schools," explained Caroline. "Hires and fires us schoolteachers. Also a member of the Council of Fifty."

The most influential men in Nauvoo belonged to the Council of Fifty. Brigham Young was head of the council, but not all of its members were Mormons. The Council made and carried out political, economic, and even religious decisions.

"What did he want with her?" I asked.

"First he talked about school business to kind of warm things up. You know Sarah. Nice, polite lass. Just sat and listened, like he was saying something important. She's nice to everybody."

Pat stopped talking and started stabbing a piece of meat with his fork, giving the impression that it was hard to say the next part.

"Go on," Caroline urged.

"This McConklin guy is old enough to be my pop, and he just leans across the desk and tells Sarah that God and the leaders of the Church want her to be his third wife."

"You're not serious," I said, hoping he might be setting us up for some kind of joke. Caroline didn't say anything, but I noticed she stopped chewing right in the middle of a bite, waiting for Pat to continue.

"No. The old bugger really did it. He told her he had had strong feelings about her ever since she started teaching at the school. He said he had taken the matter before the Lord and had received the confirmation that Sarah should be his celestial mate. He added that Brother Brigham had approved the union."

Pat stopped again, probably pondering the theological pros and cons of plural marriage.

"And what did Sarah say?" I asked.

"She decided to quit being so nice and told the old goat she was engaged to marry the only man she loved—me, Pat O'Riley. McConklin didn't give up easily. He told her about Abraham, David, and Solomon having many wives, that polygamy was God's eternal law. Sarah said she had heard the law had been restored and that she would give serious consideration to letting Pat take a second wife, but Sarah Lange was going to be his first.

"As I said, the old goat was persistent. He asked her if she wanted to go to hell—if she understood the consequences of going against God and the prophet. The lass couldn't take it any longer. Got up and ran out. Came straight to the temple, where I was working."

Pat stopped again, this time taking a bite of bread and chewing thoughtfully. After swallowing, he continued, "After she told me the whole story and I kissed away the tears, I figured there was two things I could do. I could march over to this Ebenezer's house and bust his nose. Or I could head over to Brother Brigham's and try to find out what in hell was going on. Or I could do both."

I noticed that Pat's fists were clenched, his face red, and that the vessels and sinews were bulging on the sides of his neck.

"We headed over to Brother Brigham's house. It was closer than McConklin's place. Brother Brigham was home, and seeing I was mad, invited both of us into his private office and shut the door. He just sat there, not saying a single word, as Sarah told him the whole story.

"When she was finished, Brother Brigham said he remembered Brother McConklin asking about her, but nothing had been said about the engagement to Pat. He didn't know if Brother McConklin knew about it either."

"Then Brother Brigham leaned forward, looked Sarah right in the eye, and said, 'What Brother McConklin said about the restoration of celestial marriage is true, but, young lady, you don't have to marry someone you don't love.'

"That's when I felt a lot better, like I didn't need to punch somebody. The prophet said he would talk to Brother McConklin and see that there was no more trouble.

"We were getting up to leave when he asked us when we were planning to marry. I said it would be in about a week, that our bishop was going to do it, just a private ceremony because neither of us had any family in Nauvoo.

"'Would you like me to marry you?' he asked. Not everybody gets a chance to be married by the prophet. We said we would."

"That's great!" I said. "When's the big day?"

"Brigham Young doesn't beat around the bush. He called in a couple of witnesses and married us right there on the spot."

"You're kidding!" exclaimed Caroline, speaking for the first time since Pat began his story. Pat just shook his head and smiled. He was serious, all right.

"Congratulations," I said, reaching across the table to shake his hand.

"Where's the bride?" asked Caroline, and before he could answer, I broke in with another question, "What are you doing here, buying all those supplies?"

Pat sat back, stretching out his suspenders with his thumbs, grinning from ear to ear, looking as proud as a man could look.

"We're moving to Keokuk. Got us a ranch."

With enthusiasm Pat explained the fantastic deal he had made, trading his one-acre lot and cabin in Nauvoo for a 160-acre farm west of Keokuk.

"How did you ever make a deal like that?" I asked.

"The good brother was tired of living among the gentiles. Afraid of persecution, I suppose. Wanted to move to Nauvoo. Felt he and the wife would be safer in the middle of the Saints. Couldn't find a buyer for his place, so he was tickled to trade me straight across."

Pat leaned forward, a serious look coming across his face.

"Do you know how much land 160 acres is? My daddy worked his whole life on six acres. There were eleven kids. Seldom enough to eat. Never any money to spend. My older brother got the six acres for his family, and I got pushed out of the nest with nothing but the shirt on my back, and it had four patches.

"I know how much 160 acres is," Pat continued. "It's enough to make a man a king. It'll feed all our kids and grandkids for a hundred years, and produce big cash crops, too. It's only a few miles from the Keokuk landing where boats can pick up my crops and carry them to the best-paying markets. A few good harvests and I might even pick up another 160 acres. If my daddy could only see me now. He would know how much 160 acres is. He would drop to his knees, dig his fingers into that soft black soil, and cry out his happiness."

"Do you think the Mormon-haters will leave you alone?" I asked.

"I never had any trouble getting along with gentiles. Used to be one myself. Never met one that could stay with me drink for drink in the pub. Figure I'll get along just fine once they discover I'm not pious, that I'm not trying to shove Mormonism down their throats."

Later in the day we borrowed three of Peter Weaselhead's saddle horses and a pack mule and rode out to Pat's new farm, taking along all the new supplies.

To my surprise, Pat's enthusiasm was not exaggerated. Over forty acres were already planted in wheat and corn. The cabin was sturdy, built from fat, twelve- to sixteen-inch diameter pine logs, about twice as big as Pat's cabin in Nauvoo. There was a new log barn, and most of the land was already fenced with split rails and poles. The previous owner had put a lot of sweat into the place before abandoning it for the safety of Nauvoo.

Pat and I were riding through the tall grass along the south boundary, a little ways ahead of Caroline, when I noticed that she had not been sharing our enthusiasm for the new farm. In fact, she had been keeping pretty much to herself and had spoken hardly a word since arriving at the farm. Pat and I pulled in our horses, and as Caroline caught up with us, I asked her if anything was wrong.

"Have you met any of your neighbors yet?" she asked Pat, her tone deadly earnest.

"Be plenty of time for that after we get settled in," he responded.

"Do you know who lives over by those hills?" she asked, looking across the fence to the south.

"No," said Pat. "Do you?"

"Dick Boggs," she said, still looking to the south. "The man who shot our boat full of holes."

I remembered her telling me how she had visited the Boggs place on her way to Nauvoo, at the request of a mutual friend in Philadelphia. There was an empty feeling in my stomach, knowing that if Boggs knew I was here he would come to kill me. No doubt about it. It is a terrible feeling knowing someone will kill you if given half a chance.

"I'll bet this Boggs and me are buddies within a year," boasted Pat, undaunted in his cheerfulness.

"Be careful, Pat," I warned. "He's a snake. He castrates his slaves. He's raped Mormon women. He's burned Mormon homes. If he gives you any trouble, let me know."

"And what will you do?" Pat asked, still smiling.

"I'll kill him."

A sober, silent mood prevailed as we turned our horses around and headed back to town.

Chapter 21

When Brigham Young officially announced that the Mormons would be moving west, the city of Nauvoo—almost overnight—converted into a wagon factory. There was still some doubt as to exactly where the Saints would be going—California, Oregon, Vancouver Island, or possibly the Great Basin in the heart of the Rocky Mountains. Since I had lived in the Rocky Mountains, I was frequently asked questions about the geography, weather, soil, Indian tribes, and the ability of the land to produce food crops.

I said tobacco was the only crop I had ever seen planted and harvested in the Rocky Mountains. The Indians grew little patches for their peace pipes. I told them that in the flat grasslands between Mount Timpanogos and the lake the wild grasses grew as tall as a horse's belly. I told them there were plenty of fish in the lake and streams, and that I thought the Indians would be friendly if treated with kindness. Even though I had lived there, I couldn't be sure the land would support ten thousand Mormon settlers. Only one thing was sure: when the grass turned green and the waters began to flow in the spring, the Saints would be heading west.

Even the basement of the temple was used to manufacture wagon parts. While the workmen upstairs were hurrying to complete a temple for the Saints, the workmen downstairs were hurrying to build the vehicles to carry the Saints away from the new temple.

Throughout the summer and fall of 1845, I worked ten-hour days on the temple and in the basement wagon factory. In my free time I finished my little cabin, knowing I would be leaving it in the spring. I suppose I worked on it for lack of anything better to do.

Caroline was constantly on my mind, but I saw very little of her. After our adventure on the river she had resumed her involvement in the Nauvoo social life. When not teaching school, she was off on carriage rides and attending parties and dances. When I bumped into her on the street or in church meetings, she was always glad to see me, but she skillfully dodged my efforts to spend more time together. It was totally frustrating, knowing she liked me and not understanding why she put me off.

With the coming of fall and winter I was taken away from my work with increasing frequency to perform guard duty. As the temple neared completion, at least to the point where ordinances could be performed, the gentiles increased efforts to harass Church leaders. There were so many deputies and sheriffs coming to town with all kinds of writs and legal papers that Brigham Young and most of the other Church leaders had to go into hiding. Mormons flocked into Nauvoo in increasing numbers as the mobs drove them from their farms. Hardly a day went by when the smoke of a burning cabin could not be seen from the upper floor of the temple. The Nauvoo Legion, after extensive reorganization, began to practice maneuvers with increasing frequency.

I didn't hear anything from Pat and Sarah on their new farm near Keokuk, so I assumed they were getting along all right.

Two days before Christmas I was assigned guard duty at the door of the temple while Brigham Young met with the High Council inside. Apparently President Young didn't intend to stay long, having left his carriage parked conspicuously in front of the temple.

About five o'clock, five or six armed strangers approached from the west. When they reached the bottom of the steps I cocked back the hammer on my rifle and ordered them to halt and identify themselves. Two of them said they were federal officers from Springfield, that their companions were state troopers assisting them, that they had papers authorizing them to arrest Brigham Young and Amasa Lyman. They said they had reason to believe Brigham Young was in the temple.

Without waiting for me to reply, they started forward toward the temple door. I raised the rifle to my shoulder and aimed at the heart of the first man.

"I'll kill the first man to take another step," I warned.

They stopped.

"You'd better get out of here, kid," said one of them in a calm voice. "You might get one of us; then you'll be dead."

"Then all of you will be dead," I responded, surprised how calm and firm my voice sounded. "This very moment, a hundred armed men are headed in this direction to give me a hand."

I didn't know if anyone had seen my predicament and sounded the alarm, but I figured it couldn't hurt to bluff. There was plenty of help around; all I needed was time.

"If you men value your blood, you'd best turn around and head back to the street. Do that, and I'll see if President Young wants to . . ."

Suddenly the temple door opened. It was George Grant, President Young's coachman. Seemingly unconcerned, he walked past me and the officers and headed straight for the carriage. He seemed to know what he was doing, so I didn't say anything as I lowered the rifle.

The officers watched Grant with interest as he untied the horses, crawled into his chair, and headed the team toward the front door, pulling them to a stop at the base of the steps beside the curious officers.

"Is this Young's carriage?" asked one of the officers.

"Yup," said Grant.

"Is Young coming out?" asked the officer.

"I suppose he will," said Grant brightly.

I wondered what in the devil was going on, but Grant seemed to know exactly what was happening, so I just held my ground and didn't say or do anything.

It wasn't long until the door of the temple opened again. Quickly

I glanced behind me, not wanting the officers out of my sight any longer than absolutely necessary.

It was William Miller, but he looked very different wearing Brigham Young's beaver hat and Heber Kimball's silk coat. Walking confidently down the steps, Miller greeted the officers in passing and started to get into the carriage. One of the officers stepped forward and arrested him, charging him with counterfeiting the coin of the United States.

Miller told him there must be some mistake, that he was not guilty of any such charge, but the marshal insisted the charge was right. Miller then asked if the marshals would accompany him to the mansion where legal counsel could determine if the writ was lawful. It was apparent the officers thought Miller was Brigham Young, and Miller didn't say anything to change their minds.

The two marshals climbed into the carriage with Miller and headed toward the mansion. I later learned that upon reaching the mansion Esquire Edmonds examined the writ and pronounced it legal. The marshals loaded Miller into the carriage and headed for Carthage.

When the carriage was out of sight, the temple door opened again and President Young stepped out. Looking up at the gray December clouds, he said, "Hate to walk home without a hat, but I suppose things could be worse."

Chapter 22

On February 2, 1846, Brigham Young announced a sudden change in the plan to evacuate Nauvoo. Rather than wait until late spring when there would be mild weather and plenty of grass for the stock, he told the captains of hundreds and fifties to prepare the people for immediate evacuation.

The Nauvoo Legion and police had been unable to put a lid on the local counterfeiting ring, and federal authorities seemed intent on bring Church leaders to trial on counterfeiting charges. Church leaders had no intention of giving themselves up to due process of law as Joseph and Hyrum had done at Carthage.

Apparently the arrest of William Miller had embarrassed the feds, and now there were rumors that federal troops would be coming up the river as soon as the ice was gone. Brigham Young had no intention of seeing the Saints prevented from migrating west, so he announced the westward trek would begin immediately.

That's when it became apparent to me and everybody else in Nauvoo that life as we had known it in this beautiful Mississippi River city would soon end. While many were apprehensive about moving to the unknown, uncharted territories of the West, I was eager with anticipation. I had been there, seen the snowcapped peaks, wandered the endless prairies. I was ready to participate in the largest wilderness migration since Moses led the children of Israel out of Egypt.

The only thing that concerned me was Caroline Logan. If she didn't join the migration, I would probably never see her again. She had not joined the Church and therefore would have no reason to go west with the Saints. I knew that if I didn't talk to her soon, and say the things that were in my heart, our paths would head in different directions, never to cross again.

I also knew there was a likelihood that she would reject me, as she had done in the past, for reasons still foreign to me. But I had to try. It was now or never.

I wanted her to be my wife, to come west with me, to bear my children and establish with me our own little kingdom in the tops of the mountains. Yes, that was what I wanted, more than anything—and somehow I had to figure out a way to get Caroline to share that dream with me. As far as I was concerned, Caroline was the only one who could fill that inner void I had carried in my heart since the death of Red Leaf.

On the very night that President Young announced the beginning of the migration, I cleaned up and headed up Parley Street toward the house where Caroline and other schoolteachers rented rooms. My stomach was in knots, wondering what the best way would be to present my suit. What should I say to the woman who had already told me she wouldn't marry me?

I began to feel more than a little disgust with myself for feeling such anxiety over an anticipated conversation with a woman. After all, I had fought off a grizzly without weapons, engaged in hand-to-hand combat with savages, and stolen Comanche horses, risking life and scalp. Now I was trembling like a baby in the fear that Caroline would reject my proposal.

The thought occurred to me that perhaps I should throw caution to the wind, be more bold and daring, mount my horse, gallop up to her bedroom window, call out loud enough for all to hear an invitation for her to come away to the Rocky Mountains with me. Maybe she would respond better to that than she would an intelligent, civilized conversation.

I was still wondering how to approach Caroline when I found myself standing on her porch. Plan or no plan, I knocked, hoping my instincts would lead me in the right direction.

A matronly woman ushered me into the parlor and invited me to take a seat, then quickly retreated, too quickly, leaving me in the company of an older gentleman seated in one of the chairs.

He was the first to speak, mentioning something about the upcoming migration, the most talked about subject in Nauvoo. I nodded agreement to the things he said, not wanting to get into a conversation but not wanting to be rude, either. I wasn't really paying much attention to him until he introduced himself.

"My name is Ebenezer McConklin. What's yours?"

I recognized the name immediately but at first couldn't remember where I had heard it. Then I remembered. Yes. He was the old goat who had tried to take Sarah as a plural wife, the guy Pat was going to punch in the nose. He was a member of the Council of Fifty and president of the school board. I looked at him more closely.

Ebenezer McConklin looked to be in his mid-forties, maybe older. He carried a thick head of partly gray hair slicked straight back. His face was stern and wrinkled, like a man who scowled frequently and smiled rarely. He wore a new suit and a fresh-pressed white shirt. He had a double chin, and his hands were small and white like a woman's. He was not accustomed to hard work. I figured he would have a hard time on the westward trek.

"Your name, please," he repeated.

"Dan Storm."

He jerked forward in his chair, looking at me more closely. He recognized my name. Maybe Caroline had told him about me.

"You're the fellow Caroline was with on that uninhabited river island."

"That's right," I responded, noticing an increasing intensity in his countenance. He seemed to be groping for words, not sure how to ask the next question. I sensed what he didn't have the courage to ask, so I teased him by saying, "Yeah, we were on that island, just the two of us, five whole days—and five nights."

"She said you were bit by an eel, that you were unconscious with fever."

"That's right. I did pass out for a little while, but not for long.

Caroline really took good care of me. If she ever got tired of teaching school, she'd make a great nurse. But you shouldn't be concerned about what she did on the island. After all, she hasn't been baptized and isn't bound by Mormon laws."

Ebenezer's face had turned red. At first I was amused, but then I wondered why he would be so upset over the island incident. Could it be jealousy? Could he be waiting to see Caroline too? I remembered how quickly the matron had left the room, as if avoiding an awkward situation. I also remembered McConklin's unsuccessful attempt to take Sarah as a plural wife. Could he be trying again, this time with Caroline?

Suddenly my face was red too. My heart was thundering in my chest. The muscles in my arms and legs—finely tuned from hard work in the temple and wagon factory—throbbed with eagerness to do battle with the man across the room, the polygamist who was courting the woman I loved.

"Dan, what a pleasant surprise," said Caroline as she entered the parlor.

Mr. McConklin and I both stood to greet her. I had never seen Caroline look more beautiful. Her long blonde hair was freshly washed and brushed, hanging loose about her shoulders. Her long dress was as white as the new plaster on the temple wall, with a scattered pattern of light blue flowers. The dress looked new and the fit was perfect, revealing the swell of her bosom, the curve of her waist, and just enough ankle to be interesting. Her blue eyes were alert and clear, more intense than usual. And the additional color in her cheeks might have been at least partially the result of finding me and McConklin together.

She introduced us. McConklin and I shook hands, without enthusiasm. Then, to my total amazement, she moved to McConklin's side and put her arm in his. He flushed with delight and I wanted to kill him, right there in the parlor, in front of Caroline. I figured she must be mad.

"Dan," she said in a kindly voice. "Ebenezer and I are going to be married."

I had already figured out what was on McConklin's mind, but

I had had no suspicion that Caroline was such a willing participant. I was dumbfounded.

"Do you love him?" I asked, my voice faltering.

"Yes," she said, moving a little closer to McConklin, but looking to the side to avoid my direct stare.

"He's already married. You'd be a plural wife."

"I trust you will maintain confidence," blurted out McConklin, butting into my conversation with Caroline. "If you value your place in the kingdom."

"Don't threaten me," I snarled, taking a step forward, forcing him to step back. Then to Caroline, in a more gentle voice, "I don't know why you are doing this. I don't know what game you are playing. I don't know why you want to spend the rest of your life as a third or fourth wife to an over-the-hill polygamist."

McConklin started to say something. I told him to shut his mouth, that I would soon be gone.

"But I do know one thing," I continued, looking directly into Caroline's eyes. She didn't look away. "I came here tonight to ask you to marry me."

Caroline was caught by surprise, off guard. She put her hand over her mouth, but her eyes remained on mine. McConklin started to speak. I caught him by surprise by striking him firmly in the middle of the chest with the palm of my hand, sending him sprawling into a chair which—fortunately for him—just happened to be situated two paces behind him.

I looked back at Caroline, who still had her hand over her mouth.

"Wouldn't you rather spend the rest of your life, and perhaps eternity, with me?"

She continued to look at me, without saying anything.

"I'm heading west at daybreak. If you change your mind," I nodded toward McConklin, "come with me. Be at my place at dawn."

I turned on my heels and marched out, slamming the door hard on my heels.

Chapter 23

I spent a sleepless night wondering mostly about Caroline—if she would accept my challenge, or invitation, to go west. I couldn't put my finger on it, but something deep inside told me that she loved me as I loved her, that she really wanted to be my wife. Yet I couldn't get the picture out of my mind of her standing arm in arm with Ebenezer McConklin, telling me that she was going to become his plural wife.

It didn't take long to pack my possessions. I spread out my buffalo sleeping robe on the clay floor and piled on it the things I intended to take with me—ball mold and lead, extra powder, extra pads, beef jerky, flour, my personal journals with a record of daily happenings, and some seeds for Ike, my old friend, the escaped slave, now chief of the Gosiutes. I remembered him telling me he wanted to teach the Gosiutes to farm and asking me to bring him seeds if I ever returned to the Rocky Mountains. The package contained wheat, corn, pumpkin, melon, and apple seeds. I figured if Ike could get these things to grow on an experimental basis, I would find a way to get a plow to him.

I rolled the robe into a long bundle and lashed it tight with strips of rawhide so it would be easy to carry both over my shoulder and on my saddle.

I was dressed in my buckskin shirt and leggings, the same clothing I had worn upon returning from the Rocky Mountains.

Moccasins were on my feet. The possibles bag on my belt—the same one Beaver George had given me—contained flint and steel, salt, spare lashings, a razor, several gold coins, and two writing sticks.

Around my neck I wore the medicine pouch the Ute brave Neuwafe had given me. I checked the contents—the beaver teeth, the bear claw, the gold nugget, the bundle of horse hair, and the lock of fine black hair that had once belonged to Red Leaf, my Ute bride. Each item made ancient memories seem fresh again—except the gold nugget. I couldn't remember why Neuwafe had included it in the pouch. I wondered where he had found it. Maybe there were more. I should have asked him where it came from. Maybe he would tell me when I returned to the Rocky Mountains, if he was still alive. Many things could change in five years.

It was clear in my mind what I would do when the sun came up. If Caroline showed up, it would be our wedding day. I would spend my money and possibly the gold nugget to outfit a wagon for the westward journey.

If she failed to come, I would keep my money and offer my services to Brigham Young as a scout and hunter in leading the Saints west, providing I could leave immediately to blaze the trail across Iowa. I was sure my services would be welcomed, having lived in and traveled the Upper Missouri and Rocky Mountain regions.

By the time the morning sun began to warm the gray February sky, there was still no sign of Caroline. I had wanted so badly for her to come, but apparently she had decided on McConklin, for reasons I thought I would never understand.

I was bitter and resentful as I lashed the buffalo robe onto my saddled horse. I was entering a new phase of my life and was not very happy or enthusiastic about it because Caroline was not going to be sharing it with me. I wondered how long it would take to get thoughts of Caroline, at least the painful ones, out of my system.

I returned to the cabin one last time to make sure I hadn't forgotten anything. Then I removed the cap from the kerosene jug I had bought the day before and began pouring it around the cabin walls, inside and out. I had no intention of leaving the cabin behind to benefit the people who were driving us from this beautiful city.

I might have felt differently had I been able to sell it for a fair price. But that wouldn't happen. John D. Lee, one of the Church leaders, had sold his twenty-seven-room mansion, which had cost $50,000 to build, for $12.50. He got more out of his second house, having traded it for two ox teams.

No one was going to steal the cabin I had worked so hard to build. It looked good to me on the spot Caroline had selected, in plain view of the new temple and overlooking the mighty Mississippi River. Taking the flint and steel from my possibles bag, I struck a spark onto the kerosene-soaked ground.

Within seconds the entire cabin was in flames. With my rifle in one hand and the lead rope to the horse in the other, I turned away from the roaring blaze and headed toward the river and a new life in the West—a new life without Caroline Logan.

Chapter 24

I didn't cross the Mississippi River until February 9, 1846, one week after burning my cabin. When I reported to Brigham Young and offered my services as a scout and hunter for the first wagons heading west, he asked me to remain in Nauvoo for a week or so. During the days my help was urgently needed to help build flatboats to carry wagons across the river. There were over twenty thousand Mormons in Nauvoo, and the vast majority of them would be heading west immediately. Over two thousand wagons with teams and stock, as well as twenty thousand people, would have to be ferried across the mile-wide river.

Sometimes the Mississippi froze over, allowing wagons to roll across the ice, but presently there was no ice on the river, and there was no way of knowing if a severe freeze would be coming. Brigham Young was not a wait-and-see person. He ordered the construction of dozens of flatboats.

President Young had another reason for asking me to stay and work on the flatboats. Upon discovering that I had lived with the Utes in the Great Basin, he wanted me close for a few evenings so he and some of the other Church leaders could hear everything I had to say about the Upper Missouri, Rocky Mountain, and Great Basin regions.

Their biggest interest was the farming potential of the region—the potential of the land to produce enough food to support a

Mormon nation. I honestly admitted that tobacco was the only cultivated crop I had ever seen in the area, and added that the Rocky Mountain tobacco leaves were much smaller than those cultivated in Missouri and Illinois. I was quick to explain that Indians didn't tend their tobacco crop as diligently as the white men did—that it was common for a nomadic Indian to plant his tobacco patch in the spring and not see it again until he stopped by in the fall to harvest the leaves.

I said many of the valleys seemed to have plenty of water, delivered in streams from snowcapped mountains, but that there was less rain, perhaps too little to sustain crops like corn and potatoes, although the wild grasses in the valley floors grew high. My comments about rainfall concerned the brethren.

I told them about the abundant wild game, easy pickings for a man with a good rifle. The buffalo were in greatest numbers on the plains east of the Rocky Mountains. In the valleys of the mountains, deer and elk were abundant. Many of the streams and lakes had fish, mostly trout. I also told them about the Indian tribes I had had dealings with—the Utes, Gosiutes, Shoshones, Comanches, and Blackfeet.

I couldn't answer any of their questions about possible mineral deposits of iron, lead, zinc, and copper—although I did assure them they would find plenty of salt in the Great Basin.

I also showed them the gold nugget from my medicine pouch, admitting I didn't know where it came from. Some of the men became greatly excited, asking many questions I couldn't answer. The gold nugget did much to generate enthusiasm for the westward trek.

When I crossed the river on February 9, I did so as a member of the road and bridge–building crew. My services as a scout were not needed; wagon ruts already stretched across the full width of Iowa. My services as a hunter were not needed because the Iowa settlers had already killed sufficient game to make it scarce. One could obtain more food by working for wages and buying corn than by hunting.

But my services were desperately needed on the roads and bridges. Brigham Young couldn't have picked a worse time to cross the sparsely settled Iowa Territory. With the coming of spring, the rivers overflowed their banks. When the warmer spring rains coaxed the last of the winter frost out of the ground, the land became an endless sea of mud. Wagon wheels sank deeper and deeper until the wagon boxes became boats floating on the seemingly bottomless ocean of muck.

On the frontier, people simply didn't travel in the spring, especially not in wagons. But the Mormons were doing it anyway. They had to, if they didn't want their leaders jailed and their numbers dispersed. Brigham Young saw no alternative, though I'm sure the responsibility of leading twenty thousand people into a wilderness weighed heavy on him.

As a whole the Mormons were not frontier people. Most of them came from civilized cities and towns in New York, Pennsylvania, and England. They managed shops and well-tended farms. They didn't want to leave their well-cared-for Nauvoo homes.

Although President Young announced that he would be leaving on February 3, the same day I burned my cabin, he was unable to get away. Thousands of Mormons still had not received the benefit of the endowment—an all-day ceremony and ordinance, kind of like an advanced, more complicated form of baptism, though very secret, reserved for missionaries and married people only, as far as I could tell. It was a necessary forerunner to the secret and sacred ceremony that sealed marriages beyond death into eternity.

Earlier I had entertained dreams of Caroline and I experiencing these ordinances together on our wedding day. Now I had nightmares of Caroline and Ebenezer McConklin entering that sacred building arm in arm. I was eager to cross the river, figuring that once away from Nauvoo, it would be easier to put thoughts of Caroline out of my mind.

Anyway, that's how I felt on the morning of February 9 when I led my horse onto the flatboat. Brigham Young was still in Nauvoo, administering hundreds of endowments every day. Hundreds of wagons had already crossed the river and were establishing a camp about eleven miles inland at a place called Sugar Creek.

The river was crowded with flat-bottom boats loaded with new wagons, shouting people, and nervous stock. The thought of so many people heading west to establish a new kingdom—a new country, somewhere far away in the unsettled frontier—made the hair stand up on the back of my neck. The endeavor was bold, daring. No one knew for sure what lay ahead. New sights. New experiences. Plenty of hard work, for sure. Some would die, perhaps many. Some would lose faith. Perhaps many more would find faith.

In the middle of the river my idealistic thoughts were suddenly interrupted by the alarmed cries of a man and two boys in a nearby skiff. Their load was too heavy. It was taking water, sinking.

They were rowing frantically in our direction. We stopped our forward movement in an effort to allow them to catch us more quickly. The two boys were bailing water while the man rowed.

It looked like they were going to make it. They were within thirty feet of us when a larger than normal wave washed over the side of the skiff and it disappeared. The man and boys stood up, and for a moment it appeared as if they were just standing there in the middle of the river in knee-deep water. Knowing their skiff and supplies were hopelessly lost, they had no choice but to plunge forward and swim to us. Fortunately, all three of them knew how to swim.

Their teeth were chattering when we pulled them out of the icy brown water. Blankets were obtained from the wagons and wrapped around the unfortunate victims.

The boys were about the same size, maybe fifteen or sixteen, the same age I was when I went to the Rocky Mountains with Ike. The man was heavyset and in his mid-forties. He said his wife, the boys' mother, had died of the fever the previous summer.

Many people had died of the fever in Nauvoo. It came every summer, and hundreds never recovered. Nearly everyone who lived in Nauvoo more than a year had had a friend or loved one succumb to the fever. It came with the warm summer weather and departed with the first fall frosts.

Many figured the coming of the fever had something to do with the many river-bottom swamps around Nauvoo. Over the years the number of deaths decreased as swamps were drained in preparation for cultivation. But still, with the coming of summer, the fever was more dreaded than the mobs because there was nothing you could do to fight the fever once it got into you or a loved one.

As I looked at the man and two boys huddled quietly in their blankets, I couldn't help but feel sorry for them. In the midst of winter they were leaving their comfortable Nauvoo home and heading into an unknown wilderness with nothing but the clothes on their backs.

I was contemplating giving them some of my money when out of the corner of my eye I witnessed one of the most stupid acts I have ever seen in my entire life.

An older bearded fellow was sitting on the sideboard near the stock—oxen and horses—chewing tobacco. He was the only passenger who had not helped rescue the man and boys from the water; he seemed unconcerned with everything about him. His cheeks were bulging with tobacco and juice.

Suddenly, without warning, the bearded man spit a stream of brown juice into the eye of the nearest ox. Not only is tobacco juice dirty and smelly, but it burns when it comes in contact with sensitive tissue.

The ox bellowed as it swung its head in a wide and high circle. Senseless with pain, it lunged forward, dragging its yoked companion along. The bearded man rolled to one side as the two oxen charged over the sideboard and into the river, breaking loose one end of it. The water rushed in.

I dove for the loose end of the board and pulled it toward the boat, effectively cutting off most of the influx of water. I couldn't pull the board tight or flush against the side of the boat because of the protruding nails where it had been kicked free. I called for help, for someone with a hammer or other blunt object to come over and pound in the nails.

Before anyone could respond, another team of oxen, alarmed by the departure of the first two, followed the first team over the sideboard and into the river. This time the board was broken completely free. There was no stopping the incoming water. The boat was sinking for sure.

Fortunately, we were well past the middle of the river and almost to shore, not more than a few hundred feet away. While most of the people gathered around the wagons—which they expected would float when the boat sank—I began to untie the horses and oxen so they would be free to swim to shore, saving my horse until last. He was still loaded with the buffalo robe containing my gear and rifle.

After a quick glance to make sure everything was lashed securely in place, I tossed the lead rope over the horse's neck and slapped him on the rear. He hesitated for a second, then leaped into the river. I dove in after him, grabbed the half-floating tail, and let the horse pull me to shore.

One of the wagons made it to shore. The other sank, along with most of its contents. Luckily, none of the people drowned, but the first team of oxen to go overboard was never recovered.

After everything that could be saved was hauled from the river and carried to high ground, we huddled around fires to dry our clothing and find refuge from a bitter north wind.

Everyone had been cold and wet before. That, in itself, wasn't so bad. The hard thing was being cold and wet against a cold February wind while still in sight of comfortable Nauvoo homes that had been abandoned because of religious persecution.

The cold Mississippi River water had doused any spark of enthusiasm that existed earlier. Before the boat sank, people were looking toward the western hills, wondering what was ahead, hoping the new life would be better, beginning to believe that leaving Nauvoo might be a good thing after all. Now the biggest thing in everyone's mind was surviving the approaching February night with wet gear.

The bearded man who spat in the ox's eye acted as if he had done nothing wrong. I wondered how many more stupid mistakes like that would be made before the migration ended. I wondered how many more people would overload their skiffs or wagons, thus creating problems and possible disaster for those around them. I wondered how many would become discouraged and leave. I wondered how many would die.

I tried to imagine what kind of courage it would take for Brigham Young to order fifteen thousand mostly unprepared people into the wilderness and take responsibility for their movement, nourishment, and safety. I hoped he had the dedication and commitment to see it through. I thought he did.

I wondered what part Caroline Logan would have in the migration. Would her husband-to-be give her her own wagon? Who would drive it? Or would she be assigned to the back of a wagon belonging to one of McConklin's senior wives? How would McConklin fare in the wilderness? My impression had been that he was a soft man, unaccustomed and unprepared for the rigors of wilderness survival. His wealth wouldn't be as important in the wilderness.

The thought of Caroline, perhaps pregnant and helpless on an endless, windswept prairie with no one but Ebenezer McConklin to protect and care for her, made me furious.

Damn, I thought. *Why didn't she marry me instead? How could she have made such a dumb decision?* Hoping that someday I would understand the mystery of Caroline Logan, I headed for the woods in search of more dry wood for the fires.

Chapter 25

The lack of food wasn't so bad. Many were not prepared when Brigham Young suddenly announced on February 2 that the exodus would begin immediately. The Saints had been expecting a late spring departure and had not accumulated sufficient food for the westward journey. Those few who were prepared had to share with others, and soon everyone was critically short on provisions. But the situation was bearable. Men could go to nearby settlements and split rails, chop wood, and build fences in exchange for food. Nobody was starving.

The cold weather wasn't so bad, either. There was plenty of firewood. One could keep warm by walking instead of riding. There were no bugs—no flies and mosquitoes to pester people and livestock. Of course, there were deaths from pneumonia, but in the warm summer weather, just as many died from swamp fever. When the temperatures dropped really low, rivers and swamps could be crossed easily, on the ice. While uncomfortable, the cold weather was bearable. One could always look forward to the spring weather just around the corner.

The worst thing was the mud, the endless sea of Iowa mud—black, brown, and gray. Wet, cold, and slippery; it was on everything—boots, hands, faces, jackets, bedding, even the food. One couldn't get away from it. The oxen and horses always matched in color the most recent mudhole.

Earlier, mobbers had been a threat, burning homes and beating up people. Later, Indians would be a threat, shooting occasional arrows, stealing food and sometimes a horse. But in Iowa the only important threat was mud—the endless Iowa mud that swallowed up hopes and dreams.

A group of wagons would start out in the morning with the intention of covering twelve or fifteen miles. An hour later, not one but eight or ten wagons, would be buried to the axles in an unexpected mudhole. Up to their bellies, the oxen were practically helpless. Nevertheless, sometimes as many as a dozen teams had to be unhitched from their wagons and coaxed forward to help pull the first wagon free, then the second, until all were through. Sometimes wagons had to be emptied—everything, including heavy iron stoves and plows, carried on weary shoulders to high ground.

When the oxen were in place, men and boys would gather around the wagon, lifting and pushing, sometimes up to their waists in muck. It wasn't uncommon for the mud to suck off a boot, sometimes two. If the wagon was almost free and the bootless man continued to push, sometimes he couldn't find his boot afterward.

In addition to boots, the mud swallowed up countless tools, utensils, even baby dolls. But most of all it swallowed up wagon wheels, dashing all hopes and plans of forward progress. Sometimes it took days to get through less than a mile of mud.

I was assigned to Stephen Markham, along with a hundred other men. We were the advance party scouting roads and campsites, building bridges. We didn't scout for Indians in the brush or game on the prairie. We scouted for mud in an effort to avoid it, in an effort to determine the driest path for the wagons that followed.

In checking out a beautiful meadow, we would push sticks straight down into the sod. Sometimes a ten-foot stick could be pushed out of sight. Where possible, the wagons were routed around such places.

Never was sunshine so welcome or rain so disheartening. Rain made mud, and it rained every day during March and most of April.

Historians glamorize the Mormon trek across the plains of Nebraska and Wyoming, but it was the Iowa mud that sucked a people to its knees, made boys into men, turned back the less dedicated, hardened muscles, welded lifetime friendships and loyalties, and demanded patience as endless as the mud itself. In February, thousands of frightened city dwellers entered the mud. In late April, a nation of hardened pioneers emerged from it.

The favorite story around the thousands of smoky Iowa campfires was the one about the man who was discovered up to his armpits in a very ugly mudhole. He was rocking forwards and backwards, making a clucking sound with his tongue. When asked if he needed help getting out, he said, "Yes. But first help get my horse out."

Chapter 26

For the fifteen thousand Mormons crossing the Iowa Territory in the spring of 1846, the refiner's fire was not fire, but mud. But not all the time, like on the mid-March morning when Martin Potter and I headed toward Indian Creek. We were leading two pack horses loaded with supplies to aid in building a bridge over the rain-swollen waters.

We saw an unusual sight, a wagon on high, rocky ground stalled for a reason other than mud. Several men were trying to coax a fallen draft horse to its feet. At first I figured the horse had twisted its leg in a badger hole, but when we stopped to help and got a closer look, it was apparent that the animal was sick with bloating and colic.

The wagon and team belonged to William Hall, who was bringing a load of supplies forward for Allen Stout.

Hall had tried to force some medicine down the horse's throat—a mixture of whiskey and herbs—but without success. The horse wouldn't swallow. It didn't seem to be breathing, either. One of the forefeet was over an ear, as if that's where the pain was coming from.

As we stopped to check out the situation, two other men approached from a second wagon, bringing to six the number of men gathered about the sick horse. No amount of pulling, tail-twisting or kicking got any reaction out of the animal.

William Hall explained how the horse had gone down once before, a few miles back in Indian Creek. He added that he and Lluellen

Mantle, his partner, had laid their hands on the horse and given it a blessing, the same administration Mormons gave their sick.

I had witnessed many such administrations among the Mormons. Sometimes the sick got better, sometimes they didn't. Sometimes the healings came about so quickly they seemed miraculous. But I had never heard of administering to animals before. Somehow, at first thought, that seemed almost sacrilegious.

"Maybe if you'd baptized him first, the blessing would have stuck," suggested one of the men. The humor was spontaneous.

"Could be he lost it (the blessing) when he had a lusty thought for the mare beside him," kidded another.

"Geldings don't have lusty thoughts," added somebody else. Everyone laughed.

It was Reuben Strong who put an end to the joking. "I don't see anything wrong with administering to a horse," he said, his tone deadly serious. "I never read anything in the scriptures forbidding the blessing of animals."

"But they're dumb," said another. "Animals don't know what's going on. They can't have faith. Blessings don't work without faith." The discussion was serious now, the men looking for the right answer about blessing animals.

"The Missouri pukes and Warsaw mobbers'd love to see us blessing animals," added another. "They'd call us animal worshippers. The preachers would love it. Let's leave the weird stuff alone."

"Wait a minute," persisted Reuben Strong. "We'll never make it west without healthy animals. In a way, our very lives depend on the good health of our animals. We bless our babies when they are too little to have any faith or know what's going on. I say we bless the bugger."

"Looks like he'll soon be a goner if we don't do something," said one of the men.

"Besides," continued Strong, "The prophet Joel says that in the last days the spirit of the Lord will be poured out on all flesh—not just men, but all flesh, and I suppose that means horses."

Looking around at each other, all of us nodded our agreement that we at least ought to give it a try.

A small flask of olive oil was handed to Reuben Strong, who knelt on the wet ground beside the horse's head and anointed its ear with the oil while saying a little prayer. When he was finished the rest of us knelt beside him in a circle, reaching forward to lay hands on the horse's head.

At first I felt kind of silly about the whole affair, thinking how dumb it would appear to someone looking on—six grown men kneeling around the head of a dying horse, pouring oil in its ear and saying prayers.

But in the pause that followed the anointing, while waiting for William Hall to pronounce the blessing, a surge of emotion began to swell in my chest. I couldn't help but think that a God with any kind of heart at all would respond to an act of such obvious faith.

One wouldn't be surprised to see a group of children praying over their dying horse, possibly a pet. Nor would one be surprised at a bunch of preachers or women praying over a dying animal. But a group of rough, work-hardened men on the road, away from the gentle influences of women—that was unusual, and I couldn't help but feel that a loving God would be inclined to respond to our act of faith.

There was a slight trembling in my hands, and I could feel the same trembling in the hands of the other men.

William Hall's blessing was bold and to the point. In a loud voice, he commanded the unclean and foul spirits of every name and nature to depart and go to the mobbers at Warsaw, troubling the Saints no more.

I don't know if any evil spirits ever showed up in Warsaw, but no sooner had he finished the blessing than the horse rolled over twice, seeming to be in great distress. He sprang to his feet, squealed, vomited, and emptied his bowels. The next morning he was harnessed to a load of about twelve hundred pounds and performed his part as usual.

I suppose there are those who would doubt the miraculous healing of a dumb horse. And I can understand why someone might doubt such an unusual occurrence, supposing that the horse would have jumped up without the blessing, thinking maybe the oil loosened up something in the horse's ear, allowing him to come back to his senses.

But as far as I am concerned, it was the hand of God. I was there. I felt that surge of faith, or strength, as I knelt with those men around the horse, our hands resting on the beast's head. Words can't describe the feeling of divine intervention.

I had heard many sermons in my short lifetime, from missionaries, preachers, and prophets. I had spent many hours struggling through the scriptures. I had even helped build a temple to the Lord, and I said prayers practically every day. But kneeling around a dying horse with a bunch or trail-toughened teamsters had to be the strongest dose of real religion I had ever had.

Chapter 27

It was with suspicion that the Mormons greeted Captain James Allen of the U.S. Army when he caught up with them in western Iowa in late June 1846. Fifteen thousand Mormons had fled Nauvoo the past winter, fearing that if they waited until spring, United States troops would come up the Mississippi River and arrest their leaders. It was the fault of the U.S. government that they had had to face such hardships during the muddy spring.

All remembered the last "government" deal offered to the Saints. In late February, just as the Mormons were fleeing their beautiful city on the Mississippi River, New York Mormon Sam Brannan signed an agreement that he thought would save his people from further harassment. He promptly sent the agreement by courier to Brigham Young. Amos Kendall of Kentucky, who was Postmaster General several years earlier, a Mr. A. G. Benson, and others told Samuel Brannan that unless the leaders of the Church would sign an agreement with them, to which the president of the United States was a private party, the government would not permit the Mormons to proceed on their journey westward. The agreement required the Mormons to transfer to A. G. Benson & Company the odd number of all the land and town lots they might acquire in the country where they might settle. If the Mormons refused to sign the agreement, the president would issue a proclamation that it was the intention of the Mormons to take sides with other nations against the United

States, and order them to be disarmed and dispersed. Brannan, fully satisfied that this was the secret intention of the government and that the president was a principal party, signed it.

On February 17, while encamped at Sugar Creek, Brigham Young and his council concluded that their trust was in God and that they would not honor such an unjust and oppressive agreement.

So when Captain Allen popped up at the Mormon encampment at Mount Pisgah, cheerfully seeking volunteers to help the United States fight Mexico, he was greeted with anything but enthusiasm. In fact, the only cooperation he received was a word from Wilford Woodruff, telling him where Brigham Young could be located, at the Mosquito Creek encampment, a day's journey away.

I was working on a bridge at Mosquito Creek when Captain Allen arrived. Again he received a cold reception from everyone except Brigham Young. His reaction to the call for five hundred volunteers was immediate and favorable.

I suppose later generations will praise Brigham Young for his patriotic spirit. But that wasn't the reason. It was economics. President Young had the job of getting fifteen thousand people and two thousand wagons across the plains, through the Rocky Mountains, and settled in the uninhabited Great Basin. The men could grow crops and work for corn, but hard cash was needed to buy iron, rope, canvas, gunpowder, and many other necessities of travel. Contrary to what many of our enemies believed, the Church did not operate its own counterfeit mint.

To make matters even worse, we were camped illegally on Indian land belonging to the Potowotomies and Omahas without sufficient means to go forward, and mobs of Missourians threatening to come after us should we stick around very long. We couldn't go back, and we didn't have the means to go forward. And it was against the law of the United States to stay where we were.

Foreseeing such a situation months earlier, Young had sent Jesse Little to Washington to seek government contracts to build blockhouses and forts along the Oregon trail. Such contracts would provide the necessary hard cash to see the Saints safely out of the hair of politicians worried about the "Mormon problem." Unable to arrange for the contracts to build forts, but seeing the good sense in helping the Mormons get away by themselves, President Polk saw a chance to help when Congress authorized the recruitment of fifty thousand additional troops to fight Mexico. Colonel Stephen Kearny of the U.S. Army of the West sent Captain Allen to recruit five hundred Mormons.

When President Young introduced Captain Allen, he supported the call as "the first offer we have ever had from the government to benefit us."

Brigham Young spearheaded the recruiting drive himself. And, seeing as I was an able-bodied man, without family obligations, I was one of the first drafted. I signed two papers—one agreeing to serve my country faithfully and another authorizing the government to disperse the greater part of my wages and the forty-two dollar clothing allowance directly to the Church leadership at Council Bluffs. The other 540 draftees signed the same two agreements. Brigham Young finally had the cash he needed to get his people over the Rocky Mountains, if not in 1846, for sure in 1847.

I was glad to help out by joining the battalion, as were most of the others. Caroline was still on my mind continually. Maybe going off to war and getting shot at by the Mexicans would help me forget her more quickly.

Joining the battalion was tougher on the men with families. It was agreed that some of the men, at least the officers, could take their wives and children along.

In addition to the soldiers, twenty women were hired as laundresses . . . I figured most of them would be wedded before the trip was over.

We were headed for Mission San Diego on the Pacific Ocean, and it was explained that when our enlistment was up we could keep our bedrolls and firearms, .69 caliber smooth bores. They weren't very accurate, so I declined the Army rifle and hung onto my .40 caliber Hawken. During the enlistment period each soldier was to receive eighteen ounces of bread and twenty ounces of beef, or twelve of bacon, every day.

The men were divided into five companies of about a hundred each, and Captain Allen was promoted to lieutenant colonel when he assumed command. Church leaders were allowed to choose the other officers.

After a gala party wherein Brigham Young and other Church leaders preached glorious sermons about serving one's country, we marched off to Fort Leavenworth to be outfitted.

After building bridges and pushing wagons out of the mud for three months, it was refreshing and exciting to be embarking on a new adventure into new lands, to go all the way to the Pacific Ocean—but all that excitement was short-lived.

When we stopped for the midday break on the first day's march out of Mosquito Creek, we met a wagon train headed for the main Mormon encampment on Mosquito Creek, later to be called Winter Quarters.

I was sitting on my bedroll under a dogwood tree, gnawing on a piece of bread, watching the wagons roll slowly by, when my attention was attracted to some shouting further up the road. An ox had apparently decided to stop without permission, and its driver, a tall, thick, bearded man, was shouting at and beating the beast with a rawhide whip. There was something familiar about the bearded man, but he was still too far away to recognize. I decided to take a closer look.

I hadn't gone far before my heart began to thunder in my chest. The identity of the man was unmistakable. It was Ebenezer McConklin, the man Caroline had picked to marry.

My first reaction was to turn around and head back the way I had come before I was tempted to kill the man who had taken so much from me. But I couldn't. The thought that I might see Caroline one last time before heading off to Mexico was not something to walk away from. No matter how much her rejection had hurt me, I still loved her, and I would swallow any amount of pride to see her one more time, even as the wife of Ebenezer McConklin. I just hoped she wasn't pregnant, not yet.

There were two women on the wagon seat. I lowered my hat over my eyes, hoping to get past McConklin unnoticed and ask one of the women where Caroline might be. The hat was unnecessary. McConklin was so engrossed in beating the dumb ox that Brigham Young himself could have walked by unnoticed.

"I'd like to speak to Caroline," I asked the nearest woman.

She gave me a blank look, like she had no idea what I was talking about.

"His newest wife," I persisted, "the blonde schoolteacher."

A sudden look of recognition shot over her face. She turned to her friend and whispered something. They both began to laugh.

"Where is she?" I persisted.

One of them finally stopped laughing long enough to tell me Caroline wasn't with them. They both started laughing again, but stopped abruptly when McConklin suddenly spun around like an angry bull, suspecting he was the object of their laughter.

He didn't recognize me until I stepped forward and said, "Where's Caroline?"

"I might ask you the same thing," he responded angrily.

"What?" I asked, totally confused.

"Don't pretend to be so innocent."

"Didn't you marry her?" I asked.

"You know darn well I didn't. Now get out of here before I take this whip to you."

I knew he meant business, that I would quickly be in a fight if I stuck around. But I no longer had any desire to fight Ebenezer McConklin. Caroline had not married him after all. Apparently she had backed out at the last minute. Maybe she was looking for me this very moment.

Whooping for joy, I dodged the first lash from McConklin's whip, and before he could lash out a second time, I had leaped out of reach.

Caroline is free. I will find her, I thought as I raced back to the dogwood tree where I had left my companions and bedroll.

It was the blast of the trumpet that reminded me I was in the Army and headed for the Pacific Ocean. There would be no searching for Caroline, not for a long, long time.

As we picked up our gear and headed down the trail toward Fort

Leavenworth, the excitement of going off to war with Mexico, all the way to the Pacific Ocean, was gone. Every step was taking me farther away from Caroline. I began to think maybe it would have been better if I had not run into Ebenezer McConklin and made the discovery that brought such sweetness, then such bitterness, into my life.

Chapter 28

Caroline was again in the forefront of my thoughts. I longed to see her, to talk to her, to hold her hand, to resume our courtship, to ask her to marry me. I had a strong feeling that this time the answer would be different. But the Mormon Battalion headed south along the Missouri River, taking me farther and farther from Caroline, whom I supposed was still in Nauvoo.

We arrived at Fort Leavenworth, Kansas Territory, August 1, 1846. We stayed almost two weeks getting equipped with muskets, blankets, tents, cannons, wagons, and a walking larder of stringy beef cattle. During the idle days and long nights, I yearned to head back to Nauvoo, even entertaining thoughts of desertion. It would have been very easy to slip away under cover of darkness. But there had been a lot said about President Polk sticking his neck out by calling up the Mormon Battalion. Many said the Mormons couldn't be trusted, that a Mormon army would be nothing more than a bunch of deserters and renegades. By deserting I would give credibility to that kind of talk.

Besides, as I looked among my companions, I saw men who had better reason to desert than I—men with wives and babies living in tents and mud huts at Council Bluffs—men whose women and children would soon be facing a wilderness winter without husbands and fathers to care for them. How could I desert when men like these remained faithful? I would have to leave my personal affairs in the hands of God, as these other men were doing.

I did, however, decide to write Caroline a letter. The contents were as follows:

Fort Leavenworth Kansas Territory
August 6, 1846

Dear Caroline,

I wouldn't be writing to you had I not run into Brother McConklin and his wives near Council Bluffs several weeks ago. I saw his wagon while marching south with the Mormon Battalion along the Missouri River toward Fort Leavenworth.

I approached him and his wives, wanting to see you one last time before going off to fight in the war with Mexico. I was somewhat apprehensive in doing so, not wanting to make things uncomfortable for you in your new family situation.

I can hardly describe how happy I felt when I learned that you hadn't married him after all. Had I not been in the Army, I would have leaped upon my horse and headed for Nauvoo to see you.

I hope I am not making a mistake in assuming your rejection of Brother McConklin indicates a change of heart about me. I hope you will respond to this letter concerning your disposition toward me, allowing my hopes to soar or to be put back in place. I trust your letter will reach me, but don't count on it happening very fast. We are heading into mostly uncharted territory. I anticipate a hard journey. The herd of cattle they have gathered to feed us along the way won't last very many days. I don't know how the Army anticipates getting food after the cattle are gone.

Kearney's main army is already on the way to the Pacific Ocean to take California from the Mexicans. Our job is to locate a passable wagon trail to California. It is hard to tell now whether our hardest battles will be against Mother Nature or the Mexicans, or both. President Young did promise, however, before we left Council Bluffs that none of us would be killed in battle with the Mexicans. He didn't say anything about the

Apaches, however, and that bothers me some. From my earlier days with the Utes, I remember the Apaches being a formidable enemy in the southern regions of the Rocky Mountains. I suppose we'll find out soon enough.

Again, I hesitate being forward with you since I really don't know for sure why you changed your mind about McConklin. I have to take a chance, however, this possibly being the last chance to get a note to you for many months, perhaps a year or more.

If your rejection of him had anything to do with a change in feelings toward me, I look forward to seeing you again as soon as possible. When and where that will be, I have no way of knowing at this time.

My plans are to continue with the Battalion to the Pacific Ocean, filling my one-year conscription honorably. Upon release, I will head for the Great Basin, where the main body of Saints should be settling. It doesn't appear that any will make it to the mountains this year, but I'm sure many will reach the Basin next season. I will look for a message from you there. Just send your letter to anyone at Council Bluffs, asking them to send it on with the first party to the mountains. I will find it.

If the message from you is favorable, as I hope it will be, I will head east immediately, as long as it is not too late to get through the passes before the deep snow falls. Sometime during the winter I will be at your door, whether it be in Council Bluffs, Nauvoo, or anywhere else.

Remember when we were on that island in the Mississippi River? I shared with you a dream. A dream of you and I claiming for ourselves an unnamed valley in the distant Rocky Mountains—a lush valley with plenty of clear running water, grass to a horse's belly, and fertile soil. A valley surrounded by snowcapped peaks where eagles soar out over pine forests full of elk and deer.

We could build a comfortable log home, a barn, corrals, and fences. Raise cattle, corn, and wheat. Trade with the friendly Indians. On occasion, visit neighbors in nearby valleys. We could raise a goodly number of strong sons and healthy daughters. Remember the dream? I can see it clearer than ever. I hope you can, too. Write to me soon.

Love,
Dan

Chapter 29

"Buffalo juice is good for the kidneys," laughed Lieutenant Andrew Jackson Smith as he dipped his tin cup into the green-brown water. It had been a month since we had left Fort Leavenworth, and we were in the middle of the Cimarron Desert, at the edge of what the map called Wild Horse Lake. It was nothing more than a well-used buffalo wallow. Lieutenant Smith had been in charge of the Mormon Battalion since Captain Allen's death ten days after leaving the fort.

At first the men resented a fire-eating youngster like Smith taking over the command. Not only did he seem too young for such a big command, but he seemed bent on achieving the rank of general before we reached Santa Fe. Allen's death had given Smith an unexpected opportunity to command, and he intended to make the best of it.

Grown men didn't like being bossed around by a youth who didn't need a shave more than once a week, but the initial resentment for Smith vanished quickly beneath the blistering sun of the Cimarron Desert. There the men suddenly realized a source of strength in the young lieutenant's iron will and indomitable cheerfulness.

Like on the afternoon when we reached Wild Horse Lake. It wasn't the lake we had so eagerly anticipated for two whole days of waterless travel. It wasn't even a pond or a spring, but a muddy wallow where dozens of buffalo in recent days had deposited their urine and manure while seeking relief from the relentless sun.

There was still a full day of travel, maybe two, before reaching the Cimarron River, and the map showed no other water along the way. As the first men to reach Wild Horse Lake were still looking in disbelief and despair upon the green-brown filth of the wallow, Lieutenant Smith cheerfully waded to the middle and filled his tin cup.

Nobody really expected him to take more than a sip, if that much, but he gulped down the entire cupful and scooped out another before making his comment about the health benefits of buffalo urine.

The men laughed heartily with their enthusiastic lieutenant. The initial disappointment, while still lingering, was no longer overbearing. Urine-flavored water was better than no water at all. At least we were assured of sufficient moisture to keep us alive until we reached the Cimarron River.

Along with the rest of the men, I waded to the middle of the wallow and carefully scooped up a cup of the green-brown liquid, which I siphoned carefully between my teeth, holding my breath to cut the taste as I swallowed.

I remembered my earlier trip to the Rocky Mountains in 1838, following the Missouri River to its headwaters. Plenty of water, greenery, and more game the further one went. Even most of the Indian tribes were friendly.

The southern route to Santa Fe was different. The white grass curled under the relentless sun like buffalo hair, and it wasn't much longer. Water was so scarce that even buffalo wallows were welcome sights. There was little game, except for a few antelope, buffalo, and rattlesnakes. No friendly Indians. In the Cimarron we were constantly on the lookout for horse-stealing Comanches, but the worst lay ahead. Upon leaving Santa Fe, we would enter the domain of the Apaches, reported more cunning and fierce than the Blackfeet, and that worried me.

The first of our men arrived in Santa Fe on October 9. We set up camp north of the Santa Fe River, just east of the Saint Francis Cathedral. The next morning Colonel Philip St. George Cooke assumed command, keeping Lieutenant Smith as his quartermaster. Cooke seemed intelligent and competent, though he was not familiar with the country west of Santa Fe. Fortunately, he lined up three guides who seemed to know the country—one of whom was Baptiste Charbonneau, son of Toussaint Charbonneau and Sacajawea. He had traveled with Lewis and Clark in his cradleboard, later getting educated in St. Louis and Europe.

Colonel Cooke, in his efficient manner, quickly singled out eighty-six of the men and twenty of the women and children as unfit for the journey ahead. He dispatched them north to Pueblo to spend the winter. A group of 397 men remained to continue the journey. Each of the five companies was outfitted with three mule wagons. In addition, the battalion had six large ox wagons. The quartermaster and other officers had four additional mule wagons, and four or five individuals took private wagons, making a total of about thirty.

In spite of Cooke's best efforts, he was only able to obtain short rations for about sixty days, which included the oxen pulling the wagons, twenty-eight beef cattle, and a herd of three hundred long-legged Spanish sheep called *churros*.

From Santa Fe we followed an old Spanish trail into mostly uncharted territory. Cooke had a map from Tanner's Atlas and Mitchell's map of Texas, Oregon, and California, but they didn't give enough detail to be of much use. He relied almost totally on the guides. As I said earlier, our job was to blaze a wagon road to California.

Upon leaving Santa Fe, I began to catch the excitement of our adventure. Nobody knew for sure where we were going. Nobody knew for sure when we would run into the first Apaches. Nobody knew exactly how the war with Mexico was progressing or where Mexican troops were located. We were traveling through country claimed by Mexico.

Frequently I thought of Caroline, particularly when the trail was monotonous, or during the nights while looking up at the stars. I wondered if she had received my letter and how she reacted to it. I wondered if she had written a response and, if so, where that response might be, possibly crossing the Iowa Territory in a wagon. I wondered why she had changed her mind about marrying McConklin. But even more so, I wondered why she had decided to marry him in the first place. There were things about Caroline Logan that I simply could not understand, puzzle pieces that simply did not fit, no matter how many hours I pondered them in the New Mexico wilderness.

I had followed the Missouri River to the Rocky Mountains. I had wandered through the Rocky Mountains with Beaver George. Alone I had explored uninhabited valleys of the Bitter Root Mountains. I had wandered through the huge Snake River Valley and explored the headwaters of the Green River. I had lived with the Utes in the Great Basin at the foot of the majestic Mount Timpanogos and wandered with the Utes over thousands of square miles, following buffalo.

I had seen a big portion of the American West before white men began to clutter it with cabins and fences, but never had I felt the strange, eerie, almost haunting feeling that I and the other Mormon Battalion soldiers felt during the first part of December 1846, as we left the Guadalupe Mountains, ascended a great bluff, and began crossing a huge prairie. We were traveling west along an imaginary line that later became the border separating Arizona Territory from Mexico.

The eerie feeling came over us as we emerged from a draw onto the open prairie. On a solitary rock near the edge of the bluff, a perfect vantage point overlooking the dry Guadalupe Arroyo, was a sun-warped saddle held firmly to the rock by its cinch. The saddle, by itself, though an unexpected sight, was not a disturbing one. What bothered us was the sun-bleached skull resting over the saddle horn, a sinister sentry watching and warning those who might dare to cross the plain.

It was a land like none of us had ever seen before, except perhaps the guides, who were already out of sight, supposedly scouting for any sign of Apaches. Mescale trees reaching thirty feet high, the biggest any of us had ever seen, with bristling spheres of green bayonets up to three feet in length, were scattered across the plain. There were many new kinds of cacti—from a little pink ball at our feet to some the size of trees with huge branches covered with two-inch spikes. The men named these Devilrod. Mesquite was everywhere, sometimes making travel difficult.

The mystery of the plain intensified as we found more signs of civilization—a well-worn iron horseshoe, a grove of flat-topped tree stumps where a white man's saw had been at work, and several wooden crosses with Spanish names carved on them. It was apparent the region had at one time supported a large Spanish or Mexican population.

Strangest of all was the wild animal population—not the snakes, lizards, bugs, and usual fare, but the meat-bearing animals. There were no buffalo, elk, or deer as one might expect, but cattle. Thousands of horned, wild cattle roamed this mysterious country. At the sight of men, they would stampede into the distance. And the number of bulls seemed equal to the number of cows, another clear indication the herds were unmanaged by men. We concluded from their skittish nature that the cattle were frequently hunted by Indians, much the same as the buffalo on the plains to the north were hunted by red men.

On the afternoon of December 2, we discovered what was once the center of a thriving community but was now an uninhabited ghost town. Nearby was a huge spring, maybe thirty paces across.

The guides called the place San Bernardino. Only adobe walls remained, the roofs of the buildings having caved in years earlier. There was a large, hundred-foot building with a square in the middle and a number of smaller buildings with numerous small compartments. We assumed the don, or leader of the colony, had lived in the large building, and all his peons lived in the smaller apartments. The buildings covered a space of about two acres and were surrounded by a high adobe wall with regular bastions for defense. From the walls one had a fine view of the nearby countryside.

It wasn't until the guides explained how the Mexican community had been driven off by raiding Indians that I remembered what the

Ute warrior Neuwafe had told me about his father and grandfather raiding Spanish ranches for horses. It was possible that the Ute horse herds of the Great Basin had origins in this very valley.

We stayed several days at San Bernardino, enjoying the plentiful supply of fresh water from the spring and feasting on fresh beef brought in by hunters. The hunters reported the wild cattle to be more fierce than buffalo, the bulls frequently attacking the men who shot at them—but the real danger of that ferocity wasn't fully realized until a week later.

We were traveling north along the edge of a big bluff overlooking the San Pedro River when two mounted hunters galloped out of a nearby draw, heading straight for the main battalion. There was a huge cloud of dust behind them, and at first we thought they were being chased by a huge band of hostile Indians. To our surprise, a herd of maddened bulls, not Indians, charged from the draw—not just a handful, but dozens, maybe seventy or eighty, heading straight for the Battalion.

Total confusion reigned, even among the officers. While one lieutenant ordered the men to form a line and commence firing, another was telling everyone to scatter and get out of the way. I'm sure Colonel Cooke would have arrived at a reasonable course of action had there been time, but before such a decision could be made, the raging bulls were among us. It was every man for himself.

Soon the camp was a huge cloud of dust filled with the noise of shouting men, bellowing bulls, and the frequent crack of muskets. Not only did the bulls attack the men, but everything in sight. One charged into the back of a freight wagon, actually lifting the back wheels off the ground. Another tossed a mule over the back of its teammate, then gored the teammate, spilling out a string of entrails that nearly touched the ground. Amazingly, the mule remained on its feet. Later, the battalion surgeon shoved the entrails back inside and sewed up the hole. The poor animal didn't even get sick.

Probably the most daring act of the day was performed by Corporal Frost of Company A, who became the target for a huge black bull. The beast was a full hundred yards away when it focused its attention on Frost and began its charge. Frost spotted the bull immediately and raised his musket to his shoulder. Colonel Cooke called to Frost to get out of the way, but the resolute corporal didn't budge. The course of the black bull was undeviating. He seemed oblivious to all the clamor about him as he headed for the corporal.

With the bull at a full gallop a hundred feet away, everybody started shouting at Frost to fire. He remained as still as a statue, and it occurred to me that he might be paralyzed with fear. It wasn't until the bull was within a dozen paces, and everybody figured Frost a dead man, that the musket finally exploded. Apparently Frost didn't want to take any chances on missing, and he didn't. The dead bull, a ball between its eyes, ground to a halt within inches of Frost's boots. Thus ended the only battle the Mormon Battalion ever fought. The casualties included several gored men and mules (none of which died), a damaged wagon box, and nineteen dead bulls. We had plenty of fresh beef for the next and last leg of our journey.

As we left the country of the wild cattle, I sometimes wondered about that sun-blistered saddle carrying the human skull. I also wondered about the deserted Spanish settlements—we had come across several others which appeared to be outposts to the one called San Bernardino.

I wondered why the Apaches had let us pass unmolested. Perhaps it was our large numbers. Perhaps their fighting men were somewhere else this time of year. Perhaps they were smart enough to know we were just passing through. At any rate, that haunted feeling stayed behind with the wild cattle, with the ghosts of San Bernardino.

Chapter 30

I don't know what historians will remember most about the Mormon Battalion. We didn't fight any battles, at least not any real battles, except the one with the wild bulls. I suppose the battalion might be remembered for having blazed the first wagon trail across a thousand miles of uncharted territory. Some historians will remember we were made up of volunteers who enlisted in an army that had turned its back on us a few months earlier as we were driven by mobs from our Nauvoo homes. Some historians will even remember the hockmocs, a new type of boot invented by battalion members.

I'm not sure who invented the first hockmoc, but the first time I saw a pair in service was just after the Gila River crossing. The rough, rocky trail had been tough on boots—and spare boots being in short supply, most of the men having sent their clothing allowances back home—an increasing number of men found themselves without any kind of footwear.

At first men just wrapped their bare feet with rawhide or discarded clothing. With Colonel Cooke in such a great hurry, there never seemed to be sufficient time to sit around camp making moccasins. I'm sure some of the men could have come up with a suitable moccasin pattern had there been time. Instead they came up with the hockmoc, much simpler to make than a moccasin, just as comfortable, and in the opinion of many, more durable.

Whenever an ox or a wild beef was killed, two new pairs of hockmocs were in use the next morning. A ring was cut around the hide above and below the hock joint, and then the skin was peeled off without cutting lengthwise. After this, the lower end was sewn up with sinew. Next it was turned inside out with the hair on the inside, then slipped onto a human foot, the heel finding its natural place in the crook where the hock had been.

I don't know who first called this peculiar piece of footwear a hockmoc, but I assume the term is a combination of hock and moccasin. After reaching Mission San Diego, the men were issued footwear more appropriate for seasoned U.S. Army troops, and the hockmocs were thrown to the dogs.

Although our journey ended in January, our service continued until the following July when our one-year term of enlistment expired. From January to July we were assigned to various places, including Mission San Diego, San Luis Rey Mission, and Los Angeles Mission.

The difference in leadership styles of Colonel St. George Cooke and Lieutenant Andrew Jackson Smith was evident in their parting remarks to the men. In a letter dated January 30, 1846, Cooke said, "History may be searched in vain for an equal march of infantry. Nine-tenths of it has been through a wilderness where nothing but savages and wild beasts are found, or deserts where, for want of water, there is no living creature. . . . With crowbar and pick and ax in hand, we have worked our way over mountains which seemed to defy aught save the wild goat, and hewed a passage through a chasm marching half-naked and half-fed, and living upon wild animals, we have discovered and made a road of great value to our country."

Lieutenant Smith, on the other hand, made his last remarks on July 16 when he mustered us out of the service. After calling the five companies into formation at three o'clock in the afternoon, the notorious lieutenant marched silently down one row and back the next, briefly inspecting all the troops. Upon reaching the front, he turned and faced the men.

Then in a low voice he said, "You are discharged."

That was all. It was over, and we were free to go. We were

surprised, yet pleased, at the brevity of the lieutenant's remarks. Had he given a speech, I probably wouldn't have remembered it anyway.

But there was one speech by Lieutenant Andrew Jackson Smith that I will never forget. It was not delivered on a parade ground, in a clean uniform, but in the middle of the scorching Cimarron Desert, the Lieutenant standing ankle-deep in a green-brown buffalo wallow, tin cup raised high, smiling brightly, encouraging the men to drink with the words, "Buffalo juice is good for the kidneys."

Chapter 31

Those who were mustered out of the Mormon Battalion divided into two general groups. There were those who headed back the way we had come, east across the southern California deserts and then north to the Great Basin where Brigham Young and his first wagon train of Mormons were just arriving, and those who headed north through California's Spanish settlements, finding work here and there, intending eventually to turn east through the Sierra Nevada Mountains to the Great Basin. Most of us were on foot, except some of the officers who had sufficient money to buy horses. The rest of us, having authorized the government to send our pay to Brigham Young at Council Bluffs, barely had enough money to buy food, though the California horses were the cheapest I had ever seen. A fine, well-broke saddle horse could be purchased for as little as ten dollars.

I joined the group heading north through California. The more direct route to the Great Basin was the way we had come, across the gray, desolate, waterless deserts. Those barren wastes had been bad enough to cross during December and January, but to attempt a crossing in July seemed suicidal.

Tired of the strict regulation and forced associations of army life, I soon struck out on my own. While the other men followed the coast or the central valley in their northward journeys, keeping close to the main network of Spanish settlements, I headed east to the foothills of the Sierra Nevadas. My plan was to head north along the foothills until I found a pass suitable for crossing to the east. Once through the mountains, I would head north to the Humbolt River, then east to the Great Basin.

I wasn't concerned about traveling alone, having heard no reports of hostile Indian activity near the California mountains. There were no settlements near the mountains other than a few isolated Spanish *rancheros,* but that didn't concern me. I figured there would be plenty of deer and elk to keep my stomach full. Not only had the Army allowed each of us to keep our weapons, we were also allowed to take all the ammunition we wanted to carry. I felt well-prepared for a trek across uninhabited land—as long as it wasn't the desolate desert land that had been so miserable to cross the previous winter.

California was a fascinating country in the summer of 1847. It was a rich land, a sharp contrast to the seemingly endless wastes encountered the previous winter. California was a sea of gentle rolling hills carpeted with an endless crop of rich grain—wild oats—golden in the summer and a lush green in the winter and early spring. The deer were as fat as Missouri hogs and more plentiful. Even the wild horses were fat, like Ohio farm horses before spring plowing. Scattered here and there on the hills were giant oak trees, their dark green leaves offering a beautiful contrast to the golden hills and blue Pacific sky. The land was hot and dry in July, but brown streams rushing westward from the snowcapped Sierras provided a steady flow of life-giving water to the inhabitants of this beautiful land.

I was about six days away from Mission San Diego when I spotted a huge corral in an otherwise uninhabited valley. The corral walls were high and stout, made from sun-bleached logs. I had just emerged from a grove of young oak trees on a hill overlooking the valley when I spotted the corral in the middle of the flat valley floor. More than a hundred horses rested quietly under the relentless July sun—most standing but many lying down, especially the spring colts. Several were walking along the inside of the fence line, as if looking for a way out. There were no men, buildings, or any other signs of civilization. Not far from the corral, a little creek ran lazily through a brush-filled gully.

Something seemed wrong, but I couldn't put my finger on it. Back in the Rocky Mountains, even as far east as Council Bluffs, no one would leave that many horses unattended. Too many horse thieves and Indians. Unattended horses had a tendency to disappear, quickly. In fact, as soon as I saw the corral, my first thought was to get my hands on one or two of those horses. I could travel a lot faster, and with much less effort, with a fast-walking pony beneath me. My thought wasn't to steal, but to somehow trade work or some kind of service for a horse, provided I could find the owners.

Cautiously, after checking the prime on my musket, I headed down the hill toward the mysterious corral. I hadn't gone far when I noticed that numerous white objects of varying shapes were scattered on the ground inside and in a ring around the outside of the corral. At first I thought they were branches trimmed from logs when the corral was built—but they were too white, too unusual in shape and size to be tree branches.

It wasn't until I reached the valley floor that I suddenly realized the identity of the white objects. Bones. Thousands of white, sun-bleached bones.

There was a sickening feeling in my stomach as I realized why the horses were in the corral, why they were unattended by humans, and why there were no other signs of civilization in the area.

As I approached the corral, my suspicions were confirmed by the smell of rotting flesh. And when I looked between the fence logs at the horses, I knew my conclusions were correct. The animals were gaunt from lack of feed and water. Some were already dead and bloating in the relentless sun. The stench was awful. The mares with spring colts were the closest to death, their nursing colts having increased the outflow of moisture from their bodies.

I had heard the stories of how the Spanish cowboys controlled the wild horse population. There was no market for wild horses with well-broke horses being so cheap. Nor was there any demand for their hides or flesh. In fact, most cattle slaughtered in California at this time were merely stripped of their hides, the meat left to the buzzards.

With powder and lead so expensive and cash in short supply, no one wanted to waste expensive ammunition on worthless horses. In annual or semi-annual roundups, the horses were merely herded into big, stout corrals and left to starve or die of thirst.

It seemed so cruel, such a waste. I thought of all the Indians I had known who would gladly risk life and limb for a chance to steal a few skinny desert ponies. I had known Indians who had even traded wives and children for horses. Horses made a tribe mobile and therefore stronger and richer. Those with horses could follow the buffalo herds, flee from enemies, and engage in trade with other tribes, the whites, and Mexicans.

I knew I could become rich if I could figure out a way to get a large number of these horses over the mountains. I would be a hero if I could deliver a hundred to Council Bluffs where two thousand Mormon wagons were being outfitted for the trek across the plains. Although oxen are best suited for long-distance wagon pulling, the horses would still be welcome.

But before trying anything heroic and dangerous, I decided to do the sensible thing and get a horse or two for myself. I didn't think the Spanish cowboys would mind if I helped myself, since the animals were condemned to death anyway.

Then the thought occurred to me that I might even open the gate and let the animals out. The Spanish wouldn't like that. Possibly I would become a fugitive in this strange land. I certainly didn't want to languish in a Spanish jail. I would have to think things through before I opened the gate. In the meantime, without the help of a rope, I had to figure out how to catch and break a wild horse, maybe two.

I climbed up on the fence and inspected the unlucky horses. Most of those still standing had their heads hanging close to the ground, mouths partially open, swollen tongues protruding between their teeth. Only a few lifted their heads to watch me climb up on the fence. The vast majority of these wild horses were too far gone to care.

It wasn't hard to pick those I wanted. A dozen or so, though gaunt like the others, seemed more alert and strong, holding their heads high, watching me with interest and alarm. A sorrel stallion pawed the dust and shook his head as if challenging me to come into the corral and fight him. A bay mare, her head highest of all, quivered with excitement, as if she were ready to run and leap over the high fence if I made any sudden movement. Her muscles were hard and well-defined. There was no fat on her, but the bulk of her muscles prevented her from having the skinny, bony look of most of the other animals. Her hooves were black and hard, without cracks.

I couldn't help but wonder why she looked so much stronger, with the exception of the sorrel stallion, than the other animals around her. It was as if she had just been put in the corral and hadn't suffered like the others. But that couldn't have happened. I had to conclude that she was a superior specimen of horseflesh, something I couldn't have recognized in a pasture with other well-fed horses. In a pen of dying animals, however, she was like a bright moon in a bed of twinkling stars. She was my first choice. She would be easier to break than the spirited sorrel. He was my second choice.

I sat there for a long time wondering how I could isolate and break my new horses. Without a rope and a separate corral to isolate them from the rest of the herd, it just didn't seem possible.

I walked over to the stream in the brushy draw and drank deeply of the cool, clear water. It didn't have that icy crispness of Rocky Mountain stream water, but it didn't have the filth of a buffalo wallow, either.

I couldn't enjoy the refreshing liquid without thinking of the nearby horses dying of thirst. It was a cruel thing, but this was Mexican land and the horses were Mexican business, and I had no business upsetting their way of doing things. Maybe when the war with Mexico ended, this land would belong to the United States. Some enterprising Yankee would undoubtedly find a way to get California horses to market and the senseless slaughter would end. In the meantime I had no choice but to leave the Mexican system of pest control alone.

However, every time I took another drink, I saw in the reflection of the water all those swollen tongues, the dying colts. There was also the constant reminder of the stench of the horses already dead.

I forced myself to think about my personal survival and immediate need for a horse to carry me over the mountains and across the desert to the Great Basin, and possibly the rest of the way to Council Bluffs. How could I isolate the one or two horses I wanted? How could I catch and break them?

I don't know how long I sat there by the little creek pondering these problems, but the sun was already behind the western hills when I finally reached what I thought were sensible conclusions—not only to the immediate problem of getting horses for travel, but the other, more unpleasant problem too. In fact, the solutions were inseparable.

One thing I was sure of from my previous experience with horses was the necessity of isolating the one or two animals I intended to work with. If I succeeded in separating the sorrel stallion and the bay mare by removing them from the corral, they would run away. There being only one corral in the valley, the only way to isolate my two horses would be to remove the other horses from the corral. I now had a practical reason to let the horses go. I needed to get them out of the corral so I could work with the animals that would take me to the Great Basin.

I ran to the top of the nearest hill in an effort to get a good look at the nearby countryside before dark set in. I figured if I spotted signs of a nearby ranchero, there would be an increasing risk of discovery and it might be necessary to change plans. Fortunately, I could see no signs of civilization from the top of the hill, not even a distant column of smoke from an evening cookfire.

As soon as the new moon peaked over the eastern hill, I walked back to the corral and began to untie the rawhide lashings holding the gate closed. I was grateful for the light of the moon. I didn't want any of the wrong horses to get out.

My plan was to open the gate whenever the bay mare and the sorrel stallion were at the far end of the corral. I would let the closest horses run to their freedom as long as the stallion and mare stayed away, but as soon as they came near, the gate would close. If I walked away from the open gate to haze horses through the opening, I had to be sure not to go so far I couldn't get the gate closed in time should the sorrel or bay make a break for the opening.

My plan seemed good in theory, but it simply did not work. The mare and stallion would not stay together. No sooner would one be at the far end of the corral than the other would approach the gate. When I opened the gate, the closest animals just stared at the opening as if wondering, "What new trick is this?"

Once a horse started for the opening in an attempt to escape, the strongest animals in the corral, the sorrel stallion and the bay mare, were quick to join it, forcing me to shut the gate. It would have been much easier if I'd had a companion. With one man controlling the gate, and the other hazing the horses, the task would have been easily accomplished. But as it was, it took nearly the entire night to set no more than a dozen horses free. Many of the dying animals, the ones I wanted to let out, were too far gone to recognize an opened gate, while the alert animals, the ones I wanted to keep inside, were quick to spot a potential escape route. My plan was no good. I would have to think of something else.

Chapter 32

Exhausted and frustrated after a long, fruitless night of trying to segregate the horses, I headed back to the creek to get a little sleep. I knew that if I waited long enough the horses would segregate themselves without my help. The weaker horses would die first. With time, only the strongest animals, those I wanted for myself, would be alive. But I didn't like the idea of waiting around while so many beautiful animals died of thirst.

As I approached the creek I noticed that one of the horses I had let out during the night had died. A palomino yearling had apparently swallowed too much water too quickly. It was on its side at the edge of the creek, bloated, its legs stiff and straight, hundreds of flies covering its eyes, nose, and mouth. I moved upstream to a grassy spot under the branches of a big oak tree, and by the time the sun came up I was sound asleep.

I don't know how long I slept, but I was awakened by the squawking of dozens of birds—jays, magpies, black hawks, and even a couple of red-necked buzzards—all fighting over the remains of the palomino yearling. The biggest buzzard moved about the horse at will, tearing off a piece of flesh here and there, holding his head high every time he gulped down a bite of breakfast. If the smaller buzzard got in his way, he squawked for it to move. If it was in the middle of tearing away a bite and failed to respond, the big bird stood tall and began to spread his wings in a threatening gesture as if he were preparing to attack. Whenever this happened, the other bird quickly forgot its business and got out of the way. The hawks milled about just outside an imaginary circle, one occasionally streaking in for a quick bite when the buzzards were occupied elsewhere. Beyond the circle of hawks the magpies and jays fluttered about, one occasionally darting in to steal a little piece of flesh. The pecking order was clear and distinct. There was plenty of meat for all, but there was no sharing among the selfish birds.

I had just finished a breakfast of beef jerky, a hard biscuit, and several dried peaches—provisions the Army had given me upon leaving Mission San Diego—when the fighting of the birds over the dead horse gave me a sudden idea, an idea that just might enable me to segregate out the horses I didn't want and get to work taming and training the bay and sorrel.

I hurried into the meadow, gathered a large armload of the golden wild oat grass, and threw it over the log fence into the corral at the point furthest from the gate. As I suspected, the horses were too thirsty to be interested in the hay.

Then, picking up a short, stout stick with a somewhat pointed end, I crawled through the gate and began scratching out a shallow hole.

The hole was on the inside of the closed gate, but when I pushed the gate inward six or seven feet, the hole was on the outside of the partially opened gate. As soon as the hole was ready, I climbed back through the gate, walked down to the stream, and removed my Army-issue cotton trousers.

After buttoning up the fly and tying a knot at the end of each pant leg, I pushed the trousers into the creek and filled them with water. Holding my new water bag upright with both hands so as to lose as little water as possible, I hurried back to the corral, through the gate, and dumped the water in the hole. I quickly scurried back through the gate to get out of the way.

Horses that had been too far gone the night before suddenly came alive at the sight and smell of fresh water. Every horse in the corral headed for the water. Soon the near end of the corral was a mass of squealing, kicking horses.

When the dust settled, my earlier suspicions were confirmed. The sorrel stallion was drinking the water while, at a safe distance, a tight ring of eager horses waited for him to finish. The bay mare was the closest to the stallion, but she didn't disturb his drinking. I hurried back down to the stream to refill my trousers.

By the time I returned, the stallion had finished the water and was pawing at the muddy hole. I threw a stick at him to drive him back, quickly refilled the hole, then retreated again to the outside of the fence. This time the stallion was unchallenged as he stepped forward to drink. I hurried back to the stream to get more water.

When I returned, the stallion lifted his head to look at me, water dripping from his lips. The bay mare was closer now, her head low, her nose stretched toward the hole. She took another step forward and, after no reaction from the stallion, took another. Soon her nose was in the hole, finishing off the water.

After driving the horses away again, I refilled the hole, then stood back to watch as the bay mare, the stallion at her side, drank every drop while the rest of the horses milled about restlessly.

I headed out into the meadow and gathered another armload of wild oats, making a lot of noise to attract the attention of the horses as I tossed the oats over the fence at the same place I had deposited the earlier armloads of hay. I headed back down to the stream to refill my trousers with water.

When I returned, the horses were milling about the muddy hole, pawing, squealing, and fighting—all except the two that were no longer thirsty, the sorrel stallion and the bay mare. They were at the far end of the corral, enjoying their first meal in many days, the oat hay I had thrown over the fence.

This time, instead of filling the hole as I had done before, I pushed the gate inward with one hand, holding the water-filled trousers in the other. I kept inching the gate inward until the hole was on the outside of the gate at my feet. I filled it with water and moved along the outside of the fence.

After covering about twenty paces, I climbed over the fence and got behind the mass of horses that were already crowding into the opening. Behind me the sorrel and bay continued to gobble up the hay, hardly noticing that the other horses were being driven from the corral.

As soon as the first few horses decided to abandon the wet hole and head for the creek, the rest were quick to follow. By the time the sorrel stallion and bay mare decided to follow, I had closed the gate.

I ran to the stream in an effort to drive the horses away from the water before they drank too much, as the palomino colt had done the night before, but they merely scattered upstream and downstream, keeping away from me and returning to the creek here and there almost at will. I soon gave up trying to keep them from the water. I realized some might die from too much water, but I figured most would live. That made me feel a lot better.

I returned to the corral to take a closer look at my new horses. The sorrel stallion was trotting about snorting and whinnying after his lost herd. The mare was eating hay. I still didn't know how I was going to catch and break them without a rope.

Chapter 33

Once I had the sorrel stallion and bay mare isolated in the corral, my plan for breaking them began to formulate. The first thing I did was gather more armloads of wild oats for them to eat. Then I stationed myself just outside the fence from the hay. In order for them to eat, they had to get close to me.

At first they stayed away, waiting for me to leave. When I failed to do so, the mare was the first to start inching toward the hay. I remained as still as possible so as not to alarm her.

At first she just nibbled at the edge of the pile, but soon she didn't seem to mind my presence at all. The stallion was a different story. He seemed indifferent about the hay, trotting about the corral, continuing to whinny desperately over his lost herd. Every time he came near me, he laid his ears back and shook his head as if daring me to step into the arena with him.

I was delighted at the way the mare was gorging herself on the dry hay. The more the better. I knew the yellow grass would make the mare very thirsty, as trotting around in the hot sun would make the stallion thirsty.

It didn't take long. By midday they were pawing up the moist soil where I had watered them earlier that morning. They would have been delighted had I brought them more water, but I didn't. They weren't thirsty enough to suit my purposes.

As the afternoon advanced under the scorching August sun and the horses' thirst intensified even more, they lost all interest in the hay. That was fine with me. While waiting for the sun to do its work on the two horses, I brought all my gear back to the corral and built a little lean-to on the outside of the log fence. I covered it with leafy tree branches to shade me from the blistering California sun. I wanted the horses to start getting used to my constant companionship. This new shelter allowed me to be within sight, sound, and smell of them throughout the day and night.

Just before the sun went down, I walked down to the stream, removed my trousers again, and filled them with water after knotting the legs. This time, after entering the corral, I didn't dump the water in a hole, but just stood quietly by the gate, the water bag in my hands in front of me. I figured if the horses became thirsty enough, they would drink out of my trousers, if not this time, in a day or two when their thirst became unbearable.

They could neither drink nor eat without help from me, and I didn't intend to help them without something in return. They would have to drink out of my trousers with me holding them or not drink at all. And if they wished to continue drinking, they would have to let me pet and handle them as they drank. Though they were wild, with time they would have to give in, if they wanted to survive.

The mare came the closest, but neither horse drank the first night, or the next day. After standing patiently, just inside the gate, for ten or fifteen minutes, I would dump the water on the ground and leave. By the time they got to it, the life-giving liquid had been soaked up by the ground. They found little satisfaction in pawing the mud.

I was not idle while waiting for the horses to get thirsty enough to drink out of my hands. Like the palomino colt, some of the other horses had died from drinking too much water too fast. I was busy making a couple of horsehide ropes, Indian style.

After removing the hides and pelvic bones from two of the dead animals, I stretched the hides out on the ground, using small sharpened sticks to hold them in place, flesh side up. As they began to dry, I urinated on them at every opportunity. I don't know exactly why I did this, other than the fact that I had observed the

Utes doing it and the application of urine seemed to be an important part of the tanning process. White men used tannic acid in making leather. Indians achieved the same results with urine and rotting brains.

Fresh brains have too much texture to be useful, but after a day or two in the sun, they are just right for tanning. The second day, after each of the hides had been saturated with urine several times, I returned to the carcasses of the skinned animals and cracked open the heads with a fist-sized rock. The smell confirmed that my timing was right. I scooped out handfuls of the hot, greasy mush and rubbed it into the outstretched hides.

Using my knife I cut each hide into a three-inch-wide continuous strip, starting on the outside edge and working toward the middle in increasingly smaller circles. After tying one end to a tree, I stretched the hide strip tight while twisting many times, as is done in making hemp ropes. Then I shoved the free end of the rawhide strip through the eye of a pelvic bone before tying it to another tree, leaving the strip of hide twisted and stretched tightly between the two trees. Once the hide began to dry, I started working the pelvic bone vigorously back and forth, softening the hide and removing the outside hair. With time and work, the hide became soft and pliable. When removed from between the two trees, it maintained the twisted rope form. Within a week, I had two thirty-foot horsehide ropes, strong enough to hold most animals.

It was in the afternoon of the second day that the mare took her first drink from my handheld watering trough. At first she took just a few sips, her long neck stretched to its limit, her lips barely touching the water.

I held perfectly still but let the water slosh back and forth, thinking that might make it more irresistible to the mare. After ten or fifteen minutes of quick sips and stepping back to a safer distance, the mare finally walked up to the trousers and drank deeply. The stallion stood about ten yards back, pawing the ground and shaking his beautiful head.

It wasn't until the third day that he took his first sip. I had opened the gate just a little, holding the water-filled trousers in the opening. I was fearful that he might strike out at me with one of his front feet. Several times he laid his ears back and acted as if he were about to strike out, but I always responded quickly by withdrawing the water. If he wanted to drink he would have to behave.

By the end of the third day, I was stroking the mare's neck and shoulders as she drank. It took two more days before the stallion would allow me to touch him. Eventually I insisted on petting them while they drank. No petting, no water. The need for water was the key to taming these wild horses.

I fed them hay just inside the fence from my lean-to, forcing them to be close to me while they ate. At first I was very still so as not to alarm them, but as they became used to me, I began moving about, climbing upon the fence, shouting at them, and even hitting the fence with sticks.

Within a week, I could pet both of them while they ate and drank. Most of their fear of me seemed to be gone. The loss of fear made the stallion dangerous. He was constantly moving, biting, pawing. I was forced to carry a stick, to strike his nose when he tried to bite and his leg when he pawed at me. As his strength returned with drinking and eating, he seemed to become more aggressive and unmanageable. He was always getting in the way when I tried to do anything with the mare. If I tossed the wet trousers over her back in an effort to get her used to things on her back, he would grab the trousers in his teeth and pull them away.

When the horsehide ropes were ready, I arranged the horses' feed in a neat little pile beside the stoutest post in the corral fence. As the horses fed, I rubbed their heads and necks with the horsehide line, getting them used to it. Quietly I doubled the rope in half for double strength, slipped it over the stallion's neck, tied a non-slipping knot, looped a half-hitch over his nose, and tied the other end to the fence post before he realized what was happening. Quickly, I jumped out of the way as he suddenly discovered this new restraint on his freedom. He reared, pawed, and lunged with all the fury he could muster. For a moment I feared the double rawhide leash might not be strong enough. But as his lunges became less determined, the horsehide rope continued to hold. I decided to leave him tied for the remainder of the day and through the night.

With the stallion finally under control, I decided it was time to ride the mare. She wasn't broken to the rope yet, but she was used to me, allowing me to walk up to her and pet her at will. Confined in the corral, she couldn't take me anywhere I didn't want to go, so without the aid of any kind of halter or rope, I just crawled up on her back, expecting to get a wild ride.

To my surprise, she just stood there, not doing anything except taking one quick look at my foot to see where I had gone. At first I just waited for her to do something, but when she failed to become alarmed, I began rocking back and forth, tightening knees and heels, slapping her on the rump.

When she failed to get excited about that, I began kicking her sides with my heels until she started walking. It wasn't long until I removed my shirt and waved it against the side of her head to make her turn. By the end of the day, she was trotting about the corral, turning away from my shirt whenever I waved it beside her head.

Over the years I have watched many men break horses. The usual method, at least on the frontier, was to force a severe bit into the frightened animal's mouth, then climb aboard with sharpened spurs, subduing the animal with force and pain, bloodying the mouth and sides if necessary.

I learned on the California frontier that horses can also be tamed with gentleness. I think I was successful because I allowed the mare plenty of time to get used to me, and because I didn't alarm her by trying to restrain her head or inflict pain with a bit or spurs.

The gentle method, however, did not work on the stallion. When I climbed up on his back the next afternoon, he promptly threw me to the ground. The second time, he tossed me into the fence, nearly breaking my arm. That's when I decided that one horse would probably be sufficient for my needs. I turned the sorrel stallion loose and waved a relieved good-bye as he galloped off to round up his scattered herd.

With the stallion gone, the mare responded quickly to my training. She learned to respond to my knees and heels and the end of a rawhide rope looped around her lower jaw. Rather than cut the rope to a convenient length, I left it long, looped and tucked in my belt, Blackfoot and Ute style. Should I fall from her back while galloping across the open plain, the uncoiling loops would allow me time to bring her under control before she reached the end of the rope. The bareback riders of the plains lost more horses because of short reins than any other single reason, except perhaps thieving neighbors. Falls were frequent, especially from the backs of green horses, and once a horse was free on the open plain, it wasn't always possible to catch it again.

By the time I figured the mare was ready to carry me north, I had been at the corral nearly two weeks. I was getting restless at being in one place so long. I wanted to get through the mountain passes before they filled with snow. I could have walked a long way in two weeks. On the other hand, I would travel faster with a horse under me. It was comforting to have the speed of a horse to carry me to safety in times of danger, especially once I got through the mountains into a country frequented by hostile Indians.

Early in the afternoon, the day before I planned to leave the corral, I carried the last load of water from the creek up to the corral. No more would I remove my pants to give this horse a drink. From now on she would drink from creeks and streams by herself.

The mare had gulped down about half of the water when she suddenly jerked her head up. Her ears forward, her head high, she whinnied softly at something behind me. As I started to turn, I heard a voice.

"Gringo."

Chapter 34

I'd been in California long enough to recognize immediately what *gringo* meant. I spun around to face the two riders coming through the creek, a husky young man and a long-haired *señorita*. My first thoughts were of my rifle, not more than twenty yards away in the lean-to.

I was about to scramble for the gun when I noticed that both riders were grinning broadly. At the same time I noticed that the young man's pistol was in his holster, not his hand. The *señorita* didn't appear to be armed. Forgetting about the rifle, I suddenly realized why they were grinning.

My trousers were in my hand instead of where they belonged. Quickly I shoved my right leg into the trousers, only to discover that the end of the pant leg was still tied in a knot. When I tried to slip my leg back out again, the wet material stuck to my leg like the underside of a bean leaf.

In frustration I let go of the pants and straightened up to face the two riders who were pulling their horses to a halt just a few yards away. I was grateful my shirt was sufficiently long—if I didn't bend over—to allow me to maintain at least partial modesty.

"*Habla español?*" asked the chubby young man. Though substantial in size, he appeared to be no more than a boy, a big cherub. His face and hands were pink and soft, without wrinkles, and slick with sweat. His smile was friendly and enthusiastic, without guile. He looked like he was dressed for church, or perhaps a funeral, in a black wide-brimmed hat, white shirt with ruffles on the sleeves, and black trousers. His spurs appeared to be made of silver, and opposite his pistol he wore a long sheath carrying a sword. He appeared too fat and slow to be an effective sword fighter. I figured he was probably the son of one of the wealthy land owners in the area.

When I looked at the woman, she looked down at my feet, then quickly to one side. She seemed to be more unsettled by the nakedness of my legs than I was. That pleased me. She appeared to be about the same age as the fellow, maybe in her mid to late teens. She was wearing a long brown dress that covered the top of her boots as she straddled her horse. In contrast to the young man, she had a lithe, athletic look—like Caroline Logan.

The Spanish girl's hands and face were smooth and tanned, her hair long, black, and clean—too clean for one on a long journey. That, in addition to the obvious lack of traveling gear and bed rolls, led me to conclude that the two were not very far from home. Her face was attractive, the kind that tempted a man to stare.

"*Hablo un poco español,*" I said, wanting them to know I understood a little Spanish. I had managed to learn some of the basics in my six months at Mission San Diego. "*Habla ingles*?" I added, hoping that perhaps they spoke a little English.

The young man shook his head to indicate he didn't understand my language.

"*Como se llama*?" he asked, wanting to know my name.

"Dan Storm, *y usted?*"

"Pedro Sanchez," he responded. Then nodding to the woman, "*Mi hermana,* Elena Sanchez."

So, they were brother and sister. While Elena looked away, I slipped into my trousers after untying the knots. Pedro and Elena didn't show any concern or even seem to notice the absence of wild horses in the corral. Apparently they had not been involved in the wild horse roundup. I invited them to dismount and have lunch with me.

They seemed eager to accept my invitation. It was as if they had never met a *gringo* before and were very curious to find out all they could about the mysterious stranger.

After tying their horses to the fence, they joined me in the lean-to, bringing some of their own food to supplement my scarce fare of beef jerky and hard biscuits. They had some dried plums, sweetened corn cakes, and a flask of delicious tangy grape juice.

I had a hard time explaining where I was from. They had never heard of Illinois or Missouri. It wasn't until I mentioned St. Louis that they generally understood. They knew about New York and St. Louis, though they had never visited either place. In fact, they had never traveled outside of California.

Not wanting to let what they figured to be a world traveler out of their sight, they invited me to ride with them back to their *hacienda.* Since they indicated it was only a few hours' ride to the north, the same direction I was heading, I didn't see any harm in joining them, though I felt a reluctance to complicate my life with new friends who might perhaps delay my return to the Great Basin and news of Caroline Logan.

Chapter 35

As we mounted our horses and rode away from the corral, we didn't head back to the *hacienda,* at least not immediately. Pedro and Elena explained that they were out looking for their father's lost rifle. Several weeks earlier their father, while out surveying cattle herds, had been badly gored by a bull. He had managed to get on his horse and make it back to the *hacienda,* but he had left his rifle behind. From their description it was a Spanish muzzle loader, similar in appearance to my .40 caliber Hawken.

They said their father told them he had dropped the rifle on the grassy hillside above the creek several kilometers upstream from the big corral, the one where I had caught and trained my mare.

Most of the afternoon we searched the grassy hillsides above the creek, but with no success. As the sun began to drop low in the sky signaling it was time to head back, Pedro and Elena were reluctant to give up the search. I could understand why a rifle would be so important to a family living in such a remote area. What I failed to understand was why their father had only one gun. I had visited some of the great *haciendas* near Mission San Diego and had observed arsenals of weapons. The lack of sheriffs and other law enforcement officers left the protection of the *haciendas* pretty much in the hands of the owners.

In my broken Spanish I asked Pedro why his family didn't have more guns. He explained that the family owned three rifles, but that the other two had mysteriously disappeared from the house shortly after his father's injury.

I had been in Spanish California long enough to know that something out of the ordinary was happening at the Sanchez *hacienda*. Theft and burglary were not common in this land of plenty. The vast herds of cattle, managed for hides only, provided an endless supply of practically free beef for the Spanish and Indian population. Crops of corn and squash could be grown year-round in the temperate climate and rich soil. The rivers and ocean were full of fish. Orchards and vineyards gave bounteous harvests year after year with very little care. There was plenty to eat for all. Living was easy, even for the lazy. It was not necessary to steal to live; most doors were without locks or bolts.

Even travelers found the living easy, especially in the more populated areas. Unlike the roadside taverns and inns in the states and territories, the Spanish *haciendas* didn't charge for their accommodations. There was always an extra place at the table and an extra bed in the spare room, no charge. Travelers were treated like longtime friends or even relatives. It wasn't uncommon for a traveler to find a plate of gold and silver coins on the table beside his bed. He was welcome to help himself to satisfy immediate monetary needs, but it wasn't considered polite to take a lot of the money—the less, the better.

Transportation was practically free, too, thanks to the wild horse herds that seemed to be everywhere. Free-spirited *caballeros* would catch and break a horse for several dollars or several days' wages.

The Spanish, led by their Catholic *padres,* seemed more interested in the good life than in acquiring huge individual holdings through industry and commerce. No one seemed to be terribly aggressive or ambitious. Long *siestas* and frequent *fiestas* were the order of the day.

But it would all end with the arrival of the Americans. The Mexican government was not defending California in the war with the United States. General Kearney's men already held the key sea ports. This fat land would soon belong to the United States, and when reports of California bounties and mild climates reached New York and St. Louis, thousands of Americans would catch the dream of a better life in California. Some would probably come on the road I had helped the Mormon Battalion blaze. Others would come by ship. And when the ambitious, eager Americans arrived, life in the Spanish *haciendas* would change. People like the Sanchez family would lose their large land holdings if they were not careful.

Pedro seemed reluctant to discuss the stolen guns, so I asked Elena who took them. She looked at Pedro, as if she were asking for his permission to speak to me. He said nothing, seeming to ignore her.

"Jose Lobo," she said. Then there was silence. A somber, uneasy mood had fallen over Pedro and Elena, like a heavy blanket. They didn't want to talk any more. I figured I would find out soon enough the source of their problem. I hoped it wouldn't swallow me up as it had them. I was beginning to regret meeting Pedro and Elena. I had enough problems of my own, making my way over the Sierra Nevada Mountains and across an unsettled desert to the Great Basin.

Several times during the afternoon, as their story unfolded, I felt the urge to say good-bye to them and head off toward the mountains. That urge grew stronger as we rode in silence toward their *hacienda,* but when the white walls of their home finally came into view across the yellow plain, I knew I would not be turning away. I didn't know who Jose Lobo was or what the nature of their trouble might be. All I knew was that I would be sharing it with them, at least for a little while.

Chapter 36

The Sanchez *hacienda* was similar to many I had seen in California. Inside the adobe wall was the central house where the Sanchez family lived, surrounded by huts for the servants, storage sheds, and animal shelters. All the walls were made of adobe and painted white. The roofs were made of red tile.

Approaching the open gate, we passed a big mud pit where the adobe bricks and roof tiles were made. Two naked Indians were still working, wading about the mud pit, mixing straw and dry manure into the red clay-mud. At the edge of the pit were three huge clay pots from which water was ladled when the mixture became too thick.

Two more Indians were sitting near the edge of the pit, spreading thick mud over their thighs, cutting away the edges to form curved tiles that were carefully removed from the thighs and set on beds of straw to dry. Hundreds of adobe bricks were drying in rectangular wooden frames. There were several piles of finished bricks and tiles.

By the time we entered the gate to the central square, word of our arrival had spread from hut to hut, and everyone was coming outside to see the stranger who had returned with Pedro and Elena. Women and children and several old men from seven or eight families surrounded us as we dismounted.

Immediately I noticed an unexpected lack of men. It was evening; the men should have returned from the fields long ago. I made a mental note to ask Pedro or Elena where the men were.

There was no one who fit the description of Jose Lobo, the suspected gun thief.

Upon entering the Sanchez home, Pedro and Elena went directly to their *padre's* room and left me in the care of the housekeeper, a middle-aged woman with the most common Spanish name of all, Maria. Her size, nearly two hundred pounds, led me to believe that she was probably a pretty good cook. Her greeting was friendly, but as she led me to my room, there was a quiet, worried feeling about her.

An hour later we gathered about the table for an evening meal of boiled beef, beans, fresh plums, and corn tortillas. Pedro and Elena were more worried than ever about their father, who was being attended by Maria during the meal. Apparently the old man was unconscious with fever and becoming weaker by the hour.

Although large in size, Pedro seemed too much like a boy to be taking over leadership of the ranch and all the families associated with it. It seemed doubtful that he was ready to handle the responsibility.

I commented on my observation concerning the lack of grown men at the *hacienda,* including Jose Lobo. Elena explained that the men had begun disappearing, one or two at a time, about six months earlier. Maria's husband, Juan, was the first to disappear. He had gone out to butcher a beef cow and never returned. His horse-drawn cart had returned to the *hacienda* in the night. The next morning, Pedro and his father had followed the cart tracks to the butchered beef, but there was no sign of Juan.

Jose Lobo disappeared regularly but always managed to return. No one knew where he went. None of the other men had ever returned.

It was a depressing conversation. Pedro suddenly changed the subject.

"Will you sell us your rifle?" he asked.

I tried to explain that I was headed east over the Sierra Nevada Mountains into Indian country, that it was dangerous enough traveling alone with a rifle. Without one, it would be suicide.

"Couldn't you send someone down to Mission Los Angeles to buy one?" I suggested.

"Who?" he asked. "The men are gone, except Jose Lobo, and we can't trust him."

"Maybe I could do it for you," I offered. I was worried that I might not make it over the mountains before the snow came, but I couldn't just ride off leaving Pedro and Elena without help. They were barely more than children—Pedro a big, beefy, pink-cheeked, oversized boy; Elena just becoming a beautiful woman but not yet acting like one. I figured they would both grow up quickly, now that it appeared their father would not survive.

After supper Pedro and Elena returned to their father's room. Maria returned to clean up the supper and dishes. I paced about the main floor, wondering if I should leave the next morning for the coast to get Pedro a rifle. If I hurried, I could be back within a week. Unless there was an early snowstorm, there should still be plenty of time to get over the mountains.

The adobe walls were decorated with numerous wildcat and calf hides, the floor with bearskins and bull hides. There were iron bars over the windows, and the furniture was handmade. There were no books or paintings.

Suddenly the front door burst open and I found myself looking into a rifle barrel. My rifle was in my room, out of reach.

Holding the rifle was the meanest-looking man I had ever seen, except for maybe Dick Boggs. He was a Mexican—skinny, bow-legged, long greasy hair, a patchy stubble of a beard covering his pock-marked face. His eyes were small and black, like those of a mink, and too close together. He blinked incessantly. His formerly white pantaloons and shirt were brown and dusty from many days on the trail. He motioned for me to step outside.

"*Pronto, gringo,*" he said in a raspy voice. I didn't hesitate in stepping toward the door. He looked like the kind of man who would gladly pull the trigger. I knew without asking that his name was Jose Lobo.

The next morning, hands tied behind my back, I was helped on the back of my bay mare by two of Jose Lobo's *bandidos*. I had spent the night in a pile of straw, bound hands tied to my feet. I had been treated roughly, but not with unnecessary cruelty. I had no idea why I had been taken captive.

Jose Lobo spent the night in the *hacienda* with the Sanchezes. Lamps burned throughout the night, and at one time I thought I could hear Maria crying. After a long restless night of trying to doze in my uncomfortable situation, one of the guards told me that *Señor* Sanchez had died during the night.

I hadn't been on the mare very long when the heavy front door of the *hacienda* swung open and the huge boyish bulk of Pedro stepped into the opening. Even from a distance, I could tell from the redness around his eyes that he had been crying. Unlike me, his hands were not tied behind his back. A sudden shove from behind sent him stumbling down the front steps. Jose Lobo appeared in the doorway, rifle in hand.

Pedro was ordered to get on a horse that had been brought to the front of the house by one of Lobo's men. Another horse was waiting for Lobo. It appeared we were all leaving together. I had no idea where we were going. Had they intended to kill me or Pedro, they would have done it earlier.

As soon as Lobo was mounted, he waved for the riders to move out, "*Pronto.*" As the horses began to gallop, I quickly forgot about possible destinations and gave my full attention to keeping my seat on the green mare. It wasn't easy with my hands tied behind my back.

We headed northeast at an angle toward the distant Sierras. After covering a mile or two at a full gallop, we slowed to an easy trot, a pace the horses could maintain most of the day. One of Lobo's men led my horse.

What surprised me was Lobo's failure to tie Pedro's hands. The boy's father had just died, and being forced to leave his family, the young man was bound to do something desperate sooner or later, if he got the chance. Not tying his hands was like offering an invitation to attempt an escape. Lobo didn't seem concerned. It was as if he was daring the boy to make a run for it.

We had been on the trail about an hour and were riding through the center of a large valley when Pedro decided to make a break. I had the feeling he had fallen into a trap.

Hardly looking up, Lobo uncoiled his *lazo* and dug spurs into his horse's sides. I'll never forget the delighted look on his face as he galloped by. He knew the boy would try to escape. He had been waiting.

The boy's horse was slow. Lobo had planned it that way.

The boy hadn't covered more than a few hundred yards when Lobo caught up with him, *lazo* twirling swiftly above the *bandido's* head. The loop shot forward, encircling the boy's thick torso. After taking two quick loops with the free end of the rope around his saddle horn, Lobo pulled his horse back and to the side, jerking Pedro from the saddle.

As soon as the boy hit the ground, Lobo's horse was headed in the other direction, dragging the victim back to the main group of men. After a short distance, Lobo slowed down enough to allow Pedro to get to his feet. No effort was made to retrieve the boy's horse. As we continued our journey to some unknown destination, Pedro—the big boy with the narrow shoulders, fat butt, and pink cheeks—was forced to follow behind at the end of Jose Lobo's rope.

Chapter 37

I don't know why Lobo was so cruel to Pedro Sanchez, but he seemed intent on making life as miserable as possible for the boy. While the rest of us rode along on horses, Pedro was forced to stumble along at the end of Lobo's rope. Whenever he fell, which occurred quite frequently as he became tired, Lobo would drag Pedro along the ground for a while before allowing him to get back on his feet.

When we stopped to rest, Pedro was always the last to get a drink, and sometimes during the hottest part of the afternoon, he was denied any drink at all. In camp at night, Pedro was the last to eat, receiving only leftovers, covered with ashes from Lobo's hand-rolled cigarettes.

I figured Lobo's hate had something to do with his earlier status as a servant or hired hand on the Sanchez ranch. He probably resented taking orders from Pedro and his father. He had let that resentment fester within him until he was full of poison. Now, at last, he was getting his revenge and seemed to be enjoying every minute of it. Poor Pedro passively accepted the abuse. There was nothing else for him to do. He was no match for Lobo.

By the end of the second day we reached the foothills of the Sierra Nevadas, then headed straight north. In the afternoon of the third day, we turned east, up a thickly wooded canyon along a well-used trail.

Just before nightfall we were greeted by two armed Mexicans who immediately recognized Lobo. They seemed pleased that he had brought them a *gringo,* along with another Mexican prisoner.

A few minutes later I discovered why we had been brought to this remote place. We were led into a huge, flat clearing. Up against the side of the mountain was the opening of a mine shaft. Nearby, two more guards were herding eight men into a pole cage. The men were dirty, weary, and in rags. The guards were prodding them with rifle barrels to get them to move faster. The men were Indian and Mexican. All the guards were Mexican. I was the only *gringo.*

With fresh piles of white quartz piled around the edge of the clearing, it didn't take long to figure there was a mining operation going on and that the men in the pole cage were prisoners or slaves brought here to work the mine. I figured they were probably after silver or gold. Apparently Pedro and I were destined to join the men who worked the mine.

My hunch proved correct. Without any explanation or warning, Pedro and I were shoved into the cage with the Indian and Mexican laborers. All but one of the guards retreated with Lobo and his men to a long cabin at the far end of the clearing.

I kept my back against the edge of the cage, carefully watching the other men, looking for signs of friendship or hostility.

I didn't have to wait long. Two Mexicans and an Indian stepped forward, all three smiling. I was readying myself for some kind of deceit when Pedro suddenly rushed forward and embraced one of the men, whom he obviously knew.

They talked so fast, and with such excitement, that I couldn't understand what they were saying. But when Pedro addressed the other man as Juan, the missing pieces to the puzzle suddenly fit together. The men who recognized Pedro were also from the Sanchez *hacienda.* I guessed the man called Juan was Maria's missing husband. The men from the *hacienda* had been kidnapped by Lobo and brought to the mine. Apparently Lobo was being paid to bring slave labor to the mine.

In my earlier days with the Utes in the Great Basin, I had become familiar with the Mexican custom of using Indian slaves in their silver and gold mines. Now I was going to get a chance to see, firsthand, what happened to the Indian boys, and everybody else, who were carried off to the mines.

Just before dawn, we were awakened by the awful clatter of a stick on the outside of our pole cage. The door opened partway and one of the guards handed us a bucket of boiled beef and a handful of cold corn tortillas.

Having missed dinner the night before, the food tasted good. Not a word was spoken as the men wolfed down the meat and tortillas, every last morsel. There was no fighting to see who got the most. The understanding seemed to be that everyone ate as fast as possible until all the food was gone.

As soon as the bucket was empty, we were herded out of the cage and toward the open shaft. Several of the men were accompanied by a guard to the opposite side of the clearing, to a crude mill where the ore was crushed with a huge grindstone. The rest of us, accompanied by two lantern-carrying guards, entered the shaft and began pushing a huge plank wagon with wooden wheels.

Two trenches, several inches deep and about four feet apart, guided the wheels into the shaft that headed upwards into the heart of the mountain. The wagon ruts were not centered, but several feet left of center, allowing a pathway on the right side of the shaft where the men could walk around the wagon or safely get out of the way when the wagon was thundering out of the shaft.

The incline was rather steep in places, requiring four or five of us to keep the wagon moving. I was grateful the incline was up instead of down. It would have been much more difficult pushing the loaded wagon out of the mine. As it was, I guessed the incline was sufficiently steep to allow the loaded wagon to roll out by itself. I figured the incline was not on purpose, that it was just following the vein of ore which happened to be headed upwards into the heart of the mountain.

Since arriving at the mine, my mind had been busy taking in every detail—the number of guards, the nature and locations of their guns and knives, the construction of the cage, the lay of the nearby forest and mountainside, the availability of rocks, tools, and other potential weapons.

I had no intention of spending years in a Mexican mine. Sooner or later, I intended to escape. Hopefully sooner. How, I didn't know. I had gotten myself out of worse situations than this, at least more dangerous ones. I knew I could do it again.

What probably surprised me the most was my lack of fear. I suppose I was getting older, more mature. In fact, I felt more than just a twinge of excitement at the uncertainty of my future, even a grim satisfaction in anticipating such a formidable challenge. Somehow I would outsmart these Mexicans and make them sorry they had tried to turn this *gringo* into a slave.

Chapter 38

At first I wasn't in any big hurry to escape from the Mexican mine. I was very curious to understand the business responsible for the thriving slave trade among the Indian tribes of the Rocky Mountains. There were four Indians working in the mine, one older man, and three boys in their late teens, about Pedro's age. Wondering if some of these Indians might have come from the Great Basin area, I said a few things in the Ute and Gosiute languages, but they just stared blankly at me. I concluded they were probably from one of the California or Oregon tribes. None of them understood Spanish either, just a few words they had picked up at the mine.

In the beginning, except for the long, hard work, life at the mine did not seem so bad. Twice a day we received generous portions of beef and tortillas, occasionally some dried fruit. There was no abuse from the guards for those who did nothing but sleep, eat, and work. There was no time for anything else. We entered the mine at first light and returned to our cage after dark. With the addition of me and Pedro, there were ten of us in the labor gang and six guards to make sure we did our work.

It was a hard-rock gold mine. We were following a flaky vein of light yellow gold that wound its way up into the mountain in a bed of white-orange quartz. We chipped away at the vein with chisels and hammers. Once or twice a day we interrupted our work to blast away at the bigger sections of rock with black powder. We welcomed the brief blasting breaks. The chance to stand around in the sun for a few minutes with nothing to do was a valued treat that could only be appreciated by those engaged in long periods of hard, uninterrupted work.

When we weren't chipping away at the quartz, we were loading the broken rocks into the big cart and guiding it down the shaft and across the clearing to the crusher. If we got it going fast enough, the momentum would carry it all the way across the clearing to the crusher. The hard part was pushing the empty cart back up the incline to the end of the shaft.

As a boy, I had done a lot of farm work—hauling hay, doing chores, digging ditches, and the like. I had worked as a stone mason on the Nauvoo temple. As part of the Mormon Battalion I had helped clear a wagon trail to the Pacific Ocean. But none of that work could compare in difficulty with chipping away at that endless rock, thirteen to fifteen hours a day, seven days a week.

At the end of the first three or four hours of work on the first day, my hands, and Pedro's as well, were covered with calluses. By the end of the first day the calluses were bleeding, but the pain in our aching backs, arms, and necks helped keep our attention away from the bloody hands.

Pedro was lucky that Lobo had left. The other guards weren't nearly as cruel or hard on the Mexican boy. They were Mexican too and seemed more inclined to be cruel to the Indians or *gringo* than to one of their own kind. Still, they were insistent that Pedro do his share of the work, and that wasn't easy. At home Pedro had never learned the rigors of hard physical labor. When he tried to stop for an unscheduled break, a frequent occurrence the first few days, one of the guards was quick to jab him with a rifle barrel and get him back to work.

It was in the afternoon of the third day that my attitude toward slave labor in a Mexican mine took a sudden and irreversible change for the worse. Though slow, the four Indians were steady workers. They tried hard to avoid the wrath of the guards. If an Indian took an unscheduled break, he received bruising jabs from the rifle of the nearest guard, frequently accompanied by kicks to the shins or groin.

It was in the afternoon of the third day that the old Indian suddenly threw down his tools and stoically seated himself on a large rock, his arms folded. During my three days I had seen a number of attempts to take unscheduled breaks, but never one so bold. It was as if the old man had suddenly made a decision, like he was trying to prove something.

When the guards jabbed him with their rifle barrels, he refused to go back to work. They beat him to the ground and kicked him almost senseless. Still the old man refused to pick up his tools.

Finally, the guards went off by themselves for a brief discussion. When they returned, one of them pushed his rifle barrel against the Indian's chest and pulled the trigger.

Suddenly a man was dead. Neither the guards nor the other prisoners acted like anything out of the ordinary had happened. Pedro and I were stunned to see a man's life snuffed out with such ease and lack of concern.

Pedro ceased taking unscheduled breaks. With new determination he forced himself to keep working, hour after hour, against the screaming protests of aching muscles and bloody blisters.

My attitude changed too. My earlier curiosity about the slave trade and the workings of Mexican mines had suddenly disappeared. Suddenly there were only two concerns—staying alive and figuring a way to escape. I realized I had misjudged the seriousness of our situation. I had misjudged the humanity of the guards. Men who could kill so easily had killed frequently. Pedro and I were closer to that precarious edge separating life and death than I had supposed.

Chapter 39

"Your name is familiar, but not your face."

I had just introduced myself to Kenny Scott, recently brought in by Lobo and his men. It was evening and we had just returned to our cage for the night. A week had passed since Pedro and I had come to the mine.

"I was just head'n down the pass toward the Sacramento Valley when those two gun-totin' monkeys in white bakery suits stepped out from behind a tree and ordered me to get off my horse," continued Kenny. "Before I could explain anything, my hands was tied behind my back and they was helping me back on my horse to bring me here. What is this place, anyway?"

"A Mexican mine," I said, explaining that he was now a hard-rock gold miner along with me and all the other guys in the cage.

"Go against the guards and they'll shoot you," I warned, the death of the Indian still fresh in my mind.

"I was just looking for my little brother and these monkeys decided to bring me up here," he continued.

"Your brother?"

"Yeah, think he's in California somewhere. Came out with the Mormon Battalion."

"So did I!" I exclaimed, then asked his brother's name.

"William Scott; called him Willie," he answered. "You know him?"

"Yeah, he headed up the valley for Sacramento when I headed this way. Shouldn't be too far from here."

Kenny and I talked long into the night. He was a Mormon too and had come west to the Great Basin late in the summer, expecting to meet his brother in the valleys of the mountains. But finding no brother, he continued his journey west, eventually crossing the Sierra Nevadas. Neither one of the brothers was married.

"Dan Storm. Your name is familiar, very familiar. I'll remember," he said, scratching his head.

Kenny was a strong, good-looking kid in his early twenties with black curly hair and a bronze, almost Indian, complexion. He adjusted quickly to the work schedule. Not understanding Spanish or any of the Indian languages, he tried to stay close to me. Listening to the constant prattle of the guards, our Spanish improved daily.

Kenny and I were the only ones who understood English. Without fear of discovery, we frequently discussed escape alternatives. The plan that appealed to us most was a very simple one. We figured that one evening as we pushed the last load of ore to the rock crusher at the edge of the hill, we would just take off running down the hill. The scattered trees would offer some cover against the rifle fire from the guards. It would be easy to avoid the guards once it became dark, if we could only evade them during the half hour or so before darkness set in. They would have the benefit of horses, while we would be on foot, but we figured the steep incline of the hill would nullify the horses' advantage.

There was only one thing that bothered me. The plan seemed too easy. The guards couldn't be so dumb as to leave such an obvious avenue of escape open. Surely men had tried it before. What had happened to them?

We decided to share the plan with the other men, at least with Pedro and Juan. They could be trusted.

The next evening, as I was sitting between Juan and Pedro, I casually picked up a stick and began drawing in the dirt a diagram of the camp. It didn't take but a few seconds to get their attention. I scratched out the mine entrance, the guard cabin, our cage, and the rock crusher. Using a rock as a symbol for the ore cart, I pushed it from the mine entrance to the mark indicating the rock crusher. Pointing at Pedro and Juan, then to myself, I made a running motion with my fingers, suggesting we run down the hill away from the crushers. Then I gave each of them a questioning look to see how they would respond.

Pedro nodded eager support for the plan, but Juan, who had been at the mine much longer, just smiled and shook his head. Calmly taking the stick from my hand, he smoothed out the dirt and drew another diagram, showing the incline of the hill beyond the rock crusher. He showed how the incline became steeper and steeper, eventually becoming a vertical cliff, over which there could be no safe escape. From the clearing, the cliff was not visible. I explained the situation to Kenny. We decided to look for another plan of escape.

At first I thought we would find our way to freedom in a few weeks, but the weeks dragged into months. As the nights grew cold and the days cool, even though there was no snow at the mine, I knew the passes in the high Sierras were filling with snow. I realized the time was past when I could safely cross the mountains. I would have to wait until the following summer. I had missed my chance to get over the mountains in 1847.

As fall turned into winter, I noticed a marked change in Pedro. First it was physical. The endless toil with rocks, hammers, and chisels gradually transformed the baby fat into steel-hard muscles. His fat butt disappeared, his waist narrowed, his shoulders broadened and burst the seams of his shirt. His neck swelled until it was thick as a fence post.

Even the features of his face changed as the baby fat disappeared. His cheekbones became prominent, his jaw firm and well defined. Eyes, once bulging, boyish, and fearful, withdrew beneath strong black brows. The eyelids ceased blinking, and I sensed in those black eyes an intensity of spirit that glowed increasingly brighter as the days turned into weeks and the weeks into months.

Sometimes I thought back on the whimpering boy who had come with me to the mine just a few months earlier. I would not have believed such a transformation was humanly possible had I not seen it for myself.

I pondered the change, at first marveling what hard physical labor could do to a man. I had changed too, feeling stronger, harder, more intense than at any other time in my life. The hard work agreed with my constitution. While the work was boring, my mind was active and restless, always looking for clues to an escape plan. But I was cautious and patient, always remembering the dead Indian and the guards' lack of concern for human life.

But it was more than hard, physical labor that was molding Pedro's body and mind. He was responding to intense emotional forces, too. With the sudden death of his father, the responsibility for the well-being and safety of the many families at the Sanchez *hacienda,* and his sister Elena, had become Pedro's. He was their protector and provider now. There was no one else to assume that role. He was the only one, he felt, who could stand between his loved ones and the likes of Jose Lobo. Unseen forces seemed to be working overtime transforming Pedro into the kind of man who could fulfill the destiny he was feeling for the first time in his life.

Yet there was irony in the situation, in that the only one who didn't seem to notice, or at least acknowledge, Pedro's marvelous transformation was Jose Lobo, who had been a regular occupant at the mine since bringing in Kenny Scott.

Lobo persisted in harassing Pedro—throwing dirt in his food, jabbing him from behind with a rifle barrel when he wanted Pedro to work faster, or making Pedro single-handedly push the cart up the trail to the head of the shaft.

There was constant verbal abuse, too. But Pedro never responded, even when Lobo bragged of urinating on the fresh dirt of Pedro's father's grave and violating the chastity of Elena, his unprotected sister. Pedro bore it all, without comment, without action. But inside he was churning. I knew it. The others knew it. Even the guards knew it. But Lobo kept pushing incessantly.

When we first came to the mine, the workers would turn away in embarrassment and disgust when Lobo teased and taunted Pedro. They felt pity for the helpless boy. Now they no longer turned away but watched intently, knowing that one day the taunting would cease. Pedro was no longer a frightened boy shrinking with fear, but a powerful animal waiting to strike, a raging bull waiting to be let out of the pen, a patient man with a cause that would not be denied short of death.

Every day while Lobo sat on a rock, rifle in hand, shouting his obscenities, Pedro chipped rock and loaded the ore cart, his muscles becoming stronger and stronger with each day's work.

No one knew what Pedro was waiting for, and he didn't say. Maybe he knew what he was doing, and maybe he didn't. Only one thing was sure. He would get only one chance. If he failed, he would be dead. Lobo was wicked, but he was not dumb. In fact, with time I began to believe that Lobo knew exactly what he was doing, that he was playing some kind of wicked game with death, a game that he intended to win. In winning he would finally taste total victory over the Sanchez family—the family he had once worked for and now resented so fiercely.

Chapter 40

We were thinking about a plan to work loose a pole on the side of our cage so we could escape during the night, when another opportunity presented itself quite unexpectedly.

It happened near the end of a day in late February. Pedro, Juan, and Kenny were filling the big cart with the last load of rocks for the day. I was helping Lobo and one of the guards set up a keg of black powder in a previously chipped out hole. The rest of the guards and workers had already left the mine.

We always blasted at the end of the day because after an explosion the air was full of dust, making breathing and work almost impossible. It took several hours for the dust to clear.

I was on my knees, trying to shove the keg of powder into an opening that was just a little too small for it, when Lobo became impatient with my inability to get the job done quickly. He ordered me to move away.

When—to my delight—it became obvious that he couldn't shove the keg through the hole either, Lobo ordered the guard to hold the powder in just the right position against the opening so he could tap it with the butt of his rifle. The guard leaned his rifle against the wall as he dropped to his knees to wrestle the keg into position.

In his eagerness to get the keg through the opening, Lobo failed to notice that his rifle's hammer was cocked. Nothing happened the first time he tapped the keg, but the second time the hammer was jarred free and the rifle fired, filling the shaft with a deafening explosion.

At first we thought we were goners, figuring the keg of black powder had exploded. It was with great relief that we realized only the rifle had fired, the slug ricocheting harmlessly off the ceiling. The guard let go of the keg and rolled back on his haunches, pale and sick with relief. Lobo looked at the rifle in his hand and cursed violently. Pedro, Juan, and Kenny stopped working and were looking in our direction, wondering what had happened.

It was at that moment that I discovered a once-in-a-lifetime opportunity—one that would be gone in a few moments if I didn't act fast. I was closest to the guard's rifle, the one leaning against the cave wall. Lobo's rifle was for the moment harmless, having just discharged. There were no other weapons in the cave.

I knew the opportunity wouldn't last long. I didn't have time to think out the consequences of getting the drop on Lobo and the guard. What would I do next? How would we get out of the cave and past the other guards? There was no time to figure things out.

I knew only one thing for sure. For the first time since Lobo took me prisoner, I had an opportunity to get the upper hand. I might never get such an opportunity again. I reached for the rifle.

Before the guard even knew what was happening, I was holding his weapon to my shoulder, the hammer cocked back, ready to fire. I ordered Lobo to toss his rifle to the ground in front of me. He reluctantly obeyed, smart enough to sense that his former slave would not hesitate to pull the trigger if necessary.

Next, I ordered Lobo and the guard to toss me their powder horns and ball bags. By this time, Pedro and Kenny were at my side, Pedro with a sledgehammer in his hand. Juan remained beside the cart, keeping an eye on the shaft entrance.

Kenny had just finished reloading Lobo's rifle when we heard the first shouts at the other end of the tunnel. Reinforcements were coming to the rescue.

Pedro ordered Lobo and the guard to fall on their faces so they could be tied up. While he and Kenny took care of that, I joined

Juan at the cart to see who was coming.

Two guards were running toward us through the dim lantern light. I aimed at the one on the right and pulled the trigger. He went down, wounded but not dead. While I was reloading, the healthy guard helped his wounded companion to his feet and they began scrambling back the way they had come, leaving their rifles behind.

The next thing I knew, Juan was racing down the shaft toward the spot where I had shot the guard. I wasn't sure what he was doing until he picked up the two rifles and headed back. Quick thinking, I thought, getting the rifles before the enemy had a chance to figure out what was going on. Now we had four weapons.

Juan had covered about half the distance back to the protection of the cart when several shots were fired from the far end of the shaft. Juan stumbled as if he had been hit, but maintained his grip on the rifles and continued running toward me. I fired a shot into the empty shaft past Juan in an effort to discourage those who would fire at Juan.

Juan collapsed at the side of the cart, a ball in the lower right side of his back—a nasty wound. After making him as comfortable as possible, I checked the prime on the new rifles to make sure they were ready to fire. By this time Pedro and Kenny had finished tying up Lobo and the guard with their own belts and trousers.

When they joined me beside Juan, all was quiet except for Lobo's mumbled curses. They had gagged him and the guard.

We were discussing when to make our break for freedom, in daylight or cover of darkness, when Kenny smelled the first smoke. A minute later all of us could smell it. The guards had begun to smoke us out with a brush fire at the mouth of the mine.

The decision was made for us. The oxygen would soon be gone, replaced by smoke. If we were going to give ourselves up, or make a break for freedom, we had to do it now.

"Let's ride out, in the cart," suggested Kenny.

"Get the rocks out first," I responded, knowing Kenny's idea was a good one. The thick plank sides on the cart would stop bullets. If we could get enough momentum to carry us all the way to the rock crusher and the nearby cover of trees, so much the better. Working quickly we removed most of the ore from the cart.

By this time Juan was weak and pale from loss of blood. Gently we lifted him into the cart. Kenny and I were just leaning into the back of the cart to get it moving when we noticed that Pedro was absent. We looked back and saw him leaning over the keg of black powder, carefully inserting a long white fuse. Lobo was wrestling frantically against his bonds, fully aware of Pedro's intentions. When the fuse was firmly in place, Pedro removed a lantern from the wall, ignited the fuse, then joined us at the cart—but not before giving Lobo a friendly pat on the head.

The three of us leaned into the cart, getting it off to a fast start before piling in. We crouched low in case any of the guards decided to fire upon the approaching cart.

The huge pile of smoldering brush and sticks offered little resistance and was scattered in all directions as the ore cart plunged out of the shaft. We had good momentum and nearly reached the crusher before coming to a halt. By that time we had already begun firing back at the surprised guards. They had not expected us to come so quickly or so dramatically.

While the sides of the big cart gave us protection from the guards' bullets, they had no cover to protect them from our bullets. Three of them received wounds from our first four shots. They scrambled for the nearest safe place—the entrance to the mine shaft.

"They're dead men!" exclaimed Kenny.

"What?" I asked, not understanding what he meant.

"The powder. Pedro lit the fuse."

The firing stopped when the guards disappeared into the darkness of the open shaft. We waited for what seemed a long time, and were beginning to think that perhaps the fuse had gone out, when suddenly we felt—more than heard—a giant belch from the inside of the mountain, followed by violent rumbling, and finally a loud blast of rock and dust from the mouth of the shaft—a blast which no one in the mine could have survived. The noise of the explosion was soon replaced by the cheering of the Mexican and Indian slaves, now free men.

The key to the cage was lost with one of the guards in the explosion, making it necessary to chop it open with an axe. Pedro took care of that. All the men were smiling.

The Mexicans and Indians headed out the next morning, some alone, some in twos and threes, headed in various directions to their homes. Pedro, Kenny, and I remained at the camp, having moved into the cabin previously occupied by the guards. Juan was too weak to travel, and we were determined to stay with him until he recovered, or died.

We didn't have to wait long. Two days later, in delirium, Juan called to his wife Maria, then gave up the fight. We buried him near the edge of the clearing.

Kenny and I were carving Juan's name on a cross we were fashioning for the grave when Kenny suddenly looked up at me and said, "Remember when I first came here and told you your name was familiar, but not your face?"

"I remember."

He looked back at the name he was carving on the cross.

"I saw your name written down once, on a big envelope. I remember where now."

"Where?" I asked.

"Ben Richards had it in his wagon."

"Who is Ben Richards?" I asked, somewhat annoyed at this seemingly insignificant interruption to the serious business of burying Juan.

"Came west to Salt Lake with him. He had a big envelope with 'Dan Storm' written on it."

"Do you know who it was from?" I asked, beginning to get interested, vaguely remembering how I had written to Caroline a long time ago, suggesting that she could get in touch with me by sending a letter with someone to the Great Basin.

"From a woman, I think. Caroline Lopez, Larsen . . . something like that."

"Caroline Logan!" I said.

"That's it."

I walked to the center of the clearing and looked eastward

toward the snow-covered Sierra Nevada Mountains. Soon the snow would be melting, and I would be heading through those passes. I could hardly believe that Caroline had responded to my letter, my marriage proposal.

The next morning I said good-bye to Pedro and Kenny. They headed west, and I headed east, mounted comfortably on my bay mare.

Chapter 41

I didn't know it at the time, but while I was a slave in the Mexican gold mine, some of my Mormon Battalion companions discovered gold at Sutter's Fort on the Sacramento River, less than a hundred miles to the north. I was with the first group of men to cross the Sierras in the spring of 1848, taking news of the gold discovery to the United States.

I could have traveled faster alone, but there was safety in numbers. I didn't want to take any chances of getting scalped, killed, or driven off in another direction, especially now that Caroline's letter was waiting for me in the valley of the Great Salt Lake. The man who had her letter was named Ben Richards.

After fighting through the late spring snowdrifts of the Sierras, the trip was uneventful except for several of the horses getting bit by rattlesnakes.

As we headed out of the tall sagebrush onto the barren wastes of alkali and wiry salt grass bordering the south end of the Great Salt Lake, I remembered my old friend Ike, the big black slave who had come to the Rocky Mountains with me ten years earlier. I wondered if he was still alive, if he was still war chief of the Gosiutes, if he had taught his adopted people how to use horses and grow crops. I longed to leave the party and head south into the land of the Gosiutes. Had it not been for the knowledge of Caroline's letter, I would have done so. But I continued east, following the most direct route to the city of the Great Salt Lake, eager to locate Ben Richards as quickly as possible.

In 1848 Salt Lake City wasn't much of a town. There were a few small, hastily put together cabins and sod huts. The newest arrivals were still living in wagons with crude lean-tos against one or both sides. The primary effort demanding everyone's time and effort was clearing land, diverting streams, and planting and caring for crops. There would be plenty of time later for improving homes and residences once there was sufficient food to keep everyone alive.

I didn't have any trouble finding Ben Richards. He had settled his young family in a sod hut a few miles south of the center of the city. The Richards family was glad to see me, like I was an old friend. Carrying the letter across the plains and mountains had established a bond between us, strangers who had never met before.

I was glad to answer the questions of Ben and his wife, but I don't think I was a very accommodating guest. I impatiently awaited the chance to tear open the brown envelope they had carried such a long distance.

I didn't have to wait long. Ben's wife, Mary, sensing my anxiety, retrieved the letter from a trunk just inside the hut and proudly handed it to me. I thanked them and headed for a grove of cottonwood trees bordering a nearby creek.

The thickness of the envelope surprised me. It was no ordinary letter. It was bulky enough to contain an entire newspaper. It was smooth and clean, having been well protected in the Richards's trunk.

My hands were trembling as I read the carefully written words on the envelope:

Dan Storm
Great Salt Lake City
From Caroline Logan

Inserting the point of my knife into the fold at the corner, I carefully cut the envelope open. The thickness led me to suspect that maybe Caroline was sending something else along with a letter, but as I looked inside, the total contents consisted of a folded-over wad of hand-written pages—a total of thirty-three pages with handwriting on both sides.

Never in my entire life had I ever seen or even heard of such a long letter. I remembered Caroline telling me how she had been a newspaper reporter in Philadelphia before coming to Nauvoo. She certainly hadn't forgotten how to write.

She began the letter by thanking me for writing to her as the Mormon Battalion began its westward journey. She thanked me for expressing my feelings toward her and thinking her worthy to be my wife and mother to my children. She hoped her letter would not be written in vain, but would reach me in the Great Basin.

My hands really began to shake when she said she shared similar feelings toward me, and that she had begun to entertain thoughts of becoming my wife long ago on that Mississippi River island where I had been bitten by the eel and she had taken care of me.

To my total surprise and amazement, Caroline went on to explain why she left Philadelphia to join the Mormons in Illinois. She explained that the schoolteacher job was just a cover; she'd made an arrangement with a Philadelphia publisher to come to Nauvoo as a spy to get the inside story on polygamy. Her engagement to Ebenezer McConklin was part of a plan to gather material for her book.

She tried to explain how she resisted her feelings toward me, determined to complete her mission and do the book. She thought that after I left she would gradually forget me; she was making progress in that direction when my letter arrived. Again she began to think that maybe her future should be with me in the West rather than writing books for an Eastern publisher. But she wasn't sure, even though she now realized she loved me more than any man she had ever met.

She explained how after getting all the information she could out of Ebenezer and deserting him at the altar, she fled south to Keokuk to stay with Pat and Sarah, who were now expecting a baby and planning to head west in '48.

Caroline said she had pretty much finished the book and knew it would be a top seller because it proved once and for all not only that the Mormons were practicing polygamy, but that they had been doing it for some time.

She said it bothered her at times, the fact that she was going to publish a book that would harm a people who had been so kind to her. She wasn't converted to the doctrine and the Book of Mormon yet, but she liked and trusted the people. In some ways she felt like publishing the book would be a betrayal of sorts, not only to the Mormons in general, but to me, Dan Storm.

She decided to come out west with Pat and Sarah and bring the unfinished manuscript with her. Hopefully we would meet again in the Great Basin and be able to resume our relationship. If things worked out, maybe we could build that cabin in the beautiful mountain valley I had often described to her. If things didn't work out, she could return to Philadelphia to finish her book, or she might even decide to become the plural wife of a prominent Mormon. As I read this part of the letter, I thought maybe she was trying to be funny, but I wasn't sure. She didn't think the Mormons would be so secretive about plural marriage once they got out by themselves in the Rocky Mountains.

I stopped reading. She had said so much. There were so many things to think about. The biggest thing of all, of course, was the part about her coming west with Pat and Sarah in '48. That was this summer. She was probably already on her way. Maybe I could have the cabin built by the time she arrived. There was no doubt in my mind that things would work out between us and we would marry.

I was so happy, but as I returned to the letter to read the last page, my blood suddenly turned to ice. My fists clenched, wrinkling the letter.

"By the way," she said. "Do you remember that man who was supposed to be my contact with the publisher? The same one who shot at us when we were loading our horses on the boat?"

She was writing about Dick Boggs, the meanest man alive. Except for, perhaps, his cousin the governor, Dick Boggs was the vilest Mormon hater of them all.

"He has really changed," she continued. "As you know, he is our neighbor. He helped Pat build a barn, and he even loaned us some seed and a mule. In fact, Mr. Boggs is coming over with his wagon tonight to take the three of us to Keokuk to a magic show. You would be so pleased to see the change in him."

I stood up and threw down the letter. How could an intelligent woman be so naive? How could Pat and Sarah be so careless as to get involved with Boggs? He hadn't changed. Not Dick Boggs. A man that cruel didn't just become a nice guy. He was up to something. He wanted something. Maybe the unfinished manuscript. But no, that wasn't likely.

Then I knew. He wanted Caroline. What man wouldn't want a woman like her? Of course she wouldn't feel the same way about him. When he realized he didn't have a chance with her, the real Boggs would surface.

A man like Boggs wouldn't let a prize like Caroline get out of his reach, not when she was coming to me, his most bitter enemy. When he realized he couldn't win her with pretended sweetness, he would take her by force. That was the real Dick Boggs. My instincts told me that Caroline was in trouble. Maybe she wasn't on her way to the mountains after all.

I stuffed the pages of the letter back into the brown envelope, leaped upon the bay mare, and headed back to the Richards's hut. Without dismounting I thanked them for bringing the letter to me.

When they asked me to stay for supper and possibly the night, I thanked them but said I had to be on my way immediately.

"It's late afternoon," responded Ben Richards. "Where could you be in such a hurry to get to this late in the day?"

"Keokuk, Iowa Territory," I answered, as I spun the mare around and dug my heels into her sides.

Chapter 42

Caroline was seated comfortably in a low-back wooden chair, her forearms resting easily on the edge of a small oak table. The table was covered with random bits and pieces of paper surrounding a neat stack of white manuscript pages. It was a summer evening in 1847, but little of the outside light penetrated the cabin loft where Caroline worked. A kerosene lantern hanging from a nearby rafter provided the necessary light to read the piles of notes.

Her table and chair were located in the loft of Pat O'Riley's cabin near Keokuk, Iowa Territory. At the rear of the loft was the cot where she slept. Various items of female clothing including dresses, petticoats, and undergarments were draped over a rope stretching from one side of the loft to the other. She had been living with the O'Rileys since leaving Nauvoo the previous winter.

Caroline had arrived in a snowstorm, wrapped in a buffalo robe and mounted on a horse loaned her by Peter Weaselhead. She carried two bundles, one containing clothing and personal belongings, the other a tightly wrapped bundle of papers. She explained later the papers were notes for a book.

When Caroline explained that she needed a place to stay while she worked on a book manuscript, a history of sorts of the deserted city of Nauvoo, the O'Rileys gladly offered her their loft for as long as she wanted to stay.

When asked about the book, Caroline explained that a publisher in her hometown of Philadelphia had asked her to do it. She wasn't specific about the book. She didn't tell them how the publisher had selected her because of her good looks as well as her writing skills to come to Nauvoo and get the inside story on polygamy. She didn't explain how her involvement in Nauvoo social life and her eventual engagement to Ebenezer McConklin were merely ploys to dig out the facts and hearsay on polygamy.

It wasn't that Caroline didn't feel she could trust her friends with her secret. It just didn't feel right to include them in her espionage plot. She felt it was for their own good. Right or wrong, she had gotten into this thing by herself and would finish it by herself, without dragging innocent people in with her.

Pat and Sarah were content with Caroline's general explanation, and when she didn't offer further details about her book, they didn't push. Besides, they were busy from sunup to sundown clearing land, building fences, and tending crops and livestock on their new farm. Sarah was pregnant with their first child, and working, dreaming, and planning occupied every spare moment. Their dreams included the eventual sale of the farm in a year or two, earning a sufficient profit to outfit them with enough equipment, supplies, and livestock to settle and develop a much larger farm in the Rocky Mountains. Pat and Sarah had no time for or interest in the abstract ideas of a history book—not even the one Caroline was working on.

As winter turned to spring, then to summer, Caroline was left pretty much to herself to work on her manuscript. She worked hard, too hard. It wasn't the enthusiasm of producing a best-seller that drove her as much as the need to escape, escape the uneasiness she felt about deceiving people to get her information. She felt bad about the flirting she had engaged in with prominent Mormons in an effort to get them to talk about "the principle."

She even felt bad about leading the stuffy Ebenezer McConklin to the altar when all along she had no intention of going through with the ceremony.

She was still amazed at how easy it had been. While other church leaders in Nauvoo were very tight-lipped about "celestial marriage," Ebenezer seemed eager to impress upon the attractive and available young schoolteacher that he, too, had been taught the sacred principle and was entitled to the privileges of plural marriage.

Caroline was convinced that before an angry mob, or in a court of law, McConklin would have died rather than give up his secrets. But a familiar smile and gentle touch on the arm from the blonde schoolteacher, repeated on several occasions, and he was ready to tell all.

She learned that the roots of Mormon polygamy went back to the early 1830s, soon after the Church was organized, when Joseph told some of his most trusted friends that the married brethren would take Indian wives "in the same manner that Abraham took Hagar . . . and Jacob took Rachel, Bilhah, and Zilpah; by revelation."

She learned that Joseph took his first plural wife in 1835 and many more before his death in 1844. Caroline had cried upon hearing the account of Joseph introducing the principle to his trusted friend Heber C. Kimball, then telling Heber the Lord wanted him to give his wife Vilate to Joseph. Stunned, Heber returned home to discuss the matter with his beloved wife. After much fasting and prayer, they painfully decided to obey the man they believed to be a prophet of God.

When Heber held out Vilate's hand to the young prophet, Joseph openly wept, telling them his commandment had been a test, that Heber and Vilate had passed and were now entitled to be sealed to each other for time and all eternity.

The same test, when presented to Orson Pratt, had backfired. Pratt, convinced Joseph was a fallen prophet, had gone to the press and caused much embarrassment for Joseph and the Mormon Church.

Caroline learned that even among the leading brethren there were vehement differences of opinion over plural marriage—differences which eventually led to the establishment of the *Expositor,* a newspaper founded in Nauvoo to expose the assumed wrongdoings of those supporting the principle. Those on the other side saw to it that the *Expositor* was put out of business, an action that concluded in Joseph's arrest and imprisonment at Carthage, where he was murdered.

After evenings of discussion with McConklin and others, Caroline would return home and stay up long into the night writing down everything she could remember from the evening discussion. By the arrival of the wedding date with McConklin, she had hundreds of pages of notes.

Many of the items in her notes couldn't be verified because the people involved were scattered across the continent—from Nauvoo and points east all the way to the Great Basin. Still, Caroline knew she had material for the most important and sensational book yet published on Mormons and polygamy. She really did have the inside story, thanks to Ebenezer McConklin and his friends.

But there was one other thing that bothered Caroline. The young man from the Rocky Mountains. The young man who had been married to a beautiful Indian girl named Red Leaf. The one who had fallen in love with her and talked of taking her away with him to a beautiful valley high in the Rocky Mountains to settle a new land and raise a cabin full of beautiful, independent children. She had wanted to share the dream with him—more than she had ever wanted anything else. She couldn't explain why. It was just a feeling, but a strong one, so strong she dared not think about it very often. So she buried herself in her work on the manuscript. She had rejected the young man and sent him back to the Rocky Mountains, where she would never see him again. She must get him out of her mind, and out of her heart. She must forget Dan Storm.

Then the letter arrived, the one from Fort Leavenworth in the Kansas Territory. Dan was heading west with the Mormon Battalion never to see Caroline again, but he had run into Ebenezer McConklin, who was traveling with a wagon train headed for Council Bluffs. Dan had approached McConklin's wagon, hoping for a last look at Caroline, only to discover she hadn't married McConklin after all.

When the battalion stopped at Fort Leavenworth for provisions, Dan had written a letter and sent it to Nauvoo. It was forwarded to Keokuk.

Caroline read the letter a hundred times, hopelessly distracted from her half-finished manuscript. She had supposed Dan had walked out of her life forever. Now she had a second chance, something she had never hoped for, but something that made her very happy—the happiest she had ever felt.

Eventually she discussed the letter with Pat and Sarah, who convinced her that she should answer Dan's letter and join them in their trek to the Rocky Mountains, where she could resume her courtship with Dan.

After sending the letter, Caroline continued work on her manuscript, but with less urgency. She had too much work in the book project to merely abandon it. She would finish it, but she had doubts that she would ever send it to her publisher, not when she was going to the Rocky Mountains to join the people whose secrets the book possessed. Maybe if things didn't work out with Dan, she would return to the East. Maybe then she would consider publishing the manuscript. After all, she had taken great pains to see that it was accurate and truthful. She could feel good about publishing it, as long as she wasn't living among the Mormons. She would wait and see how things turned out with Dan. In the meantime, while waiting to head west, she would finish the book.

And that's what Caroline was doing at her little oak table on that summer evening when she became aware of the distant clanking of a wagon approaching along the bumpy road.

"Caroline," called Sarah from below. "I can hear Mr. Boggs's wagon. Better get your shawl and put out the lamp."

Chapter 43

Caroline felt a twinge of excitement as she climbed onto the seat of the wagon beside Dick Boggs. Her hands were perspiring, her cheeks flushed. Her excitement was not the normal attraction a woman feels for a man. She didn't have any such feelings for Dick Boggs. He wasn't the kind of man women were attracted to.

His tobacco-stained beard was bald in places, the result of a nervous habit of pulling out hairs with his fingers. The beard was thin enough to reveal the absence of a chin—nothing more than a gradual slope of skin from his puffy lower lip to his red neck.

The hair on his head was still damp, evidence that he had tried to wash himself, but he still smelled of stale tobacco and old sweat. Filth and sweat accumulated over weeks and months didn't just disappear with a quick wash—especially when his flannel underwear and cotton trousers had not been washed with soap, ever. And Boggs was always sweating, winter and summer, not so much from body warmth caused by excess fat as by nervousness.

Boggs always wore a hat, too, possibly to hide his partial baldness. When he removed his hat to greet Caroline, she was repulsed by the soggy white skin on the top of his head, reminding her of a frog's belly. But worst of all she disliked the intense, blinking stare from the black too-close-together, ferret-like eyes.

No, Caroline wasn't attracted to Dick Boggs. Her excitement was caused by a sense of danger, a feeling that she was walking close to the edge of a cliff, a very high and dangerous one. After all, Boggs had the reputation of being the meanest Mormon-hater of them all. According to Dan Storm, the man she was thinking of marrying, Boggs was one of the cruelest men alive, capable of killing without feeling or caring.

In recent months Boggs had expressed a sudden change in his attitude toward Mormons, at least toward Pat and Sarah. He had been a very good neighbor. He had loaned Pat and Sarah a mule and equipment to help clear land and get crops in. He had helped put a roof on the barn. He even brought them supplies from town, without charge.

Caroline often wondered about the change. Was Boggs's heart softening? Was he beginning to feel bad about the things he had done to the Mormons? Or was he after something? Perhaps there was a devious purpose behind his kindness. If so, someday he would show his hand and all would know. In the meantime, it was exciting for Caroline to ponder, to try to figure out what was behind the new Dick Boggs.

When Pat and Sarah climbed on the seat, Caroline had no choice but to scoot close to Boggs. The wooden bench was wide enough for four people, but only if they sat close together, touching each other. Caroline felt somewhat frightened sitting so close to Boggs. She wondered what Dan Storm would think if he could see them.

The ride to Keokuk was uneventful, the conversation mundane. They discussed the crops, the weather, and of course the Mormon westward migration. Boggs tried to be polite, helpful, and attentive as the conversation progressed, but it was obvious to Caroline that he was not accustomed to such behavior. A man does not become civilized overnight.

The magic show wasn't very impressive, certainly not worth the nickel admission charged each spectator. The long-haired young man in the wrinkled suit and top hat did not perform magic tricks but conducted a long string of parlor tricks and games instead. Though not magic, the games were entertaining, and by the time the performance was over, the crowd of farmers and half-breeds didn't seem to mind they hadn't witnessed a magic show. Even the parlor games were a welcome distraction from the everyday rigors of frontier life.

On the way back to the wagon, Caroline decided that for the return trip she would try not to sit by Boggs, but to arrange the seating with Pat and Sarah in the middle, between her and Boggs. However, as they left the schoolhouse where the magic show had been held, just as Caroline was beginning to fall behind to allow Pat and Sarah to be first onto the bench, she felt Boggs's hand grasp her arm just above the elbow. Not wanting to make a scene, she had no choice but to let him help her up onto the bench—the same place where she had ridden on the way into town.

It was dark now and Caroline felt even more frightened, sitting so close to Dan Storm's mortal enemy. She began to wonder for the first time if Boggs's kindness in recent months had anything to do with her. He was twenty years her senior, and it had never occurred to her that his recent kindnesses might have romantic roots.

Caroline's suspicions were proven beyond any reasonable doubt when under the cover of darkness Boggs slipped both reins into his left hand and carefully placed his clammy right paw on her left hand. Caroline's first reaction was one of anger, and she thought of trying to shove Boggs off the end of the seat. But her better judgment kept her still.

After a few moments, Caroline removed her hand to point at a bright lantern shining from the window of a distant cabin. She said something about how bright the lantern was, then folded her arms so her hands would be out of reach.

Unfortunately, Boggs hadn't removed his hand when she had pulled hers away, and now his paw rested on her knee. Unfolding her arms, she took a firm two-handed grip on his grimy wrist and pushed his hand away. Quickly she folded her arms again, feeling very glad that she was leaving for the Rocky Mountains in the spring. The departure couldn't be too soon, especially now that Boggs had his eye on her. She realized that in the meantime she would have to be very careful to avoid Boggs at all costs. He was the kind of man who would do anything to get what he wanted.

Chapter 44

After the trip to the Keokuk magic show, Dick Boggs began to visit the O'Riley place with increasing frequency. It became obvious to Pat and Sarah, as well as to Caroline, that Boggs had a romantic eye for Caroline.

Through the fall and winter Caroline avoided Boggs as best she could, but living in the loft of a one-room cabin on a remote country estate made it difficult to avoid uninvited visitors. The next best thing was to make sure she wasn't alone with Boggs, that either Pat or Sarah was around. But that became increasingly difficult after the baby, Patrick Jr., was born late in the fall. With Sarah frequently nursing and tending her infant and Pat off working, Caroline often found herself alone with the unwelcome visitor.

It became a tedious situation, Boggs forcing himself upon Caroline, asking her to go places with him, to come to his place, to let him give her information for the book. Caroline's polite rejections didn't seem to discourage him. Her excuses became lame and redundant, but still Boggs persisted, refusing to acknowledge the more than subtle message of her rejections.

Pat, Sarah, and Caroline had decided to play along with Boggs as long as possible in an effort not to offend him. As unpleasant as it was to have Boggs hanging around, they certainly didn't want him as an enemy.

One evening when Boggs was asking Caroline about the book and trying to draw her into a conversation on how devastating the book would be to the Mormons once it was published, Caroline's patience finally wore a little too thin.

"It may not ever get published," she said.

"What?" asked Boggs in confusion.

"I'm going west with Pat and Sarah in the spring."

"To join the Mormons in the Great Basin?" questioned Boggs, stunned like an ox.

Caroline nodded.

"But why?" asked Boggs. "You've risked your life to write that book. It will make you rich and famous. You can't throw that away."

"Remember Dan Storm?"

Boggs's face turned red. His fists clenched, turning his knuckles white.

"I'm going to meet him there," she said, allowing a brief pause before delivering the final blow. "We're going to marry."

As Caroline looked Dick Boggs in the eyes, trying to stare him down, trying to defeat him once and for all, she noticed a different look in him—a look of surprise and painful discovery. At first she thought perhaps he was hurt deeply at finally having to acknowledge rejection from the woman he loved.

But she knew she was mistaken when she recognized a look of relief in his face, like an unpleasant burden had suddenly been removed. The look of relief became a look of fiendish pleasure, like a cat about to pounce on a cornered mouse.

With Caroline's rejection, Boggs was forced to conclude that he had been wrong in trying to be the nice guy to Caroline, Pat, and Sarah. Being a gentleman had gotten him nowhere, only wasted valuable time. His look of relief was the realization that he no longer needed to play the awkward role of a gentleman and kind neighbor. He was now free to follow the base, cruel instincts he had been following all his life.

His look of joy came from the realization that in Caroline he had a means to get revenge on the man he hated more than anything in the world—the man who had lured him into a bear trap secured to the rear wheel of a runaway wagon, the cause of his amputated foot. More than he wanted this woman, or any woman, he wanted revenge on Dan Storm. Now he could get his revenge through this woman. How, he didn't know. Not yet. But he would find a way, and his revenge would be terrible, satisfying. There was an ugly grin on his face as he climbed upon his horse and galloped off into the night.

Chapter 45

Caroline didn't forget the look on Boggs's face when she told him she was going off to the Great Basin to marry Dan Storm. It wasn't the initial look of surprise that she remembered as much as the expression of total hate, followed by a look of anticipated revenge that at last he had a chance to repay a festering debt to Dan Storm. None of these things were expressed in words, but Boggs's face read like a book; the meaning was unmistakable.

In her mind Caroline saw Boggs's face when she paused from her work on the manuscript, when she was eating, and especially when she was sleeping. As fall turned into winter, as the weeks passed, she had terrible nightmares about Boggs inflicting horrible tortures on her and Dan. And when she awakened she worried continually about what Boggs might really do—to her, to Dan, and maybe even to the O'Rileys. How would he get his revenge?

Sometimes she thought the waiting was part of Boggs's plan, because the waiting was torture, real and painful. The uncertainty was horrible. Caroline found herself longing for the spring day when they would pack the wagon and head west, never to return to Iowa and Dick Boggs again. Sometimes she began to think that maybe he would forget his revenge and allow them to leave without retribution. But as soon as she began to believe that maybe he would leave them alone, she would remember that face, the hate, the passion for revenge, and her old worries would return, more intense than ever. Sometimes she wished he would just hurry up and get whatever he was going to do over with.

Winter was beginning to give in to spring when Boggs made his first move. Caroline was taken by surprise; otherwise she could have prevented the theft. Even though she had never had any firm ideas what Boggs might do, she had always assumed he would do something physical, something that would injure, maim, or humiliate. She was surprised when she arrived home from church services with Pat and Sarah one afternoon to discover the manuscript was gone. At first Caroline didn't mention the theft to Pat and Sarah, not wanting to get into a discussion with them over the content of the book.

There was no doubt in Caroline's mind, however, that Boggs had taken the manuscript. No one else knew about it, except her publisher in Philadelphia. Nobody else had a motive to steal it. And Boggs's motive was obvious. With the manuscript he could expose her as a spy to the Mormons. They would probably be furious with her and not allow her to migrate with one of their wagon trains to the Rocky Mountains. Any chance of building a life with Dan Storm in the Rocky Mountains would be ruined.

But as she thought about it, she realized there had to be more. Boggs had too much hate to be content with such an indirect revenge on Dan Storm. Too many things could go wrong. There were too many unknowns, too big a chance that Dan Storm could come out unscathed. The young adventurer had a way of turning tough situations into welcome opportunities.

Boggs had to have something more cruel in mind, something more exact, more satisfying. But what?

There was one way to find out: go ask him. Maybe he would deny taking the manuscript, perhaps not. Maybe he was just waiting for her to come to him so he could spell out his evil intentions. Maybe he would give her the manuscript back, but what would he want in return?

One thing for sure, Caroline had already gone through enough weeks and months of uncertainty, wondering what Boggs might do. She wanted no more of the misery of waiting. Boggs had stolen the manuscript. Now it was her turn to act, her move. No more waiting and wondering. She would go directly to Boggs, confront him, see what he wanted with the manuscript, and try to get it back. After the months of worry, it felt good to make a decision, to act, to take the offensive—descending into the very jaws of hell couldn't be any worse than the senseless waiting, or so she thought.

Once she found out what Boggs was thinking, maybe she could outsmart him. She also knew that dealing with Boggs could be dangerous. The man was an animal of the basest sort. But at least the waiting was over. It was time for her to do something, and that felt good, in a fearful kind of way.

The big question was how to handle the confrontation. Should she do it alone? Or should she tell Pat and Sarah about the stolen manuscript and ask Pat to accompany her? She knew he would be glad to help, but she didn't want to drag Pat and Sarah into this thing if another alternative was possible. They had been so kind to her, so helpful, and it just didn't seem right to pull them into a feud that wasn't of their own making. They had a new baby and were looking forward to a new life in the Rocky Mountains. They neither needed nor deserved to become embroiled in a fight with the likes of Dick Boggs.

On the other hand, Caroline wondered how she dared visit the remote Boggs plantation by herself. Was it courage or stupidity that drove her to want to do it alone?

Chapter 46

"I'll blow his candles out!" exclaimed Pat, shaking his fist. Caroline had just told him about the missing manuscript and her suspicion that Boggs was the thief.

"But why did he do it?" asked Sarah, much calmer than her husband.

"I don't know for sure," said Caroline. "But other than the two of you, he is the only one who knew about the manuscript. It had to be him."

"I'll go fetch it back," said Pat, reaching for his coat.

"No," said Caroline, "I'd like to talk to him first. I want to find out why he did it and what he wants. When I came to Nauvoo, Boggs was my contact with the publisher. Maybe Sears & Chadwick is involved in this. I think Boggs will tell me."

"Would you like me to go with you?" asked Pat.

"No, I just wanted you to know where I was going."

"In case anything happens," added Sarah.

"If you're not back by noon, I'll come for you," assured Pat.

The next morning Caroline pulled her horse to a stop at the top of the hill overlooking the Boggs plantation. She was wearing a pair of men's trousers, cowhide boots, a bulky shirt, and a felt hat with her hair tucked underneath in a bun. There was no artificial coloring on her cheeks or lips. Caroline wanted to look as unattractive and unfeminine as possible. She didn't want to do anything to encourage Boggs.

She felt like a fly entering the web of a spider. She knew enough of Boggs to know she was in danger. She trusted that in catching him by surprise, early in the morning, she would have a better chance of getting the manuscript back.

The thing that bothered Caroline was knowing that she didn't have anything to trade for the return of the manuscript. She knew Boggs wouldn't just give it back for the asking. He wanted something, but what? It wouldn't be money. She had little of that.

She was determined to find out what he wanted, then try to trick him out of the manuscript if possible. She would lie if necessary. Boggs was a common thief, a bitter man, sick with revenge and hate for Dan Storm. She didn't have any feeling of guilt about using trickery on Dick Boggs.

If she couldn't get the manuscript back, at least she could find out what Boggs wanted. Maybe she could learn where he had hidden the manuscript. If so, maybe she could steal it back when he was away from the cabin.

With no reason to wait any longer, Caroline gently pressed her heels against the horse's sides and headed down the hill toward the cabin.

"I've been expecting you," lied Boggs, his cracked lips parting in an evil grin, exposing his crooked, milky brown teeth.

She knew he was lying because his reddish beard contained what appeared to be the accumulation of many days of food drippings. Had he expected her so soon, he would at least have cleaned his beard.

"Come in," said Boggs, swinging the heavy door wide open.

Caroline would rather have discussed the matter on the porch. But from outside she wouldn't be able to discover the location of the manuscript. Maybe not inside, either, but she had to try. Boldly, she marched into the cabin.

At first she could hardly see, because her eyes were adjusting to the dark. Boggs quickly closed the door. As her eyes adjusted, she noticed other things. First, the intense heat from the wood stove. No wonder Boggs sweated so profusely. Soon she would, too. She didn't care.

The smell was heavy and intense—dirty socks, frying bacon, freshly skinned hides, and dirty dishwater. When Boggs shoved a platter of slippery, half-cooked bacon strips in front of her face, she politely refused, figuring she was in no condition to swallow anything in Boggs's cabin.

She seated herself on a wooden chair next to the only table in the middle of the cabin, her eyes quickly adjusting to the gloom. Boggs seated himself across from her, chewing noisily on his greasy bacon strips.

There was no floor in the cabin, only a flat surface of damp red clay with grease, bits of food, hair from scraped hides, and other items trampled into the upper crust. The log walls were cluttered with rusted animal traps and furs at all stages of curing, stretched inside out on willow loops. His bed was a crude rack of poles and corn husks with four short tree stumps for legs. Mixed in with the corn husks was a ragged buffalo robe, full of holes and tears, much of the hair missing.

Boggs was chewing the last four pieces of bacon, all at once, when Caroline heard something scratching on the outside of the door—light and tentative at first, then louder and more insistent. She looked at Boggs to see how he would respond to the noise, but he ignored it as he gulped down the last of the bacon.

"I thought you might be com'n by," he mumbled, looking down into the greasy fry pan, beginning to doodle with his finger in the rapidly cooling grease.

Except for the scratching on the door, the cabin was quiet. Boggs was playing a game, waiting for Caroline to ask about the stolen manuscript. The quiet grew into an awkward silence, Caroline determined that Boggs should be the first to talk about the manuscript. Caroline wasn't sure why she waited. It was just a feeling that she shouldn't be too eager about getting the manuscript back. That would only encourage Boggs's devious intentions, whatever they might be.

Caroline was both annoyed and curious at the continued scratching on the door. Boggs continued to ignore the sound until a loud whining began to accompany the scratching.

Obviously annoyed, Boggs stepped to the door and jerked it open. Caroline had suspected the noise might be coming from a dog, but what surprised her was the size of the dog—a skinny, big-boned brute about the size of a pony. Brown and white and shaggy, it cowered in the doorway, whimpering, begging for something to eat. Caroline figured that with so little confidence, the dog couldn't be much more than a puppy—a young dog not yet aware of its own strength and abilities.

"Git!" shouted Boggs, attempting to shoo the big dog away. It took a step back, a deep rumble beginning in its throat, then changing to a whimper. The dog was obviously very hungry—the hunger of a rapidly growing pup. It intended to be fed.

"Git!" shouted Boggs again, annoyed the dog did not obey him. When the dog refused to leave the second time, Boggs's boot shot forward with a powerful thrust aimed at the dog's throat. But the big animal was alert, easily dodging the boot, still not retreating.

Expecting Boggs to go after the dog with a club, Caroline was surprised when he turned his back on the pup and returned to the table, leaving the door open. After seating himself in a chair, facing the door, Boggs removed the greasy fry pan from the table and placed it on the dirt floor at his feet.

"Come boy, lick the pan," coaxed Boggs, his gruff voice suddenly very friendly and inviting.

The dog looked at the pan but didn't move. It didn't want to enter the cabin. Obviously it didn't trust its master.

"I've never seen such a big dog," said Caroline. "Where did you get him?"

Without taking his eyes off the dog, or his hand off the handle of the pan, Boggs responded, "Off a ship from France. Cost me twenty-five dollars. Supposed to be the biggest dog in America."

"What kind is he?" asked Caroline, not particularly wanting to get into a pleasant conversation with Boggs, but honestly curious about the huge creature.

"Cross between a wolfhound and a St. Barnyard, the captain told me. When I get 'im trained, he'll be able to take a Danite off his horse at a dead run in the middle of the night. Mormons'll hate him before I'm through."

The dog took a cautious step forward, its eyes riveted to the greasy pan. Boggs shuffled the pan back and forth, like a pan of popcorn over a hot fire.

"Come on, boy, have some grub," he coaxed, his voice having the familiar tone he had used with Caroline before he learned of her intentions to marry Dan Storm.

The big dog could not hold back any longer. He headed for the pan, nose to the floor, tail between his legs. Boggs stopped shuffling the pan but didn't let go of the handle.

The dog stopped a few feet short of the pan and carefully stretched its nose forward, a long red tongue darting out to lap up the grease.

Boggs's free hand was as fast as the tongue, quickly grabbing the dog's leather collar. The startled pup scrambled backward, Boggs refusing to let go—of both the collar and the fry pan as he was pulled forward on his knees.

Caroline looked on with fascination, then horror, as Boggs began to beat the dog with the frypan, slinging the bacon grease in every direction. At first he hit the dog on the rump, then the side, the shoulder—even on the side of the head. Caroline was amazed that the skull did not cave in beneath the flat iron surface of the pan. The dog yelped as it tried to get away, then growled as it tried in vain to close its big jaws on the greasy forearm.

The two were completely through the doorway before Boggs finally let go of the collar. Caroline expected the dog to scamper off to the woods, tail between its legs.

Instead, the big canine backed out of reach of the pan, refusing to turn away from the man who had beaten it. The tail was no longer between its legs as the black lips curled back, exposing long rows of clean white teeth. The ears were flat against the dog's head. Caroline heard the distinct rumbling in the dog's chest, awkward at first, then steady and confident, challenging the man with the frypan.

Somehow the beating had changed a whimpering puppy into a wild beast, a bitter enemy that would never forget the beating.

Boggs was furious and lunged forward to strike the animal again, but it easily jumped out of reach and began to head for the woods, the snarl still on its lips as it looked back. In a rage, Boggs threw the pan after the dog, feeling in some undefinable way that the beast had made a fool out of him in front of a beautiful woman. He had beaten the dog with a pan, but for some unexplainable reason the dog was responding as if it were the victor, as if it were no longer afraid of him. He would take care of the dog later.

Boggs reentered the cabin and slammed the door. Caroline looked down at the table, trying to control her fear. She had seen Boggs's wrath and knew there would be nothing to keep him from abusing her should she make him angry as the dog had done. She would have to be careful. She hadn't come to please this vile man, only to confront or outsmart him. Either way there was a good chance she would make him angry. The possible consequences frightened her.

"A man's got to be firm with dogs, especially the big ones," explained Boggs, still partially out of breath. "Got to teach 'em to obey, to know who the boss is. That dog'll be a good one if I can ever beat enough sense and respect into him." Caroline didn't believe Boggs; she doubted that he believed himself. Caroline was convinced that the big dog was no ordinary hound. It seemed the beating had awakened some savage instinct—as if some kind of wild primeval power, suppressed by generations of domestication and civilization, had suddenly come to the surface and taken control of the animal. The beating had converted a whimpering pup into a fearless and calculating beast.

"Where's my manuscript?" asked Caroline, taking advantage of a chance to catch Boggs off guard while he was still thinking about the dog.

He looked at her in apparent surprise, it taking a few seconds for the words to sink in. Then his lips suddenly spread into a wicked smile, exposing two broken rows of tobacco-stained teeth spotted with unswallowed bits of bacon.

"Good work," he said. "I've been reading it. Love every word. The Mormons'll never be able to deny polygamy again. Holy Joe will roll over in his grave when that book hits the streets. Everybody in this country will be after the Mormons, as I've been for years. They'll see the light, thanks to you."

"Why did you take it?" asked Caroline, immediately regretting asking such a useless question.

"Worried about you gett'n too friendly with the Mormons, maybe decid'n not to get it published. Wouldn't want all that work wasted."

"I would like to have it back," asked Caroline, her voice sounding more timid than she intended.

"Besides, you're head'n west," continued Boggs. "Mail delivery ain't too good out there. Thought I'd just help out and get it to the publisher for you."

"But it's mine," protested Caroline, realizing she was getting nowhere.

"After making the changes, that is, I'll get it to the publisher," added Boggs.

"Changes?" This time Caroline was the one taken by surprise.

Boggs was eager to explain, eager to slip in the knife, to hurt, to frighten, to worry. But first he had to tease, like a cat playing with a mouse before eating it.

"You should know better than to hog all the credit for such a fine piece of work."

"What do you mean?" asked Caroline, having no idea what he was getting at.

"I'm not an educated man, but I know the front page of a book should give the names of the people who wrote it." Caroline still didn't know what he was trying to say, so she just waited for him to continue.

"Don't worry," he toyed. "I took care of your oversight." Caroline waited for him to continue further.

"Took the front page to town and paid a lady to write Dan Storm's name beside yours, so everybody will know he helped you. He'll get his share of the credit."

"That's not true, and you know it!" exclaimed Caroline, finally understanding what Boggs was trying to do. "Dan didn't know anything about the book."

"Everybody in Nauvoo knew you and him spent a lot of time together. Of course they'll believe you was partners."

Caroline knew he was right. If the book were published with Dan's name beside hers on the cover, his people would brand him a traitor for sure. The Mormons would drive him out; the Danites would possibly do worse than that. Boggs intended to use the manuscript to hurt and possibly destroy the man she loved.

"The manuscript is mine. I want it back," demanded Caroline, her voice full of emotion and beginning to break.

"No," said Boggs, knowing that she knew he had the upper hand once and for all.

"Please," begged Caroline, feeling completely helpless.

"No."

Looking into Boggs's face, Caroline saw a look of pure pleasure. In their brief acquaintance she had never seen him so happy. She got up to leave. Without a word she reached for the door.

He was enjoying his victory too much to let her go.

"Sit down," he asked, his voice suddenly polite. "There might be a way for you to get the manuscript back."

Caroline didn't know if she could return to the chair. Like a cornered animal, she longed to pull open the door and flee. But as long as Boggs was offering a way of getting the manuscript back, she had to listen. She returned to the chair.

Boggs didn't waste any time in getting to the point. He looked down at the table, uneasy about looking Caroline in the face as he made his proposition.

"Gets mighty lonely out here . . . living alone and all . . ."

Chapter 47

After leaving Boggs's cabin, Caroline didn't head back to Pat and Sarah's place. She needed time to think things out but was afraid if Pat found out what Boggs was up to, he would probably go after him. She didn't want that. Pat was strong and undoubtedly a good fighter, but he was hot-tempered and impetuous. Boggs was tricky and would not hesitate to kill Pat if confronted. No, she would avoid Pat until she sorted things out in her mind.

Boggs had offered to give the manuscript back, including the doctored title page, if she would move in with him until summer, when she would be free to head west with Pat and Sarah. If she didn't cooperate, he would spend the spring working on the manuscript himself. He felt she had been too kind to the Mormons. He said he could fix that, juice it up some with the help of a Missouri schoolteacher. He made it clear he would leave Caroline's and Dan's names on the title page. He would send the "edited" manuscript to a publisher and a copy of the title page to the Danites. He guessed they would be eager to take care of Dan and possibly Caroline, too.

She told Boggs she would give him an answer in a few days, then headed her horse for Keokuk. She didn't know where else to go, but as she approached the rugged river-front town, she remembered the Mandan shopkeeper, Peter Weaselhead. She had borrowed a horse from him when she first came upriver to Nauvoo. She and Dan had come to Peter for refuge after escaping the uninhabited river island.

The big Indian didn't talk much, but she liked him and sensed he liked her too. There was something about his quiet, confident nature that made her feel safe, secure. She needed that feeling now as she considered Boggs's proposition. She felt Peter Weaselhead could be trusted, that he was a friend who could be called on in time of need.

When Caroline entered the store, she was relieved to see there were no customers. She was alone with Peter, who greeted her with a warm smile.

He was busy fishing soft dill pickles out of a big pickle barrel. His right sleeve was rolled up to the shoulder, and his long brown arm was wet with pickle juice.

Peter offered Caroline one of the good pickles. She accepted, the dill smell reminding her that she had not eaten all day. It was early afternoon.

"Could I speak with you for a few minutes?" asked Caroline, after taking a bite from the pickle. Peter gave an affirmative nod as he wiped his arm dry with a damp cloth. He pointed to two stools in front of a plank table where men sometimes played with cards and dice. Before joining her, he bolted the door so they wouldn't be bothered. If Boggs had bolted the door she would have panicked, but the same act by Peter Weaselhead only made her feel more secure.

Caroline didn't feel like she wanted to spill out the details of Boggs's proposition with her first mouthful of words. She sensed a need for some small talk, breaking the ice, a warming up before more serious matters were discussed.

Peter sensed her need. When she mentioned that she had been out to Boggs's place that morning, he asked if she had seen the big dog.

"Yes," said Caroline, surprised Peter knew about the dog.

Peter explained how he had kept the big pup at his store after it came off the boat. Several days later, Boggs came to town to get it.

"Smart dog," said Peter. "Before Boggs gets through with him, he'll be chew'n the Mormons someth'n fierce."

Caroline told him how the dog had come to the door to beg for food, refusing to obey Boggs's order to leave. She described how

Boggs lured the dog into the cabin with a pan of bacon grease, then beaten the animal with the pan when he got hold of its collar. She told him how surprised she was when the dog challenged Boggs with a snarl after the beating was over.

Peter didn't say anything more about the dog; he just nodded for Caroline to continue. And she did, telling him about the stolen manuscript, how she had tried to get it back, and Boggs's promise to return the manuscript if she came to live with him.

"Do you like Boggs?" was the first thing Peter asked when she finished her story.

"He makes me sick to my stomach!" responded Caroline, wondering why Peter would ask such a dumb question—a question that didn't need asking because the answer was so obvious. Maybe she had made a mistake coming to Peter. Maybe he wasn't as wise as she had supposed. But at least he was a good listener.

"Do you want to go live with him?" asked Peter, seeming to ignore her first response.

"Of course not," responded Caroline, thinking the second question dumber than the first.

"Why are you telling me all this?"

Caroline didn't like this question, either. "I just thought you might be able to help me figure out what to do. I needed someone to talk to, besides Pat and Sarah."

"Excuse me for being presumptuous," said Peter, thoroughly astonishing Caroline with his vocabulary. She remembered he had attended school at a Catholic mission in St. Louis. "I don't see where you have a hard decision to make."

Caroline was angry. "Haven't you been listening to me?" she shouted. "That filthy mobber stole my manuscript. If I don't go live with him, he'll use the manuscript to destroy Dan Storm. He can do that, you know—especially if he rewrites it with an anti-Mormon slant. I don't want him to do that to Dan. It would be at least partially my fault. Don't you see?"

"How do you think Boggs would treat you?" asked Peter, again surprising Caroline with his line of questions.

"I don't want to live with that filthy . . ." continued Caroline, ignoring the question. Peter cut her off.

"How would Boggs treat you?" His voice was firm, insistent.

Caroline paused for a moment, forcing herself to picture in her mind what it would be like living with Dick Boggs. She didn't like what she saw.

"How do you think he would treat you?" Peter repeated the question a third time.

Caroline looked into his black, laughing eyes. She was still angry that he seemed to be treating her problem so lightly. He made her feel like she was a little girl, like she didn't know anything.

"Like that dog," she answered, getting up to leave. She didn't need any more of Peter Weaselhead's ridiculous questions. She was more confused than when she came into the store.

"Please sit down," ordered Peter. "I apologize for appearing to take your problem lightly. It's just that you surprise me so."

"Surprise you, how?"

"I am astonished that a woman intelligent enough to write a book could be so naive about human nature. That's all. I suppose I sometimes forget you are still very young."

Caroline hadn't come to Peter to be put down, but she was determined not to let her pride prevent her from learning something that might help her make a tough decision. She didn't respond to his comment.

"You said you thought Boggs would treat you like he does the dog," began Peter. Caroline nodded in agreement.

"How does he treat his dog?"

"He beats it," responded Caroline, thinking she was answering another dumb question, but determined to let Peter develop his line of questioning, wherever it might lead.

"Do you think he would beat you if you lived with him?"

"Yes."

Peter shifted thoughtfully in his chair, then continued. "How did he get the dog close enough to allow him to grab the collar?"

"He coaxed it to him with a pan of bacon grease," responded Caroline, content to be led along, not trying to second-guess Peter's next question, or his wisdom in asking any of the questions.

"After coaxing the dog to him with the grease, did he let the dog eat or lick up the grease?"

"No," answered Caroline, thoughtfully. "As soon as the dog was close enough to allow him to grab the collar, he started beating it with the pan."

"What makes you think he'll behave any differently toward you?"

Caroline was confused. "I already said I didn't think he would treat me any better than the dog."

"Then why are you considering living with him?"

"Would you please explain what you are getting at?" demanded Caroline.

"Can't you see he's doing the same thing to you that he did to the dog? Instead of bacon grease, he's using the manuscript to lure you into his grasp. Do you really think that once he gets you in his clutches he will give the manuscript back?"

"A deal's a deal. He promised."

"Just like he promised the dog a pan of bacon grease."

"You really don't think he'll keep his word?"

"Do you?"

"I don't know. Why would he want to deceive me?"

"His hate for Dan Storm," explained Peter. "With that revised manuscript he can get Dan in big trouble with the Mormons, maybe get him killed. A lot of innocent people have been hurt and killed. The Danites won't look kindly on one of their own perceived as a traitor."

Caroline was beginning to understand. "And he wants me as another way to hurt Dan."

"The icing on the cake, especially if he can get you pregnant. He knows how Dan feels about you. If you go to Boggs, he will have two ways to get at Dan, the manuscript and you. If you don't go to Boggs, he will only have the manuscript."

"Thanks," said Caroline, openly admiring the wisdom of the Indian.

"If I were you, I'd get Pat to head west as soon as possible," cautioned Peter. "When you get to the Basin, tell Brigham Young about the manuscript, the whole story, including this deal with Boggs."

"Do you think he'll understand?"

"I think so. The important thing is to get out there as soon as possible, before the manuscript gets passed around, before Boggs tries something else."

"Like what?" asked Caroline, surprised at the idea Boggs might have more tricks up his sleeve.

"Oh, I don't know anything specific, but through you he can hurt Dan. Give him enough time and he will think of something else."

Caroline thanked Peter for his time, for his help, for his wisdom. The Indian seemed embarrassed by her flattery as he guided her toward the door.

"Remember, the faster you can get your wagon on the trail, the better," Peter Weaselhead called after Caroline as she galloped out of sight.

Chapter 48

I traded my bay mare and saddle to a Blackfoot chief for a buffalo boat and some furs near the three forks on the upper Missouri, just east of the continental divide. The boat consisted of a green hide stretched inside out over a willow frame. It looked more like a big soup bowl than it did a boat, but it carried me all the way to Council Bluffs without any problem. My plan was to sell the furs and boat for enough money to buy a horse, then head east across Iowa Territory to Keokuk. Unfortunately, it being the time of year when wagon trains were heading west, there were no horses available. Nobody wanted to pay me what my furs were worth, so I climbed back in the buffalo boat and headed for St. Louis, a big mistake as I learned later. In St. Louis I sold the furs for enough money to buy passage up the Mississippi River to Keokuk, where I hoped to find Caroline. It was August 1848 when I arrived in Keokuk.

After getting off the boat I headed for the general store run by the Indian Peter Weaselhead. I figured he would loan or sell me a horse to ride out to Pat's place.

Peter seemed both glad and surprised to see me. He was surprised that I hadn't run into Caroline, Pat, and Sarah on the trail. They had left Keokuk about a month earlier. It had been a long and muddy spring, and it wasn't until late June that the roads were sufficiently dry for easy wagon travel.

I realized that if I'd stuck to my original plan to leave the river at

Council Bluffs, I would probably have run into Pat's wagon. By now they were probably already across the Missouri River. If I hurried, I might catch them by the time they reached Chimney Rock.

I gave Peter most of my remaining money, asking him to fix me up with a horse and an outfit for a journey to the Rocky Mountains. The long float trip had made me restless, and I wasn't in any mood to wait around. The sooner I got back on the trail, the better.

As we were getting my supplies together, Peter told me about Caroline's manuscript, how it had been stolen by Dick Boggs, and how Caroline had tried unsuccessfully to get it back. I began to have second thoughts about heading straight west. Maybe it would be a good idea to swing by Boggs's place. Perhaps I could get the manuscript back. I didn't figure Boggs would object to giving it to me if he was looking down the barrel of my .40 caliber Hawken.

As Peter and I were getting the last of my supplies together, we were suddenly distracted by a commotion at the far end of Main Street. There were some gun shots, followed by a lot of yelling. By the time we reached the door in an effort to see what was going on, we spotted a rider heading in our direction, his horse on a dead run. The rider was crouched low in the saddle, apparently in an effort to make as small a target as possible for the men further up the street who were firing at him.

Suddenly a different movement caught my eye. A brown and white animal streaked toward the rider from the far side of the street. At first I thought it was a small, riderless horse, or a big calf. To my amazement, I finally realized it was a dog, the biggest I had ever seen. It was on a direct collision course with the horse and rider.

It appeared the dog was going to plow into the churning legs of the speeding horse, but at exactly the right moment, the big dog leaped high into the air, front paws forward, jaws open. As the dog smashed into the side of the horse and rider, the surprised horse shied away, causing the rider to momentarily shift his weight in the direction of the dog, which had clamped its jaws tight on his arm. The dog and rider hit the ground together, tumbling to a halt in the heavy dust. The horse galloped off between two buildings.

When the dust settled, the big dog still had hold of the arm of the hapless rider. The rider was flat on his back and afraid to move, because whenever he did, the dog snarled viciously between its clenched jaws.

A group of men from the far end of the street were running toward the dog and rider. In front was the big sheriff, his silver star flashing brightly in the midday sunshine. Peter and I watched with interest. We didn't leave the porch of the store to help because our help was not needed. The dog had the apparent criminal under control.

"Good boy, Port," said the sheriff, loud enough for everyone to hear. He was obviously very proud of his big dog.

"Let go, Port," he ordered, his voice stern now. The big dog just growled a little louder, refusing to let go of the bandit's arm.

"He's only had that dog a few weeks," said Peter. "Hasn't had a chance to teach it much yet." Peter explained how Dick Boggs had shipped the dog in from Europe, thinking he would train it to help him hunt down Mormons. But Boggs had been unable to control the dog or win its loyalty, so he had sold it to the sheriff. The sheriff was a better hand at training dogs and intended to make the dog into the most feared manhunter in the Mississippi River Valley. He figured a well-trained dog of that size could play a big part in keeping the peace in and around Keokuk.

As other men gathered around, the dog still refused to let go of the arm, despite severe scoldings from the sheriff. Finally the sheriff lost his patience and used the barrel of his long pistol to pry the jaws open. The bandit jumped to his feet, his healthy arm holding the one that had been injured by the dog's jaws. He didn't take his eyes off the dog as he marched back up the street toward the jail. We gathered from the conversations of the men in the street that the bandit was attempting to escape from jail when the dog was sicced on him.

Peter and I were still standing on the front porch when the sheriff, his prisoner, the dog, and about a dozen other men walked past the front of the store on their way back to the jail. I began to get nervous when I noticed one of the men talking frantically to the sheriff while gesturing in my direction. I was just starting to head back into the store when the sheriff handed the prisoner over to one of his deputies and started toward me, whistling for the dog to follow.

I knew I was in trouble when I heard the sheriff call my name.

"Dan Storm?" he asked, as he entered the door.

I nodded.

"You're wanted in Missouri. Caught Dick Boggs in a bear trap."

"That was a long time ago, and this isn't Missouri," I argued, a helpless, sick feeling welling up in the pit of my stomach.

"I still got a wanted notice on you." The sheriff's voice was calm and firm. "You're comin' with me to jail."

Chapter 49

The Keokuk jail was located in a field behind the sheriff's office. It was a one-room structure made of huge, twelve- to eighteen-inch oak logs. The ceiling was made of the same big logs, split in halves and pushed close together to give the appearance of a rough plank ceiling. There were no windows, but in several places the chinking had been chipped away to allow occupants to get a peek at the outside. The floor was made of huge rocks that had been rolled into place before the log structure was erected. There was no way the boulders could be moved without tools. The door was made of heavy oak planks, the hinges and the big lock on the outside.

The inside of the jail was equipped with three straw mats that rested on the stone floor and a sanitation bucket with a lid. Nothing else. No table. No stove. No lantern. No fresh water. I was fortunate that the thick log walls and ceiling provided adequate insulation against the hot summer sun.

The sheriff informed me that I would stay in the jail until the Missouri authorities came for me. He suspected there was a reward on me, and as soon as that was collected, I would be on my way to Missouri to stand trial.

It had been nine years since I had lured Dick Boggs into the bear trap, and I found it hard to believe the law was still looking for me. The sheriff assured me it was, and that I shouldn't figure on getting off easy just because a lot of water had passed under the bridge. I asked him if I could see a lawyer. He said I would have plenty of time for that once my case was brought to trial in Missouri. He was just holding me until the Missouri lawmen arrived; he didn't see any good reason to get me a lawyer.

Once a day, usually in the afternoon, the sheriff would let me out of the jail to wash in a nearby watering trough. Afterward he would take me to one of the local taverns for my only meal of the day. I was always very hungry.

The big brown and white dog always accompanied the sheriff when he let me out of the jail. The sheriff warned me that should I try to escape, the dog would come after me as it had the rider on the day of my arrival in Keokuk. In fact, the sheriff had so much confidence in the dog that he seldom carried a firearm on our daily visits to the eating establishments.

When we went into a tavern to eat, the dog always curled up under the table at our feet. The dog was named Porter Rockwell, after the Mormon gunfighter who had put the fear of God into so many of the local gentiles. The sheriff called him Port. A good name for such a formidable beast.

It was just after dark, the second day following my arrest, when I heard the unmistakable sound of footsteps outside the log wall facing away from the sheriff's office. When I moved closer to listen, all was quiet.

"Who's out there?" I said in a loud whisper, suspecting that perhaps Peter Weaselhead had come to offer some assistance or give me some piece of information.

"A friend," said a strangely familiar voice, after a brief pause. It wasn't Peter.

"Want to get out?" said the voice, somewhat softer. I stepped a little closer so I could hear better. "Come to the wide space between the logs, where the chinking is missing, so you can see me," the whisper continued.

I stepped toward the opening, a cold chill in the back of my neck. Something in that voice frightened me, but I couldn't put my finger on it.

It was too dark inside the cabin for the visitor to see me, and it was too dark outside for me to get a good look at him. I stepped to the side of the opening.

Reluctant to expose my face, I held my right hand in front of the opening, then whispered, "I can't see y . . ."

Before I could get the words out, something long and sharp was shoved through the opening, severely gouging the palm of my hand. It was a pointed stick. I grabbed it with my good hand, breaking it off at the point where it passed between the logs. There was a sick feeling in my stomach, knowing how close I had come to putting my face in front of the opening. Had I done so, the sharp stick would probably have found its way into one of my eyes.

When the stranger cursed over the broken stick, I finally recognized his voice. It was Dick Boggs. I moved a few steps further from the opening and waited to see what he would do next. I was quiet, and he was quiet too, apparently trying to hear something to indicate if he had harmed me.

Suddenly I had an idea, one that could possibly revenge my injured hand.

"Help," I whimpered, barely loud enough for Boggs to hear.

"What?" he asked.

"My eye," I whimpered softly, attempting to draw him to the opening. "Out of the socket. Please, get a doc . . ."

I stepped quietly toward the opening and very cautiously peeked out through the near end of the narrow slit. It was too dark to be sure, but it appeared there was a form against the middle of the opening. Perhaps Boggs was listening to my cries.

Taking a firm hold on the broken end of the pointed stick, I was about to shove it back through the opening when I realized it wasn't long enough. The logs were as thick as the stick was long. It couldn't have been more than a split second before I had a better idea. I dropped the stick and reached for the sanitation bucket, quietly removing the lid. The bucket was about a fourth full. I whined some more about my eye. Then after making sure the dark hulk was still on the other side of the big crack, I slung the contents of the bucket with all my might against the crack. Boggs bellowed like an angry bull. I didn't know how much damage I had done, but from the spitting going on, I figured I had caught him with his mouth open. I knew that as soon as he got hold of himself he would probably be mad enough to start shooting through the cracks at me.

I ran to the other side of the jail, put my mouth to a crack facing the back door of the sheriff's office, and yelled as loud as I could, "Escape! The prisoner is escaping!"

A few seconds later the back door of the office swung open and I could see the big hulk of the sheriff silhouetted against the lantern light.

"The prisoner's getting away," I shouted. "Let the dog out!"

There was more cursing from Boggs. He knew better than I how much that big dog hated him. I could hear him running away from the jail, then the thundering of hooves as his horse galloped into the night. I listened carefully for the growls and footbeats of the charging dog but could hear nothing. Apparently the sheriff hadn't succumbed to my trickery and had decided against sending his dog off into the night after an unknown rider.

When the sheriff finally arrived at my door, the dog's leash was in one hand and a kerosene lantern in the other. He opened the door to make sure I was still there, then headed back to his office. He didn't seem too concerned when I showed him my bloody hand. Said he would take me to the doctor the next day.

I didn't sleep much that night, partly because of the pain in my hand, but mostly because I was worried about Dick Boggs and what he would do next. He wouldn't take the chance of a Missouri judge setting me free. Once free, I could slip into the woods and he would never see me again. He would probably try to get me before I went to trial. And there would be no better time than when I would be traveling to Missouri, a prisoner with my hands tied. The wagon road was narrow, with thick brush and woods on both sides. An ambush would be easy along that road.

I decided the safest and smartest thing for me to do would be to escape before the trip to Missouri. The sooner I got out of range of Boggs's hate, the better.

But how? At most, I probably had only a few weeks until the Missouri law came for me.

As we entered the tavern for dinner the next afternoon, there was a fresh new bandage covering my right hand, almost all the way to the elbow. The doctor had just cleaned and dressed my wound. As we seated ourselves at a table, Port crawling underneath, the foremost thing on my mind was not food. I was wondering how I might successfully slip a table knife, or perhaps a spoon, into the fold of the new bandage. Using the rocks on the floor of the jail as grinding stones, I figured I could fashion the tableware into cutting tools to aid my escape.

Frequently while we were eating, other people would talk to the sheriff about one thing or another, distracting his attention from me. I figured a time like that would be ideal for taking a knife or spoon.

In the meantime I was forced to concentrate on eating with my left hand. It wasn't easy. We were served a thick stew on a plate. On my first bite a big piece of meat rolled out of the spoon and across my lap, leaving a trail of gravy before it stopped on my left thigh. On a ration of only one meal a day, I was not about to let a big chunk of meat go to waste, so I reached down to retrieve it.

Just as I was about to pick it up, a big black nose poked out from under the tablecloth, a long red tongue wrapping itself around the meat. Slowly, I moved my hand back to the table, fearful the big jaws might grab it if I moved too quickly.

A little while later a piece of potato rolled onto the floor. Again the big dog was quick to lap it up. Then he looked up at me, eagerly anticipating a third bite. A little while later I purposely dropped another piece of meat. As he reached for it, I patted him on the head. He didn't seem to mind. I asked for seconds on the stew, and carefully dropped most of the meat at my feet. The sheriff was busy with some papers and didn't notice.

I remembered the old saying that a dog doesn't bite the hand that feeds it, and wondered if it was really true. I still wasn't sure how I would benefit from making friends with the big dog, but it seemed like a good idea, along with slipping a big spoon under the bandage on my hand.

Three days later, feeding the dog had developed into a routine. As soon as I seated myself at the table, old Port crawled underneath and put his chin on my knee, where it remained throughout the meal as I slipped pieces of food directly into his mouth, frequently patting him on the head. The sheriff was beginning to complain about the quantity of food I was consuming, but he continued to give me all the food I wanted, as long as I didn't take any back to the cabin.

Somehow the dog seemed to understand the need for secrecy. He swallowed quietly and never begged for food, except when he was out of sight under the table. I hoped he was becoming my friend.

I sharpened the spoon on a rock and began to chip away at the end of one of the bottom logs. I had plenty of time to myself and figured if I spent fourteen to sixteen hours a day, cutting away one chip at a time, I would eventually get through. Whenever the sheriff came to the cabin, I pushed one of the straw sleeping mats up against the bottom log to cover my work area. The oak wood was hard and the spoon had to be sharpened frequently. Progress was very slow, and after nearly thirty hours of work my gash was only a few inches deep. My fingers and palms were covered with new calluses and were very sore, but I persisted. There was nothing else to do.

After a week the gash was nearly eight inches deep and at the halfway point. Another week and I would be free, provided I could push the end of the log out and didn't have to make a second cut—and provided the Missouri authorities didn't arrive during the week.

A few days later, just as the sheriff, Port, and I were finishing dinner late in the afternoon, the sheriff stunned me with an unexpected request, one that made me sick to my stomach.

"Stretch your hands out on the table, palms up," he ordered. I obeyed.

"How'd you get all them blisters?" he asked.

"Scratch'n for lice?" I suggested.

He didn't swallow my explanation, but he seemed to enjoy the humor.

"Maybe we ought to go back and hunt down them lice," he suggested with a grin. "Bet we'd find 'em hidin' in some interestin' places."

As we got up to leave, I realized my past week's work was lost. There was no doubt in my mind that the sheriff would find the gash in the log. How he would respond, I didn't know. But with the jail weakened by my chipping, I figured he wouldn't just let things continue as usual. Maybe he would tie me up, or even worse, put me in chains.

The sheriff led the way out the door. He didn't worry about me not following, not with that big dog at his side. Again, I wondered about the old saying that a dog won't bite the hand that feeds it. I had been secretly feeding and petting that hound for over a week. Still, I couldn't get out of my mind the picture of the dog taking that man out of the saddle my first day in Keokuk. Though I had been feeding him, I just couldn't see him refusing to come after me if I attempted a break.

The sheriff was big and overweight, at least ten years older than me. From his confident air I guessed he would be tough in a fight, but I figured I could easily outrun him and be well into the woods before he could get a gun. It would soon be dark. In the woods, I would be tough to catch or find—if he didn't have the dog.

I was about to give up on the attempted escape when I realized that in trying to get away I had very little to lose and much to gain. If they caught me, I would go back to jail, probably in chains—no worse off than when he discovered the gap in the big log. On the other hand, I just might get away, if the dog would cooperate.

I was sure the dog would not hesitate to come after a running man, even me. But I had another idea, one that I felt had a good chance of working. I didn't have time to think much about it.

We were walking across the field, toward the jail, when I surprised the sheriff by shouting, "Port! Come on boy, let's go." Without waiting to see how the dog would respond, I started running for the woods. "Port, come on boy," I called over my shoulder. The dog followed.

The sheriff's first reaction, rather than try to sic the dog on me, was to call it back. But the young dog was already galloping excitedly at my side, anticipating some new adventure. He ignored his master's command to return. At each step I encouraged the dog with more kind words.

I was almost to the woods when the sheriff gave up on the dog and started running back to his office to get his gun. By the time he reached the door, the dog and I were deep in the woods, heading south along a well-used trail. A few minutes later we made an abrupt right turn. It would soon be dark, and the search probably wouldn't begin until morning. During the night—though my better judgment warned against it—I intended to visit Dick Boggs. If things went as planned, by morning I would be headed for the Rocky Mountains with Caroline's manuscript under my arm.

Chapter 50

There was still a light in the cabin window when I reached the top of the hill overlooking Boggs's place. It must have been close to midnight, and I wondered why he was still awake. At least I knew he was home. Probably alone, I hoped.

I didn't have a weapon, either a gun or a knife, so I broke off the branch of a dogwood tree. It was about six feet long and unusually straight. A stout staff made a formidable weapon. One could hit and jab swiftly, and with enough force to break an arm or a neck. I had to catch Boggs by surprise and get the drop on him before he could get to a gun. How, I wasn't sure.

The simplest method seemed very simple—merely charge through the door and catch him by surprise. But there were a lot of unanswered questions. Maybe he wasn't alone. It would be difficult getting the drop on two people if I didn't have a firearm. Maybe he would not be in the center of the cabin, but off in a dark corner close to a firearm. By the time my eyes adjusted to the light and spotted him, he might already have me in his gun sight.

Whatever I did, I had to do it quickly, before he put his lamp out. I didn't want to get in a brawl with Boggs in a totally dark cabin. I couldn't wait until morning when the posse from Keokuk would be on my trail.

I headed down the hill toward the cabin, Port trotting along at my side. As we entered the clearing, just a short distance from the cabin, the dog dropped behind and began to whine softly. At first I was surprised that he hesitated. Then I remembered what Peter Weaselhead had told me about Boggs's cruelty to the animal.

As I looked back at the reluctant dog, it suddenly occurred to me that there ought to be a way to use old Port in a plan to get the drop on Boggs. I knelt down and called the dog to me. After scratching his ears and comforting him with some soft words, I took a firm hold on his collar and led him toward Boggs's wagon, which was parked in the middle of a clearing about thirty yards from the cabin door.

Feeling around in the box under the seat, I found a short lead rope. One end I tied to Port's collar, the other to a wheel spoke. As soon as the dog was secure, I hurried toward the front porch.

I wasn't halfway there before the dog, having realized his lost freedom, began to whine. By the time I reached the porch and stationed myself beside the door, old Port was howling. He thought I was leaving him behind.

It wasn't long before I heard the shuffling of a chair inside. I tightened my hold on the staff. I figured the dog was far enough away that Boggs wouldn't be able to tell, at least not immediately, that it was tied up. But when the heavy door swung open and the lantern light flooded into the clearing, I began to worry that he would see the rope and suspect a trap.

I could see the dog chewing on the rope to get free, but apparently Boggs's eyes were not adjusted to the dark as mine were, and he didn't notice anything other than the unexpected presence of the dog. A moment later he stepped onto the porch, a rifle in his right hand, the lantern in his left.

My first priority was to disarm him, so I brought the staff down with all my might on the hand holding the gun. The blow was more severe than necessary. Not only did I hear the crunching of bone as the rifle was knocked free, but the lantern was smashed from his other hand, the coal oil spilling over the porch and beginning to catch fire from the flaming wick. My blow caused the rifle to discharge, the ball disappearing harmlessly into the night.

As Boggs bent forward over his smashed hand, his face turned sideways, looking up at me in surprise, I brought the staff down again, this time on the back of his head. The force of the blow rolled him forward off of the porch into the dust. When he failed to get up, I figured he was unconscious.

The flames were spreading quickly across the porch, and knowing the cabin would soon be engulfed in fire, I dropped the staff and hurried inside to get Caroline's manuscript.

The flames provided plenty of light, but I couldn't see anything that resembled a manuscript. There was no sign of it on any of the shelves as I swept them clean with my hand. I dumped out his grub box. Nothing there. I kicked around in the piles of hides and furs. Nothing that resembled a manuscript . . .

Finally, under the filthy bed, I found a tightly wrapped deerskin bundle. Quickly I untied the lashing. Inside was a neat stack of white pages with black writing on them. The handwriting appeared to be Caroline's. I quickly rewrapped the bundle and headed for the door, now engulfed in flames.

I ran toward the door, gaining speed for a leap through the flames, when the door was suddenly slammed shut. I could hear the angry cursing of Dick Boggs as I lowered my shoulder into the door while lifting up the latch. He couldn't lock it from the outside. I figured I was stronger than Boggs and could push him aside—but I had to do it quickly before the flames around the door frame consumed the oxygen and cooked me.

To my surprise the door didn't budge. More than a man was holding it shut. I lowered my shoulder into it a few more times without success, then backed away. I remembered the stout staff I had left behind on the porch and figured he had somehow wedged the pole between the door and one of the porch poles.

The cabin was full of smoke now, and breathing was difficult. I didn't have much time. Grabbing the chair beside the table, I bashed out the lone window, threw the manuscript out ahead of me, and began to crawl through. It was barely big enough for a man.

No sooner were my head and shoulders through the opening than I spotted Boggs just a few feet away coming toward me with the empty rifle in his good hand. I slipped back inside the smoky cabin just as the butt of the rifle smashed against the windowsill.

Had the window been just a little larger and a little lower on the wall, I could have run and dove through the opening, hoping Boggs would miss me. But as small as it was, I could only wiggle through the opening, totally vulnerable to Boggs's blows with the rifle butt. There was no doubt in my mind that he would knock me senseless, then shove me back into the cabin to burn. I knew I couldn't expect any mercy, not from my old enemy Dick Boggs.

I dropped to the floor in an effort to get better air to breathe and began looking around. I thought maybe if I could find an ax, I could chop through the front door. I finally spotted one, leaning against the door frame, the handle in flames. Breathing was becoming increasingly difficult and I was soaked with sweat in the intense heat.

I was looking around for some rags or something to protect my hands from the flaming ax handle when I heard a new sound, a kind of roar that reminded me of the giant grizzly I had lassoed in the tops of the Bitter Root Mountains.

The roar became a snarl, followed by a series of vicious growls. Boggs was swearing louder than ever. Suddenly I realized what was happening. Port had gnawed through the rope and attacked his old master and enemy. I jumped up and thrust my head and shoulders into the window. There was no greeting from Boggs's rifle butt. I could hear the sound of Boggs and Port thrashing in the dust below the window. I scrambled through the opening, gulping down the cool, fresh air.

By the time I tumbled to the ground and regained my balance, the thrashing had stopped. The growling and swearing continued, but there was no movement.

I began to see why as my eyes adjusted to the outside darkness, rapidly being pushed back as the flames above the door soared higher and higher into the night sky.

At first I thought the dog had Boggs by the throat, but as I looked closer, I realized the huge jaws were clamped on Boggs's head. The upper fangs dug through a half-torn ear. One of the bottom fangs caught in the edge of an eye socket. The face and head were covered with blood. The only movement was Boggs's mouth as he continued to shout out his curses.

I felt a little sick to my stomach and very weak. I needed to sit down and collect my senses, but there wasn't time. Neighbors seeing the light of the flames in the night sky would come to help.

I picked up the manuscript. "Come on, Port, let's get out of here."

I picked up Boggs's rifle too, a .40 caliber Hawken. I would have to get powder and lead somewhere else. Nothing more could be retrieved from the cabin, now totally in flames.

I took a step toward the woods, but the dog didn't follow, refusing to release his hold on the man he hated. It wasn't until I took Port's jaws in my hands and forced them open that he finally let go.

As Port and I trotted into the woods, I wondered if I would ever see Boggs again. I hoped not. With a wooden leg, a shredded ear, and a probable patch over his eye—all because of me—the meeting wouldn't be a happy one. Hopefully I could spend the rest of my life in the Rocky Mountains and our paths would never cross again.

Chapter 51

Bishop Glenn Hill was getting sick and tired of all the fuss over buffalo chips. He was leading a small group of Mormon emigrants west to the Great Basin late in the summer of 1848. His party hadn't left Council Bluffs, Iowa Territory, until August, but with a mild fall, similar to that of 1847, no problem was anticipated in reaching the Great Salt Lake.

The problem with the buffalo chips began just a few weeks after crossing the Missouri River. Trees became scarce, and it was necessary to burn chips in the camp cook fires. Actually, the buffalo droppings were a good, hot fuel—except when damp or soggy after a rain.

Bishop Hill had been a farmer all his life and didn't see anything wrong with burning buffalo chips. But others did. Several of the women began serving cold food to their families, refusing to cook with dung. One of the young ladies had been teased to tears by some young men as she gathered buffalo chips in the hem of her skirt. But the problem didn't get really serious until a pious elder by the name of Ebenezer McConklin got involved. It was McConklin who called a special meeting of the elders to discuss the buffalo chip problem. McConklin felt—and many seemed to agree with his emotional ranting and raving—that there was something bad or at least a little obscene about having to gather and burn buffalo chips.

Much to the displeasure of Bishop Hill, McConklin persuaded the elders to establish a number of rules to govern the handling of buffalo chips. The first was a name change; from henceforth, buffalo chips would be called prairie logs. Second, only males, specifically boys, would be allowed to gather prairie logs. And they would gather on one side of the camp only, while the women did their evening cooking on the other side. Third, the prairie logs would be stored in covered containers, out of sight of women and young ladies.

Bishop Hill couldn't understand how a group of otherwise sensible men could adopt a set of such ridiculous rules. Especially men like Pat O'Riley, the hard-headed Irishman who had been a stone mason on the Nauvoo temple. Pat had a pretty little wife to care for, a new baby, and a young woman named Caroline Logan he was taking west to meet her fiancé, who had been drafted in the Mormon Battalion. Men like Pat had a lot more to be concerned about than embarrassing women with prairie logs.

The bishop's biggest concern, however, was the late departure of the wagon train. Unexpected delays, combined with early winter storms near the continental divide, could spell disaster for the party. There was always the threat of Indians, though few had been seen so far, and sometimes thundershowers could make enough mud to slow travel for days. There were injuries, unexpected deaths, broken wagons, prairie fires, and lame horses and oxen.

The last thing Bishop Hill wanted to worry about was buffalo chips or prairie logs. He couldn't understand how McConklin could get other men to agree with him on those stupid rules. But if the rules would settle the prairie log problem, allowing the people to get their minds back on more important matters, he would go along with them. That's what he told the men when they asked for his opinion.

Bishop Hill was a practical man. He was in his late forties, partly bald, and a little too broad around the middle. But his looks were deceiving. He was a man accustomed to hard work. His shoulders were broad, his back strong, his hands hard and callused. And he liked to use his hands. He would rather fix or tinker with something than read a book any day. He didn't willingly admit it to his peers, but he had never read the Book of Mormon. He had read enough to believe it was true, and he thought that was enough. He figured he had been made a bishop more for his ability to get things done than for his knowledge of eternal principles.

The biggest thing before him now was to get these people safely to the Rocky Mountains. He would not permit anything to get in his way—especially not a lot of nonsense about the handling of buffalo dung.

But he was wrong about the rules. They did not eliminate the prairie log problem. A few days after the rules were established, Ebenezer McConklin climbed onto his wagon seat one morning to find himself greeted by a friendly smile. Someone had fingered two eyes and a smiling mouth in a fresh buffalo pie resting in the middle of McConklin's wagon seat. McConklin was furious and demanded an immediate inquisition of all the young men who might do such an offensive thing. Bishop Hill refused. There was no way he would hold up the wagon train for something like that.

A few days later, one of McConklin's wives discovered another smiling buffalo chip in a Dutch oven. Again the furious McConklin called for an inquisition. Again the bishop refused.

Bishop Hill wasn't much of an idea man, but he wrestled with the buffalo chip problem. The best he could figure was that the establishing of the rules had given importance to McConklin's silly notions about buffalo chips. The bishop supposed there were those who agreed with him that the rules had blown the whole thing out of proportion, but not wanting to fight the strong-willed McConklin, they had gone along with the pious elder.

McConklin was a forceful debater, a fiery preacher who always had a lot of scriptures to back up his arguments. As for the buffalo pies on the wagon seat and in the Dutch oven, Bishop Hill figured that one or two of those who would not dare stand up to McConklin in public were expressing their protest in secret. He wondered if McConklin would learn anything from the pranks. The bishop wouldn't admit it to anyone, but he thoroughly enjoyed the pranks and their effect on McConklin, even though he didn't know who the practical jokers were. The bishop knew one thing for sure, though. He would not let this nonsense over buffalo chips slow down his wagon train.

But it did. Late one afternoon, camp was made early in anticipation of an approaching storm. The wagons stopped in the middle of a huge meadow located between the Platte River on the south and gentle rolling hills on the north. A strong wind was blowing from the river, so the women began their cook fires on the uphill side of the wagons, thinking the wagons would offer some protection from the wind. The cattle, horses, and oxen—all hungry from the day's travel—were grazing eagerly on the uphill side of the train.

The approaching storm looked like a big one, so every available boy was sent out to help gather a two- or three-day supply of prairie logs. Since prairie log gathering was not allowed on the same side of the wagons where the women were cooking, the boys headed down toward the river. Those boys who had been tending the stock joined in the gathering. There was plenty of grass in the upper meadow, and there was no worry of the stock wandering, at least not for several hours.

Everyone was so intent on getting the chores and cooking done before the storm hit that nobody saw the Indians until it was too late. They came from the North, out of the hills, seven or eight of them, galloping their ponies quietly across the soft meadow until they formed a half circle around the grazing livestock. Then, upon a signal from their leader, they turned their horses toward the grazing livestock, every Indian whooping a shrill war cry. Instantly the cattle, mules, and horses were stampeding northward. A few saddle horses tied to wagons were the only animals not involved in the stampede.

Fortunately, several of the white riders were able to break up the stampeding herd before it had gone more than just a few miles. The rest of the men went out on foot, in small armed bands, rounding up the stray livestock. The thunder and lightning from the storm helped keep the frightened animals on the run. By nightfall, less than a third of the animals had been recovered.

The next morning the search and the storm continued. Less than half of the animals were recovered by evening, and a camp meeting was called by Bishop Hill to discuss the situation.

It was a sober meeting. Spirits were dampened not so much by the incessant rain as by the knowledge that half of the livestock had been lost. Bishop Hill began by asking questions. He asked some of the boys in charge of herding why they had not been with the stock. He didn't react when they said they were helping the other boys gather prairie logs. He asked the assigned night guards why they were not at their posts. Each responded with the same answer: they had been helping gather prairie logs before taking their posts. Had the Indians waited just a little longer, the sentries would have been in their assigned positions.

"There is one thing I am thankful for," said the bishop, after finishing his questioning. "I thank the Lord nobody was killed or scalped."

He paused for a moment, then continued, "I suppose they were so busy with half our livestock herd that they just didn't have time to kill anybody." Nobody laughed.

Then the bishop surprised everyone by walking over to the nearest wagon and reaching underneath for a prairie log, a big one. He held it high for everyone to see as he walked back to his place at the head of the crowd.

"What is this?" he shouted, anger in his voice. People were confused; nobody said anything.

"What is this?" he demanded, his voice louder. Ebenezer McConklin was the first to speak.

"Prairie log," he offered.

"What?" roared the bishop.

Several others repeated McConklin's words.

"Ain't no log," bellowed the bishop, his face getting red.

"I'm not an educated man," he continued, "and I don't have no dictionary, but I do know this ain't no log!" He shook the buffalo chip at McConklin. There was a brief pause before the bishop continued.

"It's a piece of dried buffalo shit!"

The bishop waited a few moments for his words to sink in, then continued.

"It comes out of the back end of a buffalo, wet and green and smelly. After drying in the sun, it doesn't smell anymore." He held the buffalo chip to his nose. Then he bit off a chunk.

"It doesn't even taste that bad." He spit the piece he had chewed off onto the ground. The crowd was stunned. Some of the children were laughing, but none of the adults.

"The nice thing about buffalo shit is that it burns. We couldn't cook our bread and beans and bacon without it. We're darn lucky to have it."

The bishop looked directly at Ebenezer McConklin and tossed the buffalo chip in Ebenezer's direction, asking, "Ain't that right, Ebenezer?"

"Uh huh," mumbled the startled pilgrim as he caught it.

"Furthermore," continued Bishop Hill, "the rules against swearing continue, and I'll see that any man who uses the Lord's name in vain gets a whipping. But if any man or woman . . . or child . . . wants to call shit shit, he has my permission to do it, because that's what it is!"

Bishop Hill turned and walked to his wagon. There was a weariness in his step but a determined scowl on his face as he contemplated the hardships ahead.

Chapter 52

Caroline was at the back of the wagon, pushing. The wagon train had entered a sandy stretch of trail, reported to be six miles long. The sand was loose and deep, the wagons sometimes sinking up to the axles. Pat O'Riley had strapped himself into a makeshift harness in front of the oxen, a big leather strap around his waist, pulling with all his might. Sarah was at his side, carrying little Pat, now almost a year old. Sometimes she nursed the baby as she walked.

Pat lost all four of his horses in the Indian raid, while Ebenezer McConklin lost none of his oxen. Bishop Hill ordered McConklin to loan two oxen to O'Riley, but Ebenezer didn't want to share them. In addition to two saddle horses, he had four oxen, just the right number for pulling his heavy wagon across the plains. He used the two teams together for climbing hills, crossing rivers, and pulling through mud and sand. On level ground he used one team on the wagon, while the other two animals were allowed to graze along behind the wagons with the stock herd. By rotating the teams daily, the oxen remained fresh and strong. He thanked the good Lord that none of his oxen had disappeared in the Indian raid. But when Bishop Hill asked him to loan two of his oxen to Pat, he balked. He couldn't afford to give up half his oxen. And he wasn't about to hitch his two saddle horses up to a wagon. It wasn't his fault that all of O'Riley's horses had been driven off by Indians.

But the strong will of Bishop Hill won out. Ebenezer reluctantly loaned his smallest and weakest oxen to Pat O'Riley. Pat didn't like taking animals from a reluctant giver, but Bishop Hill insisted. There was no other way; the wagon train had to continue.

The forward progress of the Hill Company was cut in half after the Indian raid. The best draft animals were no longer given frequent days off to wander with the trailing stock herd. They became weary and stubborn. The same tired livestock had to be traded back and forth to pull wagons one at a time across bogs and rivers. And the fall rains continued, making travel more difficult even for those with strong teams and light wagons.

Travel habits had to change. Sarah and Caroline no longer rode in the O'Riley wagon but walked beside the oxen—except when the going was tough—climbing hills, fording streams, or plowing through mud and sand. Then Caroline got behind the wagon and pushed with all her might, as she was doing now.

The rare October sunshine was unusually warm as the wagon train entered the sand. Caroline noticed as she leaned into the back of the wagon that big drops of sweat dripped from the end of her nose with increasing frequency. Her eyes stung with the salty sweat. Her long blonde hair was tied behind her head to keep it out of the way. The perspiration circles under her arms were growing larger by the hour.

The hem of her blue and white dress was brown with wet sand, and every time she stepped on the hem, she thought how ridiculous it was that women had to wear dresses when engaged in hard work of this sort. She wondered what the reaction would be if she changed into a pair of comfortable men's trousers and a loose-fitting shirt. Of course Pat wouldn't mind. She didn't think Bishop Hill would either, but Ebenezer McConklin would be sure to find a scripture that had something to do with how women were not supposed to look like men.

But it really didn't matter what Ebenezer and his friends thought. It was hard, dirty work, pushing a wagon through six miles of heavy sand. Trousers and a shirt would be much more comfortable. She would do it the next day, and if Ebenezer didn't like it—well, that was his problem.

Then she smiled. Maybe some of the other women would follow her lead. Some of the men would, of course, look on the change as a form of rebellion. There would be plenty of heated discussions, followed by change, she thought. The people had had to change in many ways. Caroline thought about the buffalo chips and the children's shoes.

Some of the mothers protested when Bishop Hill ordered all children under age twelve to go barefooted. The bishop tried to explain that the children's feet would soon toughen to the trail, that they could walk farther, with greater ease, free of heavy leather boots and shoes. Besides, the children would need the shoes when cold weather came, and it was senseless wearing them out during warm weather. The bishop's words made sense, but some of the mothers still refused to let their children run barefooted—generally the same mothers who disliked cooking with buffalo chips.

Caroline, upon finding Ebenezer McConklin a member of the wagon train, had gone out of the way to avoid her former fiancé. She figured he didn't know anything about the manuscript, and she wasn't about to volunteer any information. He had pretty much left her alone, too, at least until the Indian raid. But after loaning his oxen to Pat, he began to visit the camp, and Caroline, with increasing frequency. It was as if the loaning of the oxen put the O'Rileys and Caroline in Ebenezer's debt. And Ebenezer was not a man who missed collecting what he figured was due to him.

Even the ever-patient Sarah had boiled over the previous night when McConklin, without asking, reached into the O'Riley stew pot to fish out a piece of meat.

"Git your dirty fingers out of my stew," she scolded, surprising Pat and Caroline as well as McConklin. "If you want something, ask for it, but keep your hands out of my cooking pans!"

Without a word, McConklin turned and disappeared into the night. He wasn't used to being scolded by another man's wife. He knew how to maintain a submissive attitude among his own wives, but another man's wife, that was a different matter. And Pat O'Riley, known to be a good fighter, wasn't a man to rile. McConklin retreated.

"Thanks," said Caroline to Sarah. "Maybe the old goat will stay away for a few days now."

But Caroline had misjudged McConklin. Even as she pushed the wagon, she became aware that a rider approaching from the rear had pulled in his horse to stay even with her. She turned her head to see who it was. Even though her eyes were blurry with sweat, she didn't have any trouble recognizing Ebenezer McConklin.

"A wife of mine wouldn't have to push a wagon all day," said McConklin.

A wife of yours would be too brow-beaten to be able to push a wagon all day, thought Caroline. But she didn't say anything, not wanting to get into a discussion with McConklin.

"Had you married me, you wouldn't have to do that," he continued. McConklin wasn't one for beating around the bush, thought Caroline. No matter how inappropriate a comment might be, he said it.

"Had I married you," replied Caroline without looking up, "I wouldn't want to push a wagon." It would take him a while to figure that one out, she thought. Apparently McConklin was taken aback by her statement, for he turned and rode away without any further comment.

It was late in the afternoon when the accident occurred. The sun had disappeared behind dark clouds and the temperature was dropping quickly. The wagon train had managed to get through four or five miles of sand during the course of the day, but progress suddenly became very slow when they reached a series of deep ravines, some with muddy streams running through them.

The sand was deeper than usual at the top of the deepest ravine, one through which a healthy stream rushed down to the North Platte River. Pulling out front, Pat dropped over the edge of the ravine first, followed by the oxen. The wagon was still bogged down in axle-deep sand, so Pat and the oxen continued to pull, with Caroline pushing from behind.

No one figured how fast the wagon would pick up speed once it got over the edge, but Pat suddenly found himself running, the stumbling oxen and wagon coming down upon him with increasing speed. The heavy strap around his waist prevented him from jumping to either side. He had no choice but to run ahead of the oxen and wagon.

As Pat galloped into the muddy stream, he misjudged the depth of the water. He fell forward, losing his balance. The oxen could not stop, the speeding wagon pushing them ahead into the stream, over the top of Pat. The strap around Pat's waist dragged him beneath the oxen's feet as the wagon ground to a halt in the middle of the muddy stream. Pat was out of sight, beneath the muddy water.

Caroline and Sarah raced down the sandy bank into the stream and quickly unhitched the oxen. Pat was unconscious when they lifted his head out of the water and unbuckled his harness. Carefully they pulled him to dry ground, where they stretched him out on the soft sand.

He wasn't breathing, so they rolled him onto his stomach, the sand sticking to his wet clothes and skin. Both women began pushing against his back with the heels of their hands in an effort to push out the water and get him breathing. Young Pat was sitting a few feet away, wailing mournfully at the crisis he didn't understand.

Soon Sarah began to wail, too. Pat was not responding to the treatment. The back of his neck was swollen and purple. His open eyes were covered with sand. There was no breathing, no movement, no sign of life. Patrick O'Riley, the Nauvoo stone mason, was dead.

Chapter 53

Pat O'Riley's funeral was short, taking place the same evening he was ground to death beneath the feet of his oxen. After Bishop Hill read a few verses from the book of Alma in the Book of Mormon, words about the resurrection, Pat was wrapped in a wool blanket and lowered into a sandy hole near the banks of the North Platte River, his widow and infant son tearfully looking on.

Rather than allow Pat to be covered up with sand only, the bishop ordered some of the men and boys to carry big rocks from the nearby river. The rocks were carefully rolled in on top of the dead Irishman. The big stones would prevent prairie wolves from digging up the corpse. No marker was put on the grave, either, in order to keep it hidden from Indians who sometimes robbed graves looking for valuables or easy scalps.

The next morning Caroline emerged from the wagon dressed in a long-sleeved shirt and men's trousers held up by a pair of black suspenders. Her long blonde hair was tied in a knot on top of her head and covered with a wide-brimmed felt hat. Sarah was dressed in similar fashion, her gray shirt and brown trousers not the customary black for a widow in mourning.

There was no time for mourning, at least not during the day. Winter was approaching quickly, and the Great Salt Lake was still hundreds of miles away. With the help of two scrawny oxen, the worst in the herd, the two women were determined to get their wagon across the Rocky Mountains.

Caroline buckled herself into the harness that dragged Pat to his death, leaned forward, and clucked for the oxen to follow. Sarah followed behind, leaning into the back of the box when the going was tough. Little Pat was free to crawl around in the box and look out the tailgate at his mother.

At first, Caroline thought she and Sarah would get a lot of help from the other families in the train, but as long as the women managed to keep their wagon moving, little help was offered. Everyone was busy with their own problems. Only when their wagon got stuck in mud or sand did the others help them get going again.

And they were stuck frequently. Twenty streams were forded in the week before reaching Chimney Rock. The streams were characterized by steep banks, sand, and mud. The two women pulled and pushed until their strength was gone and there was nothing left but willpower and the determination to force one foot ahead of the other. Still nursing her baby, Sarah wearied quickly, but she never complained.

As the two women rested by their campfire at night, Sarah sometimes talked about Nauvoo and the good times she had had with Pat. She seldom mentioned the future in the Great Basin. The dreams she and Pat had created together were shattered, and it was too early to think about new dreams.

On the other hand, Caroline wondered frequently about her possible meeting with Dan Storm in the Rocky Mountains. She wondered if he would be there when she arrived, if he would still want to marry her, if she would still want him, and where they would want to settle. Perhaps he had already picked out a beautiful mountain valley with clear streams and green grass surrounded by snowcapped mountain peaks. It was hard to discuss her dreams with Sarah, who had lost hers. Most of the time the two women were silent, except when discussing repairs on the wagon and obstacles to cross the next day.

It wasn't very long before Caroline noticed that Ebenezer McConklin always seemed to be on hand when the women needed a hand getting through a mud or sand hole. And his after-supper visits became a regular occurrence.

At first, most of his comments and attentions were directed toward Caroline, but with time he showed an increased interest in Sarah. That he was courting the two women was obvious. Sometimes after he left, Caroline and Sarah would discuss how they might discourage the eager suitor. It was a tough problem. They needed the use of his oxen, and they appreciated his help when the wagon bogged down.

"I wonder how his wives feel," remarked Sarah one evening. "He drops in to see us almost every night. Do you think they're jealous?"

"Could be," responded Caroline, "but I'll bet they're glad to get him out of their hair. Pushiest man I've ever known."

"But remember," reminded Sarah, "his oxen are pulling our wagon, and nobody else has as much time as he does to help us through the mud holes."

"I really don't mind him coming around," smiled Caroline, "now that he's more interested in you than me."

"He's not," blushed Sarah, then added seriously, "Pat's only been gone a few weeks."

"That doesn't mean anything to Ebenezer," responded Caroline. "He's got you in his sights, and if you don't want to be his third wife, you'd better start lining up your defenses right now."

"Do you really think so?" asked Sarah.

"No question about it," replied Caroline, "but don't be too hard on him. We need his oxen and his strong back. Try to hold back the big 'no' until we get to Salt Lake. We need him."

"But Caroline, I couldn't lead him on, let him believe I share his romantic interest."

Caroline thought about Sarah's remark for a moment, then continued, "I feel bad having used Ebenezer to get information for my book. It was so easy. But you know," her voice became louder, "he came right back for more as soon as he found out I was on this wagon train. I think he likes it."

Both women laughed for the first time since Pat's death. It felt good to both of them.

Caroline was the first to get serious again. "But remember, things can get awful nasty when a man like Ebenezer discovers he's been made a fool. The longer it takes, the better. Don't let him get his hopes up too fast."

"I don't think I can do it. It's just not right."

"Think of the alternative, where we are. We may not make it over the mountains without the help of an old fool like McConklin."

"Bishop Hill wouldn't leave us behind to perish."

"Not on the trail, of course," answered Caroline quickly. "But if we start holding things up, slowing the train down, there might be a lot of pressure on the bishop to leave us behind at Fort Laramie or Fort Bridger. How would you like to spend the winter with a bunch of worn-out mountain men and drunken half-breeds? We can't become a burden to the rest of the families. We need McConklin to help us along."

The next morning Caroline's and Sarah's worst fears were the subject of Ebenezer McConklin's morning greeting.

"We'll reach Fort Laramie in a few days. Lot of the men think both of you should be left behind to spend the winter at the fort. Trail will be tougher up ahead. Some figure you two'll be slowing the rest of us down. Got to git over the pass before snow flies."

"We don't want to stay at Fort Laramie, or Fort Bridger either," said Sarah.

"How can we convince the bishop and the others to let us continue?" asked Caroline.

She knew what McConklin was hinting at, but she wondered how much he would say.

"With Pat gone, there's no man to watch out for the both of you and the young'n," he began, then paused, looking away at the hills, anxious to get the next phrase just right.

"If one of ya don't marry up with a good man right soon," he said, his eyes remaining on the distant hills, "there's no way the men will let you continue beyond Fort Laramie."

Caroline responded immediately, a note of anger in her voice.

"I'm promised to a man in the Rocky Mountains, and Sarah's Pat is hardly cold in the ground. Surely we wouldn't be expected to abandon our promises and obligations."

"The decision would be a practical one," resumed McConklin, his confidence growing. "Two women by themselves could hold the rest of us up. This is a wild, cruel land, and winter's nearly upon us. Sometimes circumstances require that earlier promises and obligations be abandoned, if one is to survive."

Having said his piece, McConklin pulled his horse around and galloped back to his wagon.

Sarah and Caroline looked at each other, neither laughing. They had underestimated Ebenezer McConklin and his ability to bring matters to a conclusion very quickly.

That night Caroline and Sarah asked Bishop Hill for an interview. They had to get his feelings on the possibility of being left behind at Fort Laramie. They asked him if he agreed with those who wanted to leave them behind.

"What?" he said. "I haven't heard any talk about leaving you two behind, certainly not in the hands of those over-the-hill mountain men and drunken half-breeds."

"But if a lot of the men felt we would slow up the train . . ." Caroline began to explain.

"Now that could be a consideration," acknowledged the bishop, "but it would take someone to stir things up. Nobody's been talking about leaving you two behind, not to my knowledge."

"Someone will," said Caroline. Then turning to Sarah, added, "Ebenezer is a snake."

Chapter 54

It was a gray day in late October 1848 when the Glenn Hill wagon train left Fort Laramie. The yellow prairie grass shivered before a brisk wind sweeping down from the north. The risk of snow was increasing daily, but the Mormon pioneers in the Hill Company were determined to reach the Salt Lake Valley before winter.

Caroline and Sarah had not been left behind at Fort Laramie, but Ebenezer McConklin was no longer helping them get through the tough places. The man who had offered so much assistance earlier was now their enemy.

Caroline wondered why it was that one's enemies frequently came from the ranks of former friends. It had been that way with Dick Boggs and was now that way with Ebenezer McConklin. Many of Joseph Smith's and Brigham Young's worst enemies were former members of the Church.

The change in Ebenezer had occurred at Fort Laramie when neither Caroline nor Sarah would respond favorably to his hints of offered matrimony. Even Ebenezer's subtle hints that they would probably get left behind at the fort if they didn't tie up in a permanent way with a man failed to produce results.

Upon reaching Fort Laramie, his awkward courtship suddenly became a vicious attempt at revenge. It was McConklin who went from wagon to wagon arguing that the two women should be left behind at the fort. It was McConklin who went to Bishop Hill and demanded the return of his oxen, claiming he had to have them to get over the mountains.

The bishop refused. The oxen would stay where they were as long as the women needed them. While the bishop acknowledged the fact that the two women might slow the party down, he refused to force them to remain behind at Fort Laramie against their will.

The cold wind was incessant, sweeping down from the north and sometimes the west. Every morning the ground was frozen, making travel easy, though the wagons rattled and shook as the frost refused to give way under the iron-rimmed wheels. Sometimes the ground thawed out and became muddy by afternoon, sometimes not. Nevertheless, the Hill Company made good time until it reached the Sweetwater River.

One evening after crossing to the south side of the Sweetwater near Independence Rock, the company made camp in a gently sloping valley that formed a chute between the steep southern hills and the river. It wasn't until the last people were retiring for the night that someone spotted a yellow glow in the western sky. People were roused from their beds to see the strange but beautiful sight. Some suspected the distant glow was from a prairie fire, and the hint of grass smoke carried on the wind confirmed their belief.

The grass in the chute-like valley was mostly green, so there was little concern of immediate danger from the fire. The biggest worry was that the fire would destroy grazing for the stock at future campsites.

Gradually the weary pioneers retired to their beds, leaving two sentries to keep an eye on the stock and their sleeping companions. When all should have been quiet, however, an increasing number of voices were heard throughout the camp, especially from under the wagons where some of the people were sleeping on the ground.

The voices were discussing a distant rumbling, or vibration, that seemed to be coming through the ground. One couldn't hear it as much as feel it, but it was there. And unlike the glow in the western sky that was remaining fairly constant, the trembling in the ground was getting stronger.

Soon everyone in the camp was awake—wondering, listening, feeling. No one had ever experienced anything like this before. Some thought it was an earthquake, but the ground wasn't shaking. Some of the babies began to cry, including young Pat O'Riley. It probably wasn't the rumbling as much as the concern in their parents' voices and faces that alarmed the children.

After a while a distant thunder could be heard, a continuous thunder growing gradually louder. It was coming from the west. In the dark, moonless night, scouts were sent upstream to investigate the strange thunder. Bishop Hill ordered that all livestock hobbled outside the circle of wagons be brought inside the circle.

The camp was quiet, except for the distant rumbling, but no one went back to sleep. It seemed like the scouts had been gone a long time, too long, but they finally returned, all of them, running through the blackness, shouting, "Buffalo! Thousands! Stampede!"

The camp came alive with activity. A huge herd guessed to number in the tens of thousands was stampeding down the valley between the hills and the river, and the circle of wagons was in its path.

"Pull the wagons closer together!" shouted the bishop. "Make the circle smaller."

"Get ropes on the horses," shouted someone else. "Tie them to the wagons."

"Women and children, get in wagons on the downstream side," shouted the bishop. "I don't want anybody in the upstream wagons. The buffalo will hit those first."

By the time the bishop's orders were carried out and everything was ready, the thunder of thousands of hooves permeated everything—the ground, the cold night air, and the ears and hearts of every pioneer. It seemed the herd would be on them at any moment. But the delay continued, the thundering growing louder and louder.

Suddenly the bishop shouted, "The fires! Build up the fires! Pile on all the wood!"

His order made sense. Why hadn't anyone thought of it earlier? If there had been a full or even half moon, the buffalo could have seen the circle of wagons possibly in time to avoid it. But in the blackness of a moonless night, the panicked animals leading the herd would not see the wagons until it was too late. Their companions would push them headlong into the wagons.

So it was. The bishop's last order came too late. The fires were not yet blazing when the first of the stampeding buffalo smashed like a huge tidal wave into the upstream side of the circle, rolling over the wagons as if they were toys. The bishop had acted wisely in ordering people out of these wagons. Had he not done so, many more would have been injured.

As the wagons rolled over, stampeding buffalo charged in among the frightened oxen and horses. Confusion reigned. Babies cried. Women screamed and prayed. Men shouted. Many blindly fired rifles at the stampeding buffalo. It being too dark to see, they merely pointed in the direction of the thundering hooves and pulled triggers. It was too dark to reload for all but the most practiced riflemen. The air filled with the smell of dirt and sweat until it was hard to breathe.

Several of the downhill wagons were pushed over too, finally making an opening for the buffalo to get through the corral of wagons and join their companions in the stampede down the valley. The oxen and many of the horses broke their lead ropes and joined the flow of stampeding buffalo. Many of those who could not break their ropes lost their footing and were injured or killed beneath the thundering hooves.

It seemed like hours before the last buffalo trotted through the circle of battered wagons. The dust had already begun to settle, and the stars were fading before a gray dawn. For the first time in many mornings, the ground around the wagons was not covered with frost.

Exhausted people began to crawl out of their wagons to inspect the damage. Half the wagons were unfit for travel, but that didn't matter. There were not enough horses and oxen remaining to pull more than two wagons. Fortunately, no one had been killed. A man had broken a leg when his wagon overturned. Several buffalo had broken their necks and legs in tangling with the wagons. Those still alive were quickly put out of their misery. There would be plenty of fresh meat for a few weeks.

Bishop Hill called a council meeting to decide what to do. The alternatives seemed clear. Without oxen and horses, the wagon train could not continue. The people could walk back to Fort Laramie and spend the winter there, or they could continue on foot, using the two remaining wagons to carry the babies and old people, food and bedding. Several of the young men could be left behind to guard the valuables left behind with the wagons.

The people voted unanimously to continue on. From Salt Lake, teams could be sent back to get the wagons, still before winter if the weather cooperated. With the two wagons to carry food and bedding, they could expect to make at least twenty miles a day on foot.

The next morning, seventy-four people of the Glenn Hill Company began the final stretch of their two-thousand-mile migration. Several of the old people, who felt they would slow down the walkers, stayed behind with the young men to guard the wagons.

Sarah and Caroline joined the marchers. A place for young Pat was arranged in one of the wagons.

The group covered nearly a hundred miles the first four days. Pacific Springs and the continental divide were far behind. The fourth night, many of the tents caved in on the sleeping pioneers, as the snows that had been threatening for many weeks finally came, dumping just over twenty-four inches in one night. The next day travel was impossible.

Chapter 55

The big dog Port was no longer with me when I reached Fort Laramie. In fact, the last time I saw him was on a moonlit night just after crossing the Big Muddy, or Missouri River. We were passing through the last of the thick woods just a few days away from the open prairie. We were staying away from the main trail, not wanting to risk running into a law enforcement officer who might have a warrant for me.

Several times during the day I caught a glimpse of a fleeting shadow in the nearby timber. I figured it was a wild dog or a wolf. Old Port noticed it too, and on several occasions charged into the woods after it. When I called to him he always returned.

That night as we crouched close to our little fire for warmth, I noticed a change in Port. Instead of resting his big head on his paws and going to sleep, as one would expect a dog to do after a long day of travel, his head was high, looking this way and that way into the dark woods.

When the moon came up, the animal that had been following us began to yap in the nearby woods. It sounded like a wolf, not a dog. Port was on his feet, looking at me and whining, then looking in the direction of the yapping wolf. It was as if he was asking permission to leave.

I figured the wolf was a female, probably in heat, and my first reaction was to tie up Port and keep him on a leash until we were out of range of this enticing female. A man just didn't let his dog run off with a wolf in heat, not if he wanted the dog back again in the near future.

But as I reached for the rope, I had second thoughts. I didn't like thinking of Port as my property. Of his own free will he had run away from his master, the Keokuk sheriff, to join me. He had willingly attacked Dick Boggs, who was trying to club me as I climbed through the little window in his burning cabin. Port was my friend, not my possession. I called him to me.

"Port, old friend," I said, patting him on the head, "you run off with that wolf and she'll probably lead you to others. They'll try to kill you. You'll have to fight and win to be one of them. You'll have to find your own food, because I won't be here when you get back."

Port looked at me as I talked. When I finished, he looked back to the woods.

"Go, if you want to," I said.

He looked back at me one more time before charging into the darkness. I waited at the camp most of the next day, thinking he might return, but he didn't. As far as I know, old Port and his offspring are still roaming the Kansas prairie with their wild cousins.

At Fort Laramie I traded my horse for a pair of snowshoes. Nearly two feet of snow had fallen out of the sky by the time I reached the fort. The Glenn Hill Company had left several weeks earlier, and I was certain the same storm had stalled the wagon train somewhere along the trail. Several feet of new snow made horse or wagon travel next to impossible, and it being November already, there was a good chance the snow wouldn't melt away until spring. I was glad to get the snowshoes.

Word of the buffalo stampede had not reached Fort Laramie, so no one at the fort knew that the majority of the people in the Hill Company had left their wagons behind and were walking to the Salt Lake Valley with minimal supplies. No effort was made to send out a rescue party.

I made good time because I was traveling light. Besides my rifle and possibles bag stuffed with buffalo jerky and corn, the only extra weight was a buffalo robe over my shoulders and Caroline's manuscript stuffed inside my shirt. A few pounds of jerky and corn could keep a man going for weeks. The meat provided the strength; the corn, the bulk. A small handful of corn would swell in your stomach to make you feel stuffed.

After the snowstorm had blown over to the west, the air became cold and clear, with a little fog in the river bottoms. The snow was soft and powdery, making travel difficult even with snowshoes, but I pushed ahead, eager to reach Caroline, Pat, and Sarah as quickly as possible.

One gray afternoon, upon reaching the crest of a hill, I spotted the Hill Company wagons in a little valley on the other side of the Sweetwater River. I knew something was wrong when I noticed the absence of livestock, the single campfire, and snow still piled high on wagon seats and wheel rims. Except for a few stragglers, it appeared the bulk of the people and their animals had left the wagons behind. It occurred to me that maybe there had been an Indian massacre. Some of the wagons had been turned over, but none showed signs of burning.

I hurried down the hill, waded across the Sweetwater, and called to the young men who were huddled around the lone campfire. They waved for me to join them.

I told them who I was. Then, as I was drying my clothes, they brought me up to date on the progress of the Hill Company. They told me about the Indian raid on their livestock and the buffalo stampede, how the company had gone ahead on foot, leaving them behind to guard the wagons and goods until teams could be sent from the Salt Lake Valley. With the new snow it now appeared they would have to wait until spring, but they had enough buffalo meat and seed grain to see them through.

When I asked about Pat O'Riley, they suddenly became quiet, realizing I didn't know about Pat's death. They reluctantly explained how the Irish stone mason had been trampled to death beneath the feet of his oxen, and how he was buried on the banks of the North Platte River.

One of the young men explained how Caroline and Sarah had continued on with the company despite efforts by one Ebenezer

McConklin to leave them behind at Fort Laramie. I remembered Ebenezer McConklin, Caroline's former fiancé, the pious fellow she had used to get information for her book.

"After Pat died," began one of the young men, "Old Eb became a regular companion to those ladies, always on hand to help 'em out. But it weren't service to others that put the gleam in his eye and a new bounce in his step." They all laughed.

"Everybody could see old Eb was no Samaritan, just out to double the size of his harem," continued the same young fellow. "But I guess the ladies would have nothin' to do with him, 'cause when we reached Fort Laramie, it was Ebenezer who argued to leave 'em behind with those old trappers and half-breeds. Bishop Hill would have none of that."

They showed me Pat's snow-covered wagon, still loaded with tools, seed grain, a cook stove, plow, and boxes of supplies that the former owner would never be able to use. I reached inside my shirt and pulled out Caroline's manuscript, still wrapped in the deer skin, and shoved it into one of the boxes.

"Take good care of this stuff," I said to the fellow who had accompanied me to the wagon. "We'll be back for it."

I declined their invitation to spend the night under one of the canvas wagon tops. There were several hours of daylight remaining. I was beginning to worry about Caroline, Sarah, and little Pat. It appeared more storm clouds were blowing in from the northwest. There was a good chance the snow had come for the winter, and the marchers didn't have sufficient supplies to weather a prolonged storm. I had to reach them quickly.

As I pushed upstream along the Sweetwater River, I thought it strange how game could disappear with the first snow, especially the buffalo. There had been thousands in the area just a few weeks earlier. Now there were none.

I remembered ten years ago when my old friend Beaver George had told me about the white buffalo. "When snow flies, and the brown buffler disappear to the south, look to the tops of the mountains for the white buffler," he said. Over the years I had sometimes wondered what he meant by "white buffler." Albino buffalo, I supposed, or some other kind of animal that lived in the snow-covered mountains, perhaps goats or sheep.

When it was too dark to travel, I carved out a little snow cave in the underside of a big snowdrift. At the mouth of the tiny cave I built a small, smokeless fire of willow twigs. Overnight camping was easy in the snow. Snow caves were so easy to keep warm, and I never ceased to be amazed that things didn't get wet. The inside walls of a snow cave would evaporate before the warmth of a fire but never melt and get things wet.

The next morning when I crawled out of the cozy den, there was another ten inches of new snow. I had hoped that maybe the first snow would disappear before warmer fall weather, but the new snow and the accompanying cold temperatures were convincing evidence that the winter of 1848 had come early and was here to stay.

Chapter 56

The snow had covered the Hill Company trail, but I knew the general direction they were headed and the streams they would be following, so I didn't figure there would be any problem staying on their path.

Not finding them at Pacific Springs, I crossed the continental divide and headed toward the Big Sandy, a tributary to the Green River. I was entering familiar country, the place where I had met the young Ute chief Neuwafe nine years earlier. This was the country where I had hunted buffalo with the Ute band, the land where I had fallen in love with the beautiful Red Leaf nearly a decade ago. The memories flooded back. Old wounds I thought had healed were reopened.

Sometimes when I thought about Caroline, I felt a tinge of guilt, like she didn't belong here in this wild land, not with me. I was haunted with the feeling that I was somehow betraying Red Leaf by following another woman into the land of the Utes. Even though I kept telling myself that Red Leaf had been dead for nearly five years, the feelings of betrayal would not go away. The memories that had been dulled with time were suddenly very real again, especially those concerning Red Leaf's abduction—me leaving her alone to face the raiding Comanches, her being tied like a dog to a post in the Comanche village, the tortures and cruelties, the escape on the roan stallion, hiding in the huge beaver lodge—and her death.

Sometimes I felt like turning back, leaving this land of so many painful memories, but I didn't. Another woman, one still alive, had helped heal my wounds, had helped me forget the painful past and find hope in a better future. Caroline was different than Red Leaf; she was an educated woman, a writer. A rare woman with unusual courage who infiltrated the Mormon stronghold at Nauvoo to gather material for a book. A woman who was now crossing a continent in winter to find me. I had to continue. I couldn't just turn my back on her. She was alive and needed me. Red Leaf was buried under a sandy ledge near the big beaver lodge. I would have to figure out a way to handle those painful memories, find a way to live with them.

Trudging along through the deep snow, day after day, followed by long dark nights in snow caves, I had plenty of time to think about Red Leaf, to remember the past, to try to concentrate on the future. But my inward thoughts suddenly ended one clear morning when I spotted smoke far away to the west.

I shuffled ahead on my snowshoes, almost at a trot, a pace I could maintain for hours, especially on the gentle downhill slope. About noon I reached a hill overlooking the encampment. With a brisk breeze sweeping down from the north, the sun offered little warmth. The two wagons and a dozen or so tents were scattered among snowdrifts next to a rushing stream, not yet frozen over. There were no oxen or horses.

There was a large manmade pile of snow just outside the camp. Two boys were seated on top of the mound, sticks in hand, keeping some magpies away. The rest of the people were out of sight, in the tents and wagons I supposed, trying to keep warm. As I headed down the hill, I wondered why the snow pile was so attractive to the birds.

I hadn't gone far when one of the boys spotted me and shouted the news to the camp. People began crawling out of the tents—hungry, ragged, dirty people—their hands and faces gray and black from huddling around tiny, smoky fires in an effort to stay warm. Some had rags wrapped around their feet and hands. Some started waving to me, while others cheered at what they thought was a rescue party.

I wished I had brought food with me. The jerky and corn in my possibles bag wouldn't go very far in feeding so many people.

I recognized the first man to come out to greet me. He recognized me too. It was Ebenezer McConklin.

"You bring food?" he asked, without any kind of greeting.

"No," I said, responding in kind. He turned and walked away.

Then I was among the rest of the people, who milled about asking almost all at once about an imagined rescue party from Fort Laramie. I hated telling them that none was coming, and when I did, many returned to their tents, heads down, feet dragging.

"I'm Glenn Hill," said a strong-looking man, who stepped forward and offered his hand. "You look at home in this God-forsaken country. Sure like to pick your brain for a little while."

"Sure," I said, "but first there are a few people I want to . . ."

"Dan!" shouted a familiar voice, a female voice. Caroline.

For months I had imagined what our meeting would be like, wondering whether it would be awkward. Would she reach out to me and come into my arms? Upon seeing her, would my feelings for her remain the same?

Caroline was wrapped in a green wool blanket, her face gray and charcoal-smudged like the rest of her companions. Her long hair was tied behind her head, not matted like that of many of the women, but just as dirty from many days without bathing. Her legs were covered by a pair of baggy trousers, and her feet were wrapped in rags to protect them from the cold.

Her initial call to me had been one of surprise, a spontaneous reaction to my unexpected arrival. Instead of coming to me, however, as I thought she might, she began to back away, realizing how awful she looked. Her expectations, like mine, hadn't included this kind of a meeting. She had anticipated a more romantic setting, both of us on our best footing for what could be a very important event in both of our lives.

I wasn't sure how to respond to her when I first recognized her voice. I was even less sure when I saw her, knowing she would want to look her best for me. But when she started to back away, fear of rejection on her face, I knew exactly what to do.

"Caroline!" I called. "It's so good to see you." I ran to her and put my arms around her. When she looked up into my face, I could see the beginnings of tears in both of her beautiful eyes. I held her close, repeating my earlier words, "Caroline, it's so good to see you," followed by a long pause. It felt so good to hold her, to touch her, to be with her again. Things would work out.

It was Caroline who was the first to break the silence. She had control of herself. "Would you like to join us for a bowl of soup?"

"Sure," I said cheerfully. Then, "Where's Sarah and little Pat?"

"Over this way, at the tent." She took me by the hand and led me to their tent.

Chapter 57

The soup didn't taste like soup. The flavor could best be described as salty barnyard.

"Glue soup," said Caroline, noticing my dislike for the contents of her kettle. She explained the simple recipe—boiling a chunk of rawhide for a few hours. The last of the meat from the oxen had been eaten the day before. I reached into my possibles bag and tossed a handful of buffalo jerky into the kettle. She smiled. I tossed one more chunk to the back of the tent for little Pat to chew on.

We were crouched over a smoky sagebrush fire in front of the little canvas tent occupied by Caroline, Sarah, and little Pat. Sarah was in the back of the tent keeping the baby warm. The little boy had a deep, raspy cough; the women called it croup. Half a dozen people had died of this croup. Except for one pregnant woman, the victims were children and old people. The cold was taking its toll on the Hill Company.

"What have you got to eat when the rawhide's gone?" I asked.

"Bishop Hill says the rawhide will last until reinforcements arrive," Caroline responded. I didn't remind her that no reinforcements were coming from the Fort Laramie direction, and I doubted any were coming from the other direction, either.

"Got to have a chat with the bishop," I said, standing up. Caroline and I had not discussed our future together, the subject that had occupied a large share of our waking moments for many months. I felt relieved she didn't bring it up, and she probably felt that way, too. The time wasn't right. I was beginning to wonder if there would ever be a right time.

There was a brisk breeze coming out of the North, and the afternoon was gray. It appeared another storm was brewing. The food was almost gone, and the snow was going to get deeper. Few of the people had good enough footgear to travel through the snow without freezing their feet. Up to now the people had kept their hopes up by talking about reinforcements, but I knew better.

As I stepped away from the fire, my nostrils filled with the smell of rotting flesh. I looked directly into the wind to see where the stench was coming from and spotted the big manmade pile of snow I had seen on the way in.

"What's the big pile of snow?" I asked, turning back to Caroline.

"The dead," she said. "The ground is frozen and our only two shovels are broken. Those who've died are buried in that pile of snow until they can receive a proper burial. I don't know why they stink so."

I didn't respond to her remark, though I knew the answer. I was surprised the men in the camp didn't. One or more of the bodies had apparently been packed in the snow before they'd had time to cool. I knew that when snow was packed around a warm body, man or animal, it acted as insulation. Instead of cooling the body off and slowing the decaying process, the snow held in the warmth and sped up decay. That's why the Utes would leave a body out in the open for a night before burying it in a snow bank. A frozen body packed in snow would remain in its frozen condition until the spring thaw.

"I'll be back in a little while," I said in parting, "to fix you a snow cave. Tonight you'll be as warm as toast."

When I reached Bishop Hill's tent, I suggested he assign a detail to drag the bodies out in the open as soon as it was dark so they could freeze solid. He seemed to appreciate my suggestion.

"Keep think'n the snow will melt and we'll be able to go on," he said, a worried look on his face. "But it just keeps gett'n deeper, and no break in the cold. Food's about gone. Have any suggestions on what we ought to do?"

"Might start by sending a couple of men back to the wagons for supplies. They've got lots of seed grain and a fair amount of buffalo meat."

"I tried that yesterday but couldn't get any volunteers. You can understand why none of the men want to leave their families. All the single men were left behind with the wagons. Besides, the people think a rescue party is coming—at least they did until you came along."

"Tell 'em there's no rescue party unless they go get one," I advised. "I was at the wagons three days ago, and nobody was talk'n about comin' after you. They figured you were further along than this, possibly far enough down the west side of the divide to be out of the snow.

"Ought to send a couple of men the other direction, too," I continued. "Get word to President Young that we've been caught by the snows. He'll send help from that direction. I'll give each man enough jerky and corn to keep him a week, and I'll get some game to feed their families while they're gone."

"The game is gone," added the worried bishop. "We've sent out hunters every day, but the buffalo are gone. So are the deer and elk."

"Tell 'em I'll do my best, but remind 'em there are no rescue parties. If they don't go, the whole company'll starve. Can't just sit here and die. We've got to do something while we're still able."

"I'll ask for volunteers when we gather for prayer this evening," responded the bishop. "Hopefully this time we'll get some."

"I'm curious as to why you haven't insisted on sending men out earlier," I added, not wanting to sound critical, but really wanting to know why a group of intelligent adults would wait until I came along to adopt such an obvious course of action.

The bishop was silent for a while. I could tell by the look on his face that he received my question not as a challenge, but as a sincere inquiry to find the heart of a problem that needed to be solved.

"I suppose the problem is one of piety," he said, a thoughtful expression on his whiskered face.

"I don't understand."

"Seems every time we get together in a council meeting to decide what to do, some of the more pious brethren get all excited over how the Lord is punishing us for not keeping the commandments. We spend hours arguing repentance, fasting, prayer, cursing, reading scriptures. I don't know why, but we never seem to get around to selecting couriers."

The bishop explained the problem with the buffalo chips and how it led to the loss of half the stock.

"I thought we had learned a lesson about piety and practicality. But then the buffalo stampede ran off the rest of our stock, and we got caught in the snow. Brother McConklin began to get some listening ears when he started preaching how the Lord was punishing us."

He paused for a moment, looking down into the little sagebrush fire. "I suppose I began to believe it myself."

"Ebenezer McConklin, is he the one you are talking about?"

"He's the one," replied the weary bishop. "I embarrassed him over the buffalo chip rules and refused to let him talk me into leaving Caroline and Sarah behind at Fort Laramie. He's been fighting me ever since. Wish I could quote scriptures like that pious old goat. He's got a lot of people listening to him."

I told the bishop about my Indian bride Red Leaf, about the carefree life we enjoyed the summer of our marriage. How happy we were, two people in love, living together in a wild, beautiful land. No concerns for the future.

I told him how I had left my bride behind in our wickiup as I climbed the great mountain Timpanogos, seeking a religious experience with the Great Spirit, and how from the side of that mountain I had spotted the smoke from my burning wickiup and helplessly watched the Comanches carry off Red Leaf. I paused, looking down into the fire.

"What happened to her?" asked the bishop, compassion in his voice.

"They raped her!" I said. "They tortured her! They burned her eyes out with flaming sticks! She died in my arms inside a cold, muddy beaver lodge!"

I apologized for the outburst, tears in my eyes.

"It's all right to be pious," I continued, my voice now under control. "But a man has responsibilities that can't be neglected. You've got some dead children in that pile of snow out there. How many more will there be before McConklin and his friends roll up their sleeves and do something? It's November! You can assume the snow and cold are not going to go away until spring."

"Thanks," said Bishop Hill, standing up, a determined look on his face. "I knew what to do all along, but I guess I got confused, needed a second opinion. Glad you came along. Those couriers will be on their way at daybreak, two east, two west."

Chapter 58

The next morning I waded into the icy waters of the Big Sandy and gathered mussels, as I had seen the Utes do during hard times. I worked quickly until my hands and feet were numb beyond feeling. Some of the men joined me. While the mussels alone wouldn't prevent starvation, the mussel chowder would be a welcome supplement to our meager diet.

While showing some of the women how to prepare the mussels, I pointed to the lodge-pole pine forest on the nearby hillside and told them the black moss hanging on the north sides of the trees could be kneaded into a bitter bread for those who had diarrhea and couldn't eat the mussels. I told them I had known Indians who had lived for months on the awful-tasting bread. Some of the women headed toward the woods to gather moss.

I had given most of my jerky and corn to the four scouts who had left at first light, two east and two west. I figured it would be at least a week, and possibly two or three, before reinforcements arrived from either direction. In the meantime there were about seventy people to feed.

I had built a comfortable snow cave for Caroline, Sarah, and the baby the night before, using their canvas tent to cover the entrance and for a ground cover. As I was putting the finishing touches on the cave, the women and baby already inside, Ebenezer McConklin stopped by to remind me of the camp's strict moral code. He said he hoped I had the good sense not to share my snow dwelling with the two single women. I felt like punching him in the nose.

"You're too late," I responded with a wicked smile. "They're already inside." He turned and stalked toward Bishop Hill's tent. I quickly forgot the incident.

The cave warmed up quickly, thanks to a small fire. Caroline, Sarah, and I spent a pleasant evening discussing the recent past and our questionable future. Little Pat's croup seemed to be improving, so our spirits were high.

During the afternoon the women had braved the icy waters of the Big Sandy and washed away the ashes and dirt. I was sure that had something to do with their good spirits. For supper we sipped on hot chowder, thickened with the last of my corn.

During the evening Bishop Hill paid us a visit. He was surprised and obviously pleased at the warmth of the cave. Said he was going to build himself one the next day. I was sure the bishop had heard from McConklin, but he didn't express any concern over my sharing the snow cave with the two women. His biggest concern was the improving health of young Pat, whom the bishop had blessed several days earlier.

He asked about Sarah's health, then surprised me by saying, "I'm not worried about Caroline catching anything, not after Pacific Springs."

"Pacific Springs?" I inquired, curious as to what he was referring to.

"Didn't you tell him?" asked the bishop, looking at Caroline.

"No," she answered, then looking at me said, "I was baptized."

Before I could respond the bishop blurted out, "And I did the baptizing. Had to chop through two inches of ice, and the wind was blow'n twenty knots out of the north. A testimony of the truthfulness of the gospel. Neither of us got even the sniffles."

"Now I can call you Sister Logan," I interjected, finding the bishop's good humor contagious.

"I prefer Caroline," she responded, trying to be serious, but it was obvious she was enjoying the attention and good humor of our lively banter. Conditions had been so serious for so long that everyone was thoroughly enjoying a chance to laugh a little.

After Bishop Hill departed I told Caroline that she no longer needed to worry about Dick Boggs publishing her manuscript. I explained how I had taken it from Boggs and brought it west with me, how this very moment it was resting safely in a trunk in Pat's wagon back on the Sweetwater.

Caroline leaned over and kissed me on the cheek as she thanked me. Those old romantic feelings began to return. I began to feel like things were going to work out just fine.

During the evening conversation, Sarah occasionally mentioned Pat and his untimely death. There was no bitterness in her voice, but one could tell she missed him deeply. Her heart still ached. Nevertheless, she seemed to maintain absolute control of her words and emotions. It would have been easy for her to let go of herself in grieving over her lost husband and become a burden for those around her. She had wisely denied herself that luxury. I respected her strength. I liked her.

The two women slept at the back of the cave, little Pat between them. I huddled by the fire, rekindling it whenever the cave became a little chilly.

The women were tired, and sleep was welcome. For the first time in weeks, they slept through an entire night without shivering with cold before morning. Whereas the tent had offered little protection from the icy wind, the thick walls of the snow cave held in the warmth of the sleeping occupants.

I didn't sleep much, mostly worrying about the food situation. The most hardy could survive a few weeks on mussels and moss cakes, but not the children, the sick, the old, the pregnant. They needed good food, grain or meat.

My thoughts kept returning to Beaver George's statement about the white buffalo.

"When snow flies, and the brown buffler head south, look to the tops of the mountains for the white buffler."

The buffalo, deer, and elk had left this high, cold country, but what about George's "white buffler"? Surely he must have known what he was talking about. I had seen white mountain goats on the high peaks in the summer months, but I had never seen any in winter. If they migrated to lower elevations like other animals, one would see them. Apparently they stayed in the mountains, even in winter. I didn't know for sure if there were any goats in the nearby mountains, but I intended to find out the next day. The white animals would be hard to spot against a background of snow, but if there were any around, I was sure I would find and shoot them.

The next morning our cave was inspected by many members of the company. Some began to fashion their own snow caves. Little Pat was crawling about, his health better than ever.

It was midmorning when I put on my snowshoes, picked up my rifle, and headed for the mountains in search of white buffler.

Chapter 59

As long as the snow was deep and the incline not too steep, I had no trouble moving along on the snowshoes. The hardest places to travel were the rocky areas where the wind had blown most of the snow away. Sometimes there was so little snow that I had to carry my snowshoes.

I was continually on the lookout for game—any kind of movement, tracks, places where snow had been pawed away. I listened for the clatter of hooves over distant rocks. By early afternoon I had found no signs of life. My eyes hurt from the never-ending glare of the sun reflecting on the white snow. My neck ached from looking skyward, scanning the craggy cliffs and peaks. I continued my journey, higher and higher into the mountains.

Some of the windswept faces had moss on them, particularly the moist surfaces where water was seeping through. Occasionally there was a clump of frozen grass among the moss patches. There was feed for goats, but still no goats.

I was getting far enough from camp that if I didn't start back soon, I would be forced to spend the night on the trail. I would have preferred another night in the comfortable snow cave with Caroline and Sarah, but foremost in my thoughts was the need for fresh meat. I had to find out if there were white buffler or goats in these mountains. I didn't want to climb up through the foothills again a second day if there was no game to be found. I continued my upward journey through the late afternoon.

It wasn't until the wind began to blow that I discovered the first hint of game. I didn't hear or see anything, at least not at first, but suddenly I noticed the unmistakable odor of goat on the wind sweeping down from the slopes above. I headed directly into the wind, welcoming a new cloud bank that was beginning to block out the blinding rays of the sun.

The sun was down and I was at least a thousand feet higher when I discovered tracks in the snow where two or three animals had passed beneath a rock outcropping. The fact that I had smelled the animals convinced me the tracks couldn't be more than a few hours old.

There was no turning back now. Making sure my rifle was primed and ready to fire, I stalked carefully along the trail left behind by what I figured were two or three mountain goats. Darkness overtook me before I found anything.

Using one of my snowshoes for a shovel, I dug out a snow cave, praying fresh snow from the approaching clouds would not cover the trail during the night. Had there been a full moon, I could have continued my hunt during the night. A full moon on all that snow would have provided plenty of light for shooting. As it was, the night was cloudy and dark, and I had no choice but to wait for daylight in my little cave, nibbling on the last of my food.

First light found me hurrying along a nearly vanished trail, washed away by the incessant wind and drifting snow.

By midmorning the trail had all but disappeared, and I was about ready to head off in another direction when again the wind carried the smell of goat to me.

I looked up just in time to see the tail end of two goats walking out of sight around the side of a distant hill. They were as white as the snow, and had they not been silhouetted against the gray sky, I probably would not have seen them. They looked too clean to have such a strong smell.

With the goats out of sight I broke into a run. I didn't follow their trail but headed straight to the top of the hill they were circling. Neuwafe had taught me that. In the mountains, the hunted were most accustomed to being stalked from behind and below. The wise hunter who could get in front of and above his game was less likely to be discovered. My objective was to get on top of the hill and pick off the goats as they came around the other side, assuming they continued on their present course.

The hill was steeper and higher than I had supposed, and it took me the better part of an hour to get to the top. There being no sign of the goats, I continued cautiously along the crest, looking ahead and below for any sign of the animals. I moved slowly, like a stalking animal, doing more looking and sniffing than walking.

When I finally spotted them, they were working their way through a rocky draw, headed straight for me. They were coming slowly, sniffing and pawing around windswept rocks for bits of moss and grass. They were less than a hundred yards away.

When both of their heads were out of sight behind the same rock, I sat down in the snow and rested my elbows on my knees, getting a steady aim with the rifle. When the first goat stepped from behind the rock, I aimed at his shoulder and squeezed off a round.

The animal dropped in its tracks, and I leaned back, out of sight, to reload. When I sat up again, I was pleased to see the second animal nervously prancing about its dead companion. It didn't know which way to run. The blast of my rifle had echoed back and forth, from canyon walls to rock faces, and the animal still did not know from which direction the bullet had come.

I squeezed off a second round and, though the animal did not drop immediately as its companion had, it didn't go far before its mouth filled with blood and its legs buckled.

"Beaver George, thanks!" I yelled to the winter sky. He had been right about the "white buffler."

Stalking the goats had taken longer than I had supposed. It was past midday by the time they were dressed out and ready to be dragged down the mountain.

The hiking of the past day, at high altitudes in the extreme cold with little to eat, had made me very weary and hungry. There being no fuel to build a fire, I ate the two hearts raw while I was dressing the goats out. I didn't particularly like the raw meat, but it did satisfy my hunger and give me strength for the long journey back to camp. I chose the hearts because they were not attached to the carcasses and would have been awkward to carry.

By the time I was ready to head back, it was midafternoon, and heavy black clouds were blowing in from the west. It looked like another good snowstorm in the making. With my rifle strapped to my back, I grabbed a rough, black goat horn in each hand and began to drag the goats down the mountain.

I made good time on the steep inclines, the carcasses sliding easily behind me. But on the level places the pulling wore me out. The going was slow. The clouds became blacker, the snow thicker, the wind fiercer. I was cold and tired and decided to start looking for a place to spend the night—a good place for a snow cave. As long as those goats were with me, there would be plenty to eat.

That's when the worst thing that could have happened, happened. I had taken off my snowshoes and was checking out a flat place under a rocky ledge as a possible place to make a snow house. The ground beneath me suddenly gave way. Too late, I realized I was not on ground but the frozen surface of a small but deep pool fed by an underground spring. Before I had time to react, I was totally submerged in icy water.

Knowing I couldn't last long in the freezing water, and figuring that with the water over my head I couldn't crawl out of the hole in the ice, I swam away from the hole until I could feel the ground beneath me. Then, pulling my legs up under me, I pushed myself up, forcing a new opening in the ice. My teeth were chattering when I crawled from the water.

Knowing my hands would soon be numb, I quickly lashed the snowshoes back onto my feet. There was no way I could build a fire, even with the makings and fuel. The feeling was all but gone in my hands. I was soaking wet in subfreezing weather.

My only hope was to run, as fast as I could, all the way to camp and the warmth of someone's fire. I guessed the camp was at least three miles away, not a distance too far to run, but it would soon be dark. I might not be able to find the camp. I started running, leaving the goats and my rifle behind at the spring. I could come back for them, if I survived the night.

First my hands went numb, then my feet. Soon my buckskins were frozen hard and stiff, like a coat of armor. I could feel blisters forming where they had never been before. In the beginning there was some pain, but none after a while. I felt tired, so tired. All I wanted to do was just stretch out and sleep for a little while in the soft white snow.

But I knew about the white death, the preferred way to pass on for old Indians. It was as easy as taking a nap, once you became cold enough. I knew the first rest I allowed myself would be my last.

One foot in front of the other, again, again, and again, never stopping. Eventually I would reach camp; then all would be well. I would get out of my frozen clothes and bask in front of a warm fire.

I ran for what seemed an eternity. The storm began to break up and some stars began to appear, meaning the night would get even colder. I ran so long that I began to worry that I had passed the camp and was widening the distance between me and my only hope of survival.

Suddenly the ground dropped swiftly away as I stumbled over the crest of a steep bank. I was rolling forward, unable to stop myself, and not sure I wanted to until I realized I had stepped over the bank of a river and was headed toward the black rushing current.

I didn't stop until I was waist-deep in water. I still don't know how I managed to keep my footing, but when I tried to take a step, I fell forward and the current began to drag me downstream over rocks and boulders. At first the water felt warmer than the freezing wind. But soon it felt colder. My teeth were beyond chattering.

For the first time I had thoughts of giving up. What was the use? Soaked again. No idea where camp was.

Then I realized I must have fallen into the Big Sandy, the river that ran by the camp. I also realized there were no steep banks—like the one I had come down—downstream from camp for many miles.

I knew where I was. Upstream from camp. Probably not very far. If I could get out of the water and run along the bank, I would reach camp. I would live.

The camp was dark, and it appeared everyone was retired for the night. I wasn't aware that anyone was watching when I dropped to my knees and rolled forward into the snow cave, passing out in front of Caroline and Sarah.

Chapter 60

When I awakened I was curled up under my buffalo robe beside Pat O'Riley Jr. He was still asleep, breathing deeply. Caroline and Sarah were gone. The sun was shining against the partly opened canvas doorway to the snow cave. My first concern was for my toes and fingers that had been without feeling the night before. They were red and sore but otherwise healthy.

My wet and frozen buckskins were nowhere in sight. Then I spotted them through the partly drawn-back canvas, hanging over a sagebrush just outside the cave, freeze-drying in the winter sun now midway through the sky. I had slept nearly half the day. There being no food in the kettle, I figured Caroline and Sarah were probably down by the river gathering mussels.

I smiled at the thought of surprising them with goat stew. I remembered leaving the goats by the spring. My rifle was there, too. It would be several hours before I could find the goats and drag the carcasses to camp. I would have to work quickly to make it back before dark.

Carefully removing the buffalo skin from the sleeping baby, I draped it around my waist and crawled outside to fetch my buckskins. The sun was bright and warmer than it had been in many days. Still, the snow was not melting.

After gently covering the baby with the buffalo robe, I slipped into my buckskins, still a little damp in places, but mostly dry. As

I was dressing, I heard some shouting coming from the direction of the main camp. Men's voices in heated discussion. The loudest had a familiar whine, Ebenezer McConklin. I wondered what he was stirring up now. Before lashing on the snowshoes, I scratched a message in the packed snow for Caroline and Sarah. "Gone to get rifle. Be back by dark." I didn't say anything about the goats, still wanting to surprise them.

I followed the Big Sandy upstream to the steep bank where I had tumbled into the water, then backtracked along my trail of the previous night until it led me to the two goats and my rifle. The carcasses were right where I had left them, untouched by predators. After strapping the rifle across my back, I grabbed one of the rough black horns in each hand and began dragging my bounty back to camp.

The goats were frozen solid and dragged easily over the snow, but with each one weighing over two hundred pounds, I had my work cut out. It was dark by the time I reached the entrance to the snow cave.

Leaving the goats outside and crawling through the entrance, I was surprised to find Bishop Hill.

"Hi, Bishop," I greeted him brightly, my spirits high in anticipation of a feast on the fresh meat.

"Hello," he responded, his tone sober. Caroline and Sarah, though looking at me, did not speak. Something was wrong.

"What's wrong?" I asked, forgetting about the meat.

The bishop looked down at the packed snow between his legs. He was sitting cross-legged like an Indian, and with his knife he was scratching something in the snow. After what seemed like a long silence, he looked up at me.

"McConklin's at it again," he said. "And this time he's got a lot of people agreeing with him."

"I saw the gathering and noticed the noise when I headed out this afternoon. But I didn't catch what it was all about."

"I'm surprised they didn't wave you down," continued the bishop. "Maybe they didn't see you."

"That's possible. What's the problem?"

The bishop scratched in the snow again for a minute, then continued.

"First we lost the stock; then we got trapped in the early snows. McConklin's got a lot of people convinced the good Lord is punishing us."

"For what?" I demanded, feeling more than a little angry at the pious Ebenezer. "These people have given up their homes, their land—in many cases their loved ones—to follow their God and his prophet into a wilderness. Certainly no one would believe God would punish people for that kind for dedication."

"For adultery, allowing fornicators to live among them."

The silence was heavy. He hadn't said it, but I suddenly knew that my sharing the snow cave with Caroline and Sarah had something to do with Ebenezer's wrath. I felt a blush come over my neck and face as I looked over at Caroline and Sarah.

"Are the three of us included in those accusations?" I asked quietly, looking down at the snow.

"Yes." He nodded.

"Well, I'm innocent," I said, looking him straight in the eye. "And so are Caroline and Sarah."

"We told him that," said Sarah.

"Then what's the problem?" I demanded, anger in my voice. "You're the bishop of this company. Tell Ebenezer to keep his damn mouth shut. Tell him to go dig mussels."

"It's not that easy," said the bishop. "He demanded to be heard by the bishop's council. His arguments were very convincing. I had to confirm that you spent the first night in the cave. And he says he saw you sneak in after midnight when you returned from hunting. What really upset him was this morning when he saw Caroline bring your clothes outside and hang them over the sagebrush to air out."

"They were soaked! I nearly froze to death! Let me testify before your council! Any man calls me a liar and I'll . . ." I reached for my rifle.

"That won't be necessary," said the bishop, his tone calm and firm.

"Why not? I've nothing to hide!"

"Before I tell you that, would you like to know what Ebenezer proposed we do to you?" To my astonishment, the bishop was smiling. I nodded, seeing no humor in the situation, and wondering how the bishop could.

"It is common knowledge that Brigham Young had some men at Winter Quarters tied to wagon wheels and whipped with green willows."

"Ebenezer proposed that?"

"Yup," smiled the bishop. "And after the whipping that you be sent away without your snowshoes and rifle."

"Why are you smiling?" I demanded. "I don't see any humor in the situation. In fact, if I see Ebenezer before you do, you may have more than adultery to worry about. How about a murder!"

"I'm sorry," said the bishop. "I suppose it seems humorous to me now that it's over."

"Over?"

"Yes. The council dropped the charges. There won't be any more trouble."

"Wait a minute!" I said. "Why didn't you tell me that earlier? Why did you lead me on, like I was going to be dragged out and whipped at any moment?"

"I wanted you to appreciate," the bishop said, without hesitation, "what I went through today while you were on a carefree hike in the hills." He looked over at Caroline and Sarah, both nervously returning his glance.

Something was wrong. Something was going on between Bishop Hill, Caroline, and Sarah that I didn't know about. I realized it hadn't been by accident that Caroline and Sarah had remained silent during my conversation with the bishop. They should have had plenty to say, especially Caroline. She was a fighter, like I was. What were they up to? Where were they leading me? What kind of game was this?

"How did you get the council to drop the charges?" I asked coolly, figuring the answer to that question might help me get to the bottom of this thing.

"I lied," he smiled.

This was no ordinary bishop. First the incident with the buffalo chips. Now he was admitting to a lie.

"Tell me about it," I said.

"Remember the first night," he began, "when I visited you in the cave?"

"Yes."

"I told the council about that visit."

"And?"

The bishop gave a quick, nervous look in the direction of the two women.

"I told them I performed a marriage ceremony, you and Caroline."

I could hardly believe I was hearing this. "So the whole camp thinks Caroline and I are married?"

The bishop nodded. I began to laugh; I didn't know why. I looked over at Caroline. She was smiling.

"Looks like you got yourself in a corner," I said to the bishop. "When people find out the truth, you might get excommunicated." I don't know why the situation seemed so funny.

"That's why I'm here now," said the bishop, his tone very serious. "I need your help."

"My help?"

"Will you make an honest man out of me?" I started to ask him to explain. Then I suddenly realized what he was getting at. I looked over at Caroline. As our eyes met, her expression was serious, too. I had crossed half a continent of wilderness to catch and court this woman, but I had never imagined things coming together quite like this.

"Will you help me make this lying bishop an honest man?" I asked, not taking my eyes away from hers.

"I will," she said. "I do. Yes."

"Can you do it without a ring?" I asked the bishop.

"Yes," he said. "But there's another problem."

Again I had the feeling that everybody else knew something I didn't. Women friends customarily went to pieces when an engagement was announced. Caroline and Sarah were mysteriously quiet.

"What's the other problem?" I asked.

"I told another lie," responded the bishop, looking down as he scratched in the snow.

"What do you mean?" I asked, having no idea what he was getting around to.

"Ebenezer was concerned about you sharing the cave with *two* women, so I told *two* lies." I could hardly believe my ears, but there was no doubt about the meaning of his statement.

"And you want me to make a totally honest man of you?" I asked. He nodded.

I looked over at the two women. Sarah was looking down at her hands. Embarrassed, no doubt. I didn't blame her.

As Caroline's eyes met mine, I asked her what she thought of a double marriage to erase a double lie. As much as I loved Caroline and liked Sarah—though I had never had any romantic ideas concerning her—I felt like I was in some kind of a trap, with the jaws closing too rapidly.

"Do you understand what we'd be getting into?" I asked Caroline.

"I wrote the book on it," she said. "Remember? You risked your life to get the manuscript from Dick Boggs." I remembered.

"I helped Sarah bury her husband," she continued. "Together we have pushed and pulled that wagon through nearly a hundred miles of sand, mud, and treacherous river crossings. Together we resisted McConklin's attempts to marry us. Together we fought off McConklin's efforts to leave us behind at Fort Laramie. Together we shivered through many nights in that flimsy tent, not knowing if little Pat would be alive when morning came.

"I have shared a lot with Sarah, and she a lot with me. And, yes, I would even share my husband with her, gladly."

I felt bad about my earlier feelings of being trapped. I realized I would be the loser, not Caroline or Sarah, if I walked away.

"Sarah," I said. "How do you feel about making the bishop a totally honest man?"

She looked up at me. There were tears in her eyes.

"Pat passed away less than a month ago," she said, followed by a pause that seemed an eternity. No one else spoke, waiting for Sarah to finish.

"Pat and I loved—I mean love—each other very much. He thought a lot of you. You were his best friend." Again there was silence as she reached down and patted little Pat on the head. The baby was asleep.

"If Pat could speak to me now," she continued, "I know what he would want me to do. I know who he would want to be a father to his only son. If you want me, I would like to make the bishop a totally honest man."

"That settles it!" shouted the bishop as he headed for the door of the cave. "I'll be back in five minutes with my prayer book and two rings. Wish I could bring something besides mussels for the wedding feast."

"I'll provide the feast," I called after him. "Don't trip over the goats."

Epilogue

The morning after the double wedding and goat meat wedding feast, warm chinook winds blew in from the south, beginning to melt the crusty snow. By the time the Hill Company was ready to travel, a rescue party arrived from the Salt Lake Valley, bringing plenty of food, clothing, and extra teams. While the main body moved ahead to the Valley, some of the men took the extra teams back to get the wagons. The warm weather continued for several weeks, allowing everyone to reach the Salt Lake Valley by early December.

After a brief stop in Salt Lake, Dan Storm took his new family south to the big valley at the foot of the majestic Mount Timpanogos. They settled there, building a cabin, clearing land, and sinking roots for future generations.

About the Author

Until someone else steps forward, it appears *Storm Testament* series author Lee Nelson is the only man in modern times to kill a bull buffalo from the back of a galloping horse with a bow and arrow.

No, Lee is not a lunatic bent on suicide, but a best-selling author intent on gathering authentic research. Digging through dusty journals, starting fires without matches, even chewing on raw buffalo is part of Nelson's research in writing historical/adventure/romance novels unparalleled in authenticity and originality.

Lee was born high in the Rocky Mountains in Logan, Utah, later graduating from high school in California. After studying at the University of California at Berkeley, he served a mission for the LDS Church in Southern Germany. Lee has a bachelor's degree in English literature and an MBA, both from Brigham Young University.

Lee Nelson has over thirty published books, including ten historical novels in the *Storm Testament* series.

0 26575 76570 0